1969

"In *1969 Love and Promised Peace,* I love how the characters struggle to stop an insane war, save the environment, and learn to love each other. Sounds very familiar to me. These issues are as important today as they were fifty years ago."
    Graham Nash, two-time Rock and Roll Hall of Fame inductee
    Author, *Wild Tales: A Rock and Roll Life*

"I loved *1969* for all the personal memories it provoked and for giving me access into the mind of a man in those days. I was just 23 that year, and recently married to a guy who had joined the Naval Reserves to escape the draft. There was so much cultural and political turmoil then, in addition to my own uprooting and my beginning a career as an English teacher, that I barely knew, let alone understood, the complex dilemmas facing all the boys and men around me. John Addison's protagonist, David, gave me a male perspective that put some puzzle pieces in place, and helped me understand how the lot of us survived — and thrived, in 1969."
    Pamela Travis-Moore

"Reading *1969* sparked so many memories of those early years of my youth. I was 25 then and, man, it was sex, drugs, and rock 'n roll! But it was more, wasn't it? All the struggles of being young, wondering what kind of mark we might make in the world, battling it out with our parents and the culture of expectation we were born into, the moral crisis that was Vietnam — I revisited that time as I read Addison's book. If you were around then, you'll laugh, remember, and maybe cry a little. And if you never lived those experiences, take my word for it: 1969 is a great blend of fact and fiction, an authentic historical novel that brings that time back to life."
    Tim Flood
    Author, *Islands Apart*

"This novel is almost historical in the way it captures the end-of-an-era, the Vietnam War protests, the start of the environmental movement and the influences of drug experimentation and the sexual revolution. But different than other creative works on the period, this story is about those who lived it, survived it and took the positive effects to heart. Tragedy, insecurity, internal conflicts and excesses are overcome and the joy and hope of young people prevails. If there is a message for future generations from those turbulent times, this novel is an uplifting one: question the powerful, protect the planet, embrace change, reconcile with family, and trust the ones you love."
    John Adsit
    Class of 1969

1969

Love and Promised Peace

John Addison

Copyright © 2019 John Addison. All rights reserved. No part of this book may be reproduced or transmitted in any form or by means electronic, or mechanical, including photocopying, recording or by any information storage and retrieval system, without written permission from the author, except for the inclusion of brief quotations with attribution.

This is a work of fiction. Names, characters, places, and incidents are used fictitiously and sometimes invented. Resemblance to actual persons, living or dead, corporations, events, government agencies or locales is coincidental.

Arcane Book Covers.

Published in the United States by John Addison

ISBN 9781092856867

FIRST EDITION

Literature and Fiction / Genre Fiction

1. Coming of Age 2. Historical 3. Psychological

Contents

The Winter of Our Discontent 1

Haight-Ashbury 22

Rites of Spring 29

People's Park 48

Like Father, Unlike Son 66

The Trip 72

Party Animals 81

Guns and Flowers 88

A Funeral 97

Busted 101

Collateral Damage 110

Father's Day 114

Secret Service 120

Laguna Beach 133

Call of Duty 144

Peeing Envy 159

Santa Barbara 174

Cliff Rescue 179

Walking on the Moon 188

Woodstock 197

Laurel Canyon 211

Together 218

Chokehold 228

Celebration at Big Sur 234

Vietnam 240

Thanksgiving 242

Pandora and the Pusher 249

New Beginnings 265

Prodigal Son 275

Farewell to the Sixties 290

1969

1
The Winter of Our Discontent

Half crazy, almost naked, and broke, David dove into the icy water. The 21-year old ignored the risks of hypothermia and cold-induced heart failure. Nixon's Secret Service watched from the president's beach mansion on that icy March morning of 1969.

Only one thing mattered to David, swimming this thousand-yard ocean course in under twenty minutes to get his job back. David wanted a fourth and final season as a lifeguard in San Clemente, California. He needed another paycheck for food, rent, and his final tuition at the university.

The 54-degree water shrank his lungs. He wished that wetsuits were allowed as he gasped for enough air to take him under the next eight-foot swell. Waves of thought tossed in his head. *Do I go to Vietnam? Dad would love that. If I got killed, he could brag about his son, the hero.*

David's thoughts came in urgent flashes. *Swim faster. Put your head down. No, too cold.* The freezing ocean constricted his breathing.

If David got off course, then finishing within twenty minutes would be impossible. There would be no job and no tuition to finish college. *Don't get off course!* He scanned for the orange buoy, 500 yards in the distance and disappearing behind the giant swells. *Now I see it. This hurts. I should have trained harder.*

Perhaps it was the extreme conditions that caused David to examine his life. *After the summer, I'll put on a suit and take a paycheck from the military-industrial complex.* Working for The Man almost seemed acceptable now that his father had ended all financial support. The financial shock treatment had worked. Bank of America had moved ahead of the Dalai Lama on David's priority list. Speaking of priorities, there was David's sex life.

My sex life. My almost sex life. David almost had sex seven times. He was the quiz show contestant that never won. After making out while listening to the Moody Blues, getting to the semi-finals listening to The Doors, there was always some Big Question. He always missed. Who did he vote for? Was he going to the protest? How did he feel about the women's movement? Wrong answer. I am sorry, but we must move on to the next contestant. Even if he answered one important question correctly, he always froze when hearing, "Do you love me?"

He swallowed water in the choppy sea but kept swimming. *Put your head down and swim faster. I'm twenty-one and a virgin. Summer of Love. Not my summer. Free love? Where?* David was convinced that he was the world's oldest living male heterosexual virgin. Lurking like a shark in the deep was a fear that he could not be both a 21-year-old virgin and be heterosexual. David wanted to eliminate all thoughts and finish this trial by ice. He again tried to focus on the swim.

To finish in less than twenty minutes, David used his knowledge of the ocean gained from previous summers as a lifeguard. He had started well. Instead of running directly into the waves in front of him, he ran thirty yards to the right and dove into a riptide, using the current to pull him out past the waves and most of the other hundred swimmers, both returning guards and new competitive swimmers fighting for a few new job openings.

He judged the side drift correctly and stayed on course most of the time. At the top of the eight-foot swells, David precisely timed lifting his head to spot the buoy. David swam smart, but not fast. After his early lead, he was falling behind. When he reached the halfway buoy in a little over ten minutes, most of the others had passed him. He was tired and sore. As he swam toward shore, he now welcomed the massive swells to push him forward.

He struggled to ignore the fiery jabs of pain in his legs. *You can still beat twenty minutes.* Swim, swim, stroke, stroke. He thought of his fantasy rescue. *He, David Eliot, would rescue the president. It could happen. Nixon's summer home was in San Clemente where David lifeguarded. Nixon's daughters had given the president a surfboard as a Christmas gift. Nixon would wipe out. David would save the president who would gratefully pardon David from the draft. David would be on television. He would be on quiz shows. There would be a final question that would transform him from poor to rich. As always, he would make the wrong answer. Think happy thoughts. Swim. Faster!*

In the last one hundred yards, David raced the clock by catching a wave and passing many competitors. He bodysurfed to the beach and then staggered to the finish line shouting his last name to the man with the clipboard. *Did I beat twenty minutes?*

Wearing only his Speedo racing trunks in the 48-degree air, David wrapped himself in a wool navy blanket and sat alone. He shook from the near hypothermia that penetrated to the bone. He also shuddered from thoughts of his life ruined before it had started.

Lost in thought, David stared at the ocean. A distant fishing boat pitched in the merciless waves in a desperate struggle to stay upright as the wind slashed the steel-gray water into a million whitecaps. David could not tell where the ocean ended and the gray-black storm clouds began. He stared at the dark horizon, remembering T. S. Eliot, "I have heard the mermaids singing, each to each. I do not think that they will sing to me."

He thought of the argument with his father on Christmas at

officer's quarters at Miramar. David had arrived wearing a beard, longer hair, and jeans. He had no intention of another suit-and-tie formal dinner with other officers. His father, an admiral, delivered an up-tight lecture about Vietnam, the navy and the moral obligation to prevent the spread of communism. David felt a knot in his stomach.

As always, he didn't ask about me; he doesn't give a damn. He joked that I had long hair like a girl. Criticized my beard, beads, and bell-bottoms. Called me a hippie. He talked at me, but didn't listen to me. He doesn't even know me; only his lifelong dream that I would become an admiral like him. Reach the four stars that he aspired to and never achieved. Typical navy, he expected me to take orders and not speak my mind. Conversation over.

David recalled how he had stayed up, angry, trying to read, but too distracted. He walked into his father's closed study. Maps were spread out on his desk; detailed maps of bombing scenarios. Pentagon stuff. CINCPAC and B-52s on the maps. Then he looked up to the crimson face of his father who screamed, "Get out of this room!" David could still taste his anger and fear.

I didn't move fast enough, so he shoved me out. Not the first time that he got physical with me. When was the first? Age five? Age two? He yelled that I was looking at documents classified Secret. How would I know that? Probably new bombing flight plans from the aircraft carriers in Vietnam. The whole scene wasn't my fault. He should have had secret documents locked up. He knew I'd be there for Christmas. Probably too much drinking. More bombs, more booze.

David shivered as he recalled the argument where he denied seeing secrets, his father calling him a liar, and his shouting back. His father, Admiral Dex Eliot was furious.

Subordinates don't talk back to admirals. I'm only his son, which makes me lower than a new seaman. He goes into this tirade about how they're saving the free world, his sacrificing to raise me by himself, and how bitterly disappointed he is to have an ungrateful hippie son spying on him. The room had the smell of danger.

Before last Christmas, David was always careful with his father, but in that confrontation he was too angry to worry about how it would play out. He said, "I'd rather wear a beard and beads than kill innocent people."

Admiral Eliot had the last word, "I didn't work and sacrifice for years so that you could throw it in my face."

David was kicked out that night. That ended all money from his father. Since then, he scrambled to pay for tuition, rent, car, and food.

David walked to the campfire on the beach where his good friend Carlo shivered under layers of clothes and blankets. Carlo and David met playing water polo for the University of California at Irvine in 1965. They shared a long bus ride back from UCI's victory over USC. The conversation flowed from water polo to college classes to growing up. They discovered a common love for surfing. After the bus ride, they grabbed their surfboards and drove to Laguna to ride some hot waves.

Each summer when they lifeguarded in San Clemente, David and Carlo were roommates. This would be their last summer of living together. They looked the parts of lifeguards. David was now clean-cut with short hair, having removed his beard and cut his hair for job interviews. Carlo's haircut had subdued his curls and his mustache made him appear to be smiling; he usually was.

Mike joined. Removing his swim cap, his long hair fell to his shoulders and complemented his full beard. He removed his trunks under the towel wrapped around his waist, put on bell-bottom jeans, a tie-dye shirt, and a frayed leather jacket. Mike was the lifeguards' spiritual leader, inspiring daily discussions about the meanings of their lives, eastern religion, and philosophy. Since guard towers had telephones, they could discuss potential rescues when busy, and the meaning of life when idle. Mike said, "That swim hurt. How did we ever qualify as guards in the first place?"

David replied, "We were all once hot-shot competitive swimmers. Anyone compete after their freshman year?" Everyone just shrugged. No longer did they compete nor have time for the required twenty hours of weekly training. There were other priorities for each, such as making money, stopping the war, and spiritual journeys.

Over one hundred returning and aspiring waited for word from their potential employer, the State of California Parks system. All were men because the state did not allow women to be lifeguards in 1969, and Governor Reagan had no interest in changing the regulation.

Rob Martinez, San Clemente lifeguard captain, dropped by to notify the three, "You all qualified." He looked at David. "Some just barely. Good to have you back." David was ecstatic inside but acted with nonchalance. In 19 minutes and 47 seconds, thanks to catching a wave, he qualified and could enjoy a final summer of saving lives, meeting bikini clad girls, and making enough money for food and rent.

Captain Rob added, "You can all start working weekends in two weeks. I assume that you will all arrive in regulation short hair and clean-shaven. Right?"

"Yes sir," the three replied in unison with bearded Mike snapping to attention and saluting smartly.

"Smart ass." Captain Rob walked away.

David Eliot, Carlo Abruzzo, and Mike Hume watched the potential first-year lifeguards complete an added run-swim-run competition.

"Now the interrogation begins." Mike looked at the aspirants nervously standing in line to be interviewed inside a windowless office. "They will use techniques carefully handed down from prisoner-of-war camps."

The three reminisced about their first-year interviews, where one state executive fired tough questions, while six took notes and grilled with tough questions. The waiting potential lifeguards, most aged 18, would be asked increasingly difficult questions about first aid, rescue scenarios, and enforcing the law. Although the interviewers were interested in the answers, they were more interested in getting someone to freeze or panic during the interrogation. They were looking for levelheaded lifeguards.

Carlo, Mike, and David, stood facing the turbulent ocean, not each other, while they talked. Their heads slowly scanned back and forth as they unconsciously looked for swimmers in trouble. They were lifeguards trained to the point of instinct.

"Fierce swells and side currents. Lucky no tourists are out there. We'd be making rescues," David said and then pointed. "Look at that rip."

"Must be two hundred yards," Mike observed.

David said, "The worst was last summer during the big south swell, with ten-foot waves. During a lull, this woman is out with an inner tube around her. I looked outside and saw a ten-foot set coming. I took after her while she was still swimming out. First wave ripped that tube right off her. When I got to her seconds later, she was already under water. She would have been a goner."

They reminisced about the previous summer, as they revisited days of surf so big that they made a dozen rescues. They talked about surfing, road trips, and where each would live in the summer. Eager for warmth and uncensored conversation, they left the beach.

The three climbed into David's Volkswagen bus with the grace of hungry gorillas, and drove north on Coast Highway. Into the headwind, the VW bus maxed out at 50 miles per hour. They looked at favorite surf spots as they drove from San Clemente to San Juan Capistrano to Dana Point, following the path of the early Spanish explorers on El Camino Real.

An explosion of flowers, art shops, and boutiques announced South Laguna. The hillside was a post-impressionistic landscape of large and expensive beach homes mixed with two-bedroom cottages from the twenties. On sidewalks lined with eucalyptus and palm trees, church goers in dark suits and long dresses commingled with beach lovers in swimsuits on that Sunday morning.

The guys jumped out of the VW to look down on the beach as Rachel dove for a volleyball that was a comet blazing toward Earth. Her long tan body extended parallel to the ground as her right arm reached. Spectators held their breath as the speeding ball hit her clenched fist. One guy on the beach dropped his drink while looking at her breasts reaching for freedom from her Barely Legal bikini.

Sam, known to all as Sam the Shaman, watched, mesmerized. Tripping on LSD, the Shaman saw Adam reaching for God's hand in the Sistine Chapel. He contemplated the glistening perspiration on her Amazonian body, the Navajo white sand, and the arbitrary boundaries of the ocean, the horizon, and the infinite.

The volleyball ricocheted from Rachel's fist eight feet into the air. Linda crouched and then set the ball above the net. Darrel's driving spike scored. Point. Game. Match.

The guards turned their gaze from Rachel and Linda and

walked to Tortilla Flats, a Mexican restaurant named for the novel of Steinbeck fame. They waited in the crowded reception area for a table.

Heads turned as Rachel and Linda entered the restaurant. The receptionist called David's name, and the guys were seated. Tortilla Flats was perfect for starved college students. Generous plates of Mexican food were priced from $1.89. The combo plate at $2.49 was exceptional. You could determine each student's relative wealth by whether the ordered drink was a margarita, beer, or water. Carlo ordered the combo plate and a large margarita. David ordered water and fish tacos. Mike ordered a vegetarian tostada with black beans, no cheese, and a beer.

Minutes later, Linda and Rachel followed the hostess to their table, walking past the staring guards. Tall and tan, Rachel moved like a samba. Not much was hidden by her skin-colored mini skirt and translucent blouse. By contrast, Linda was fair with her clean-scrubbed face free of make-up. She wore a purple-gauze Indian blouse, a pale blue sweater, and white bell-bottoms. The turquoise in her Navajo earrings and necklace suggested the color of her eyes.

Rachel took the seat that faced away from the guards who could be heard four tables away, while Linda could view them from her seat. The two women sat at one corner of the large room, and the three guys at the other.

The restaurant was like a vast Mexican hacienda with white stucco walls, a high arched ceiling, and vases of hydrangea, purple dahlias, and lavender carnations. The Southern California sun streamed through the windows. The room was alive with casually dressed beach goers, families dressed for church, and a birthday party of bouncing seven-year-olds.

"I love this place," Linda said. "Sun. Sea breeze. Beautiful flowers everywhere."

Rachel tossed back her dark hair. "Yes. Too bad we couldn't

go with the others to the Oar House. Can't drink today. You've got finals. I've my research report about the Santa Barbara oil spill."

"It's wonderful that you're saving the birds covered with oil-tar."

"I go there every week and save as many as I can," Rachel said. "It's so sad. In my report, I detail how the oil spill spread over eight hundred square miles, destroying thousands of birds, seals, and dolphins."

"You should've told me when I called last week that this would be too busy for you."

"No, no. It's fantastic that you flew down to spend the weekend. I miss you. I miss Berkeley."

"Yeah, I've missed you since you graduated," said Linda. "Love your place. Can't wait to be your roommate this summer. So, tomorrow you drive us to Santa Barbara? Then I'll help you clean the birds."

"Sweet of you to help," Rachel said. "After Santa Barbara, you're still determined to hitchhike to Big Sur."

"For sure. I hitch all the time. Alicia will meet me in Big Sur and we'll spend the night in one of those funky cabins."

"I'd never hitch. It's dangerous."

Linda shrugged.

"There's a conscious-raising workshop at Big Sur next month that looks fabulous. I'll show you the flyer when we get home. I'd love to have you join me there."

"I can dig it. In Berkeley, I go to a weekly conscious-raising workshop for women."

"Still involved in civil rights?"

"Yeah, but since King was murdered, the Panthers don't want any help from people as white as me. I'm focused on stopping this insane war." Linda paused and stared out the window. "Now I'm a Berkeley activist; no more girl in a poodle skirt at the high school sock hop."

Rachel listened and nodded her head in support. The two paused to give the waitress their orders.

"So, we'll have to party at the Oar House this summer," said Linda.

"Agreed, plus I'm just not in the mood for the whole scene. It's so loud, and guys won't leave you alone, which I must admit is sometimes fun." Rachel paused. "You cannot escape aggressive guys, even here. That loud one over there already hit on me."

"Which one?" Linda asked as she looked over at the table with the three lifeguards.

"Don't look!" Rachel exclaimed with a hushed urgency. "It will only encourage them."

Linda shrunk in her chair. She put on her sunglasses, and spied at the guys through the table vase of African violets, as she mocked Rachel's caution against looking. "So, which one?"

"The big, loud one with dark, curly hair."

"He's gorgeous. When did he talk with you?"

"When I went to the restroom while we were waiting for a table. He followed me!"

Linda acted shocked. "He followed you into the ladies room?"

"He said his name was Carlo, and that he could not resist meeting me because I'm beautiful."

"He immediately said that you're beautiful?"

"Immediately," Rachel said.

"So then what?"

"I said, 'Hello, my name is Linda.'"

"You're not Linda! I'm Linda. You're giving strange guys my name?"

"Only your first name. He was being forward. I didn't want to give him my name, and yours came to mind. Besides, what's the problem? You said he's gorgeous."

"This blows my mind." Linda sat upright, removed her sunglasses, gave Rachel a stern look, and said, "He could be some serial killer and now he has my name! Tonight, you'll need to stay awake guarding the front door." She paused and looked out the window at the cottages lining the Laguna hillside. "What if he calls and asks for Linda? This is terribly confusing."

"He won't call."

"Then you didn't give him your phone number?"

"Of course not. After trying to charm me, he did ask for my number saying something about how we might be perfect for each other, but we would never know unless we got together. I had to end the conversation because I really needed to pee. So I gave him a phone number. He now has a piece of paper that says 'Linda' and the phone number of the Laguna Beach Police Department."

"You've memorized the police number?"

"Yes. I've had to use that number several times."

Linda said, "Rachel Perez, you don't make it easy on men. You're wearing a see-through blouse over a Barely Legal bikini-top, and guys can see ninety-nine percent of your legs with that mini skirt. Of course, guys are going to stare at you and ask you out."

"A woman should look her best. When I visit my grandparents and relatives in Venezuela, all the women, even the poor, dress beautifully. I don't mind the attention of men, but if they think that I will go out with them after talking for 30 seconds, forget it."

Linda took another look at Carlo. "Did you give that gorgeous guy more than thirty seconds?"

"Well, no, I really had to pee."

The waitress delivered their salads.

Linda said, "I remember when you had the entire class in stitches talking about male and female animal behavior."

"It is amazing what you learn by studying primate behavior. Some men are chimps, always demanding attention; some, silverback gorillas pounding their chest to signify authority. For me, I prefer a bonobo who accepts females as equal and is attentive in grooming his mate."

"Have you shared these theories with Wesley?"

"Not with words, but I know how to turn Wes into a caring bonobo, and I know how to put him into heat."

"Wes is starting Yale Law School next fall?"

"Yes, he's soon leaving for Connecticut, and your Brad is off to Columbia Law School."

"He's moving to New York in June," Linda said. "Brad has ambitions about being a U. S. Attorney, then entering politics. I had fleeting hopes of eventually marrying, but Brad's not the one. Did you have hopes with Wes?"

"No. I wonder if I'll ever marry. Part of me wants to be a famous professor who changes the world; part of me wants to be a loving mother."

"You can be both. I know that I'll have a good career, good marriage, and wonderful children. You need to be an optimist, not a pessimist."

"*Dios*, save me from my optimistic friend. You should be a hippie and wear hexagonal rose-colored glasses. This is you. Everything is rose colored. Thank god, I am a realist."

"The bright side of life looks quite nice. Thank you very much."

"You trust men too much, and I have experienced their deception too often. Monogamy is not in their DNA. Men can be my lovers, my colleagues, my friends, yes. But a husband to honor and obey, no."

"Men were deceivers ever, one foot in sea and one on shore, to one thing constant never," Linda quoted Shakespeare.

"This is very good. Who are you quoting?" Rachel asked.

"William Shakespeare – a man."

"Shakespeare, the world's most brilliant writer about sex and killing, two favorite subjects of the chimpanzees. By the way, how are those three primates doing in the far corner?"

Linda looked over at the table. Carlo was doing a pantomime of swinging from a tree. The other two were howling.

Rachel observed the expression on Linda's face with smug satisfaction.

"OK, they're primates. The gorgeous guy is acting like he's swinging from a tree. How did you know? You can't even see them."

"I know men," Rachel said and continued with her salad. "You want to attract men, but you make fun of my blouse and skirt, while you wear a drab sweater and jeans."

"It's cold," Linda defended herself.

"Show them you are hot. Show your legs. Show your body. With a little makeup, you would be beautiful. In your head, listen to the salsa music when you walk."

"If you insist, I'm off to powder my nose." As Linda walked away, she allowed her hips to sensually sway. She looked at David as she walked by.

At the same time that Linda and Rachel had been talking, this is the conversation that unfolded between David, Carlo and Mike.

Carlo asked, "Mike, will that be enough for you?"

"Yes. I'm now a vegan. I eat nothing from animals."

Carlo devoured his tamale, while emitting great-ape grunts of satisfaction. "Why no meat?"

"I'm healthier. With my studies of Buddhism, I have gained a respect for all sentient beings."

David asked Mike, "Are you staying out of the war with that fifteen-dollar diploma you got from the Universal Life Church?"

"I sent them fifteen bucks, and they mailed me a certificate, making me a legal minister," Mike answered. "I have married people. We still have the Bill of Rights in this nation."

"Do we?" David asked. "A million guys have been drafted against their will. Nixon talks about troop reduction, but there are five hundred thousand in Vietnam with an average age of nineteen. One hundred thousand have been wounded and thirty thousand killed."

"Most too young to vote, but not too young to die," Mike said.

"So, is being a minister keeping you out?" David

persisted.

"My local draft board is claiming that because I don't preside over a church made of brick and mortar, I don't qualify for an exemption," said Mike. "I wrote them a letter reminding them of the First Amendment and that a church is whenever two or more of us are gathered in His name."

"Well, it's Sunday and this sounds like a sermon," David said.

"Hallelujah and amen, brother," Mike said. "I'll follow the process of appealing to the local board, then state board, then national, and then I can start a new appeal process by taking the conscientious objector route. If all else fails, I'll move to Canada. I won't join the army; I won't kill."

After devouring their lunch, David asked Carlo, "Are you graduating this year?"

"No! I thought I had it nailed. Then the registrar sends me a letter that I'm twenty-four credits shy of graduating! Incompletes! I don't need the fucking degree! I'm dropping out and starting my own business."

"You'll be great in business," David said. "Look at all you've learned by selling drugs. Never underestimate the value of a college education." The three laughed, with Carlo laughing the loudest.

Carlo ordered a pitcher of Margaritas for all. Then he continued his tale of woe about 24 missing credits. "OK, I forgot about the incomplete in fencing class. The teacher was pissed when she walked in and saw me brandishing a saber as I swung from the gymnastic class rope. I was a pirate, man. No extra credit for the bandana and eye patch. I offered to walk the plank if she'd let me stay in class." Carlo was Peter Pan and Captain Hook as he stood and acted out the scene in detail, as witnessed across the room by Linda.

"Carlo's very good at groveling," Mike was laughing as he tried to talk. "And groveling is his standard foreplay."

"True. True. When it comes to sex, I have no pride. I have mastered twenty-seven variations of begging. It beats those lonely nights with my left hand, the beast with five fingers." Carlo enjoyed the audience, "Dig this. I got an incomplete from the psychology course about sensory deprivation. The fact that I forgot to show for the final is a testimony to how well I did in the lab." In a series of stories, Carlo tallied the 24 missing credits. Carlo was done with the university. He would start working the beach full time in April, and start a business in the fall. Carlo was a born entrepreneur like his father.

At this moment, Linda walked by and looked at David. Carlo pushed David out of his chair, causing David to almost fall. He shrugged his shoulders, looked back at Carlo, and then followed Linda. *What if she rejects me?*

When David got to the restrooms, there was no sign of Linda. He felt relieved and entered the men's room, urinated, and exited. There she was. David first panicked and then tried to pull himself together with meditative breathing. Linda was admiring the glazed pottery hanging from the roof, with bright impatiens overflowing. David walked to her and said, "They're a beautiful celebration of an early spring, aren't they." He smiled, blushed, and awkwardly waited for a reply.

"Yes, they're lovely,' Linda replied. "You're a poet – celebration of an early spring."

"I guess my writing classes at UCI paid off."

Linda beamed. "I'll be going to UCI next fall to get a teaching credential and master's."

"Next fall?"

"Yes, right now I'm at Berkeley. When I graduate in June I'll move in with my friend here   in Laguna."

"Far out. I graduate in June then lifeguard for my last summer in San Clemente." David hesitated, and then extended his hand. "Hello, I'm David."

Linda automatically extended her right hand as they shook. "Hello David. I'm Linda."

"You're also Linda. My roommate, Carlo, was talking with your friend. Linda and Linda."

Linda blushed. "Quite a coincidence."

David knew it was his turn to talk, but silently censored each half-formed phrase.

Linda asked, "You're a lifeguard at the beach?"

"Right on. It's the perfect spring and summer job while going to UCI. Most days are relaxed, but about ten days every summer, we earn our entire pay for the year. You're on edge every minute, looking for weak swimmers to rescue in rips."

"Rips?"

"Riptides."

"It must feel wonderful to save someone's life."

"I dig it. Most would probably make it back to the beach, but a few wouldn't if we hadn't saved them," David said as Linda looked at him with fascination. "So where will you be living this summer?"

"With my friend…" Linda almost said Rachel but caught herself. "She's renting a cute cottage here in Laguna. I'll be working with kids at a Montessori school while I start my credential courses."

"You must be patient and have a good heart to work with those little kids."

"I'm excited about it."

David again lapsed into silence. Finally, words came. "Good to meet you, Linda. I'll look for you this summer."

"Please do."

As they walked together toward their respective tables, then separated, a voice in David's mind shouted, *'Please do.' Ask her out, you idiot.* He walked in an awkward silence and hoped that he would see her again. *Oh well, at least Carlo has her friend's number.*

When David returned, Mike and Carlo were talking about the Vietnam War.

"This is really getting scary," Carlo said. "They're dying faster than ever. We could all get shipped to Vietnam this summer and shipped back in body bags!"

Mike started singing Country Joe's "I-Feel-Like-I'm-Fixin'-to-Die Rag."

"Don't worry, Carlo. I'll save you in the jungles," David said with mock bravery.

"Right. I really want my life in your hands. Like you're going to rescue me while machine guns are blazing? This guy hides under the bed when a car backfires." Carlo continued, "I've joined the army medical reserves."

Mike cut him off. "You joined the army reserves! Are you out of your mind? The medical reserves are the first being activated. They'll call you up, drop you in the jungle, and you will come home in a box!"

"If they're going to nail you, they're going to nail you," Carlo countered. "I'm hoping the reserves will keep me out of Vietnam."

"OK, Alice, welcome to Wonderland," Mike said. "You've

got to fight *against* this war, man. No way that I'm going to die in some infested jungle fighting a non-war that's illegal."

David said, "Mike's right about the reserves. They keep calling them up. You need a backup plan. The whole thing's a mind-blower. If they draft me, I was thinking of joining the coast guard. As a lifeguard, I'd be a natural."

"Are you nuts?" Mike countered. "Coast guards patrol the rivers in Vietnam. They're sitting ducks. Do you have a death wish?"

David looked discouraged as he listened. "OK, I need a plan to stay out of this. I want to save lives, not kill people."

"Your dad is some heavy in the war, isn't he?" Mike asked David.

"Yeah, he's a rear admiral in the navy." David felt his face redden. He hated talking about his dad. "Kills commies for Christ," David tried to say it as a joke. He heard a little nervous laughter and saw the empathetic looks of his friends. "You guys may remember that he got me accepted by the naval academy, and then I turned it down. Last Christmas we had a real blowout when I said that the war in Vietnam was wrong. He exploded. He was already pissed about my beard and longer hair. He totally cut me off. I pay for tuition and everything. We haven't talked since."

"Totally groovy, man," Mike said. "It's not easy having a dad who's a heavy in the war machine. It's righteous that you stood up for yourself, man. Stay out. No coast guard. No navy. No reserves. Fuck 'em. You're a bright guy; you're a computer scientist, so make a plan to stay out!"

David leaned back in his chair, rubbed the scar on his left cheek, and stared at the ceiling lost in thought.

"American Friends," Mike said. "They offer free counseling on your legal options to stay out of the war. They're a volunteer organization of the Quakers."

"Good idea." David had spent the past year living in denial, somehow thinking that he would be spared from dealing with Vietnam. *I need a plan!*

The three fell into silence until Carlo exclaimed, "Obviously, we need more tequila. Eat, drink, and be merry for tomorrow we may die! Our regiment leaves at dawn! Carlo ordered another pitcher of margaritas for all.

After returning his buddies to San Clemente, David drove to a favorite cove in Laguna. He navigated the narrow side streets with cottages almost hidden by massive eucalyptus, cypress, and overflowing rhododendron. He parked then descended the rickety stairs to the beach to wait for sunset. Gliding along the cliff were a formation of pelicans, traveling north without effort.

On the white sand, he sat in a half-lotus. The horizon was a singularity of blue ocean intersecting with blue sky. David's thoughts drifted like the overhead clouds. *Will we save lives this summer or be in Vietnam ending lives?*

When David started lifeguarding, he believed that he would be forever young and that life would be an endless summer. The year 1968 was a knife that severed his youth from youthful ideals. Now, in 1969, he wondered if a death certificate would follow his graduation diploma. He could not see a future; he could only try to create one.

2

Haight-Ashbury

Haight-Ashbury was a rite of spring, an edge of violence, an orgy, a panhandle, and a trip. The San Francisco neighborhood got its name from the two streets that intersect at its navel. Linda and Alicia walked barefoot in the Panhandle - the long thrust of grass, trees, and flowers that extended from Golden Gate Park.

The grass wiggled between Linda's toes, caressing, massaging, and dancing. She walked through crowds celebrating a Sunday in the park. Young couples picnicked with their naked children. Cops smiled. People bicycled and roller-skated. She deeply inhaled fragrances of lilacs, pine, and marijuana.

Alicia, a dancer, pirouetted around panhandlers, since she had no more money than they.

"Far out. The Indian Arts store," Linda said as she and Alicia raced into the store, soon looking in the mirror while sampling earrings and beaded necklaces.

"Did I tell you I posed naked for Brian?" Alicia asked. "Can you dig it? Shocking and so much fun."

"I don't think there's anything you'd do that would shock me," Linda said. "Tell me about it."

"Brian sits next to me in Portraits. He's a gifted artist. I should have his talent. He makes me laugh and he definitely has a perfect ass."

"I can guess where this is going."

"Brian tells me that I'm Botticelli's Venus. You know - the naked goddess on the giant shell."

"I can see that. Lovely face. Long wild hair. Yes, we covered that painting when I took art history. Someday, I want to travel the world, seeing the greatest works up front and personal."

Linda watched Alicia hold one of the store's earrings next to her face. Linda said, "You know, I think that you are more the blond in Botticelli's Primavera - flowers in her hair, floral dress, the embodiment of spring. Brian called you Venus because he wanted to get you naked."

"True. I was a willing model. He got an A+ for the work. The class loved it."

"The entire class saw you naked!"

"Not exactly. Brian made my hair long enough to cover me down there. Besides, it's just a painting."

"But Brian saw you naked?"

Alicia's hands covered her mouth in feigned embarrassment, and then she threw her hands in the air. "Yes, Brian saw all of me. He caressed. He pleasured. He exhausted. I also gave Brian an A+, and it wasn't for his performance as a painter."

"I can dig it. Sex, drugs, rock and roll."

"I want you to meet Brian. We're going to Led Zeppelin next weekend. You and Brad wanna come?"

"I love Zeppelin. Can you get tickets?"

"Yeah, but they're expensive," Alicia replied. "Eight each."

"Let me ask Brad."

Alicia hesitated before saying, "I always see you two together. Brad's great, but why get hung up on one guy?"

"OK, I see him a lot. I love him, sort of. But we're trying not to get too heavy. When we graduate in June, he's off to New York and Columbia Law School. I'm off to Laguna to live with Rachel while I get my teaching credential. You and I are different. I couldn't handle the roller-coaster ride of sleeping with different guys, like I did when I was younger."

"Yeah, you're now so old at twenty-one."

"And you're so young at nineteen," Linda said and then fell into silence.

"I'll miss Brad, but he's gotta get out of here with the FBI following him."

"It's getting bad, isn't it?"

"Scary. The Man wants him in prison or in Vietnam, like there's really a difference."

"It's totally unfair. The Bill of Rights is supposed to guarantee free speech." They fell back into silence. Alicia slowly walked around Linda, studying her face. "Raphael's Madonna."

"Madonna!" Linda laughed and said, "Madonna has fallen far from a state of grace. Did Madonna wear white bell-bottom Levis?"

"You are Madonna. I'll prove it with an art book. The Psychedelic Shop sells books."

"Maybe I'm Madonna that needs to lose seven pounds."

"You make me so mad. You always say that. You're beautiful. It's such bullshit that women are treated this way. You wrote that wonderful article on equality for women. You shouldn't sell out to this Madison Avenue thing. The pressure to be ultra thin is one reason I changed majors from dance to art."

"Maybe I'll go with the Madonna thing if I get pregnant. Would I be eligible for welfare if it's an immaculate conception?"

Cars moved slowly through the mass of people. A van of tourists drove by, windows sealed, and doors locked, as if they were touring a wild animal preserve.

Alicia asked, "Speaking of conception, you're taking the Pill aren't you?"

"Of course. You?"

"Certainly. The Pill has made life deliciously interesting."

The smell of incense pulled them into the Psychedelic Shop. One wall included posters of groups local to the Bay Area including Jefferson Airplane, Big Brother and the Holding Company, and the Grateful Dead. Alicia flipped through albums, wishing that she could play each vinyl record - Moody Blues' *Days of Future Past*, Cream's *Wheels of Fire*, and Aretha Franklin's *Lady Soul*.

Linda was browsing through recent best-selling books such as *The Electric Kool-Aid Acid Test*, *The Population Bomb*, and *Soul on Ice*.

"No art books," Alicia announced. "But I'll show you the Madonna back at Berkeley."

"I can hardly wait."

Alicia pulled Linda outside while singing the Beatles, "Dear Prudence." They walked down Ashbury until they were standing between the home of the Grateful Dead and the headquarters of the Hells Angels. Linda said, "It's hard for me to picture the Hell's Angels living in this beautiful Victorian Mansion."

"I love this area. Beautiful homes and cheap rent."

"And cheap thrills," Linda added. "Let's not linger in front of the Hell's Angels." They doubled back.

They returned to the Haight and walked toward Golden Gate Park, taking in the colorful hippies, aggressive panhandlers, and prematurely old men shouting obscenities to imaginary ghosts. Passing the Free Clinic, they stepped over heroin addicts gazing into space.

"The Haight is groovy, but better in 67, the Summer of Love, with The Grateful Dead and Jefferson Airplane giving free concerts in the park," Linda said. "Now the Haight has this hard edge with the Angels, gang rapes, and meth."

"The Haight has definitely lost its innocence."

They entered Golden Gate Park, inhaling the green grass. Alicia brightly announced, "I brought you a present." Smiling, Alicia presented Linda with a brownie wrapped with a ribbon.

Linda was grateful. "You're so sweet. Brad and I can't keep dope at our places with the FBI circling."

"I don't know how you stand it. I'd freak."

Linda divided the large brownie and each devoured her half while sharing conspiratorial smiles. They followed a path that headed north through the park. Alicia looked at a woman who was changing her baby's diapers, and asked, "Did you ever dream of marrying Brad?"

"Sometimes, yes. No. I don't know. Marriage is so fifties. So Ozzie and Harriet." Linda became thoughtful. "I like being with Brad. He can be serious and intense, but he can also be romantic. Things aren't perfect; he is a guy. There's this unspoken expectation that I cook and clean."

"That's gotta change."

"I'm working on him, but he clams up and gets defensive when I try to tell him my side."

"I hate it when guys won't talk with you," Alicia said. "I refuse to be like my yes-dear housewife mom."

"We're the new role models."

"I always wanted to be a model."

They walked for a while, taking in the scene, until Linda ended the silence. "I want a lifelong journey of growing. I cannot imagine being like my mother. She's bright and creative, but she doesn't work. She lives in her square house, fixing square meals for my square dad, then watching TV programs on a square box."

"We've been studying TV and commercials in my Media and Culture class. We're the first generation to be brainwashed with these commercials. We're buying enough crap to turn planet Earth into a trash dump!"

"And boys are trained to play with their guns. All these little boys, insecure about the size of their penises, trying to have the biggest gun."

"We even have a Dick in the White House who's telling Asia to fuck off because his is bigger than theirs."

At the edge of the park, the two stared at a massive Victorian home painted black. An electric guitar was playing a song that they had never heard. This was the home of Jefferson Airplane.

Alicia announced, "Linda, I'm promoting you from Madonna to Grace Slick."

Linda laughed. "Thank you. I'm honored. She's beautiful." They stood in front of the home, listening in reverence to the guitar and a muted voice.

"Let's stroll to hippie hill," Alicia said. "We can hang out with the freaks, paint our faces, and score some good dope."

The two sat on hippie hill in the park smoking a joint. Looking out at the meadow, Linda remembered being at this park on January 14, 1967, for the human be-in. The day was a gathering of tribes, a prelude to the Summer of Love, and to her new life as a flower child.

A man, rumored to be Owsley, parachuted, dispensing LSD to the crowd. Timothy Leary preached, "Tune in, turn on, and drop out." Linda dropped Orange Sunshine for the first time. While peaking on acid, she and Brad disappeared into the forest and made love. She started that morning living up to her Ohio nickname of Little Miss Sunshine. A few hours later, she had lost her virginity and emerged a barefoot Berkeley hippie. Linda Hope became Linda in the Sky with Diamonds.

3
Rites of Spring

Friends joked that David and Carlo were the pair in the *Odd Couple*, then a hit movie. David was Felix and Carlo was Oscar. David loved having everything clean, tidy, and in its place. Carlo lived in a disaster area of dirty clothes, towels, and dishes scattered randomly in the tiny house that the two had rented. Visitors were amazed to see that a tornado had struck only half of the 700-square-foot house that they rented for $125 per month.

One day, David had chanced upon a building being demolished. He took a "condemned" sign and some of the fluorescent-orange warning tape, and then attached both to Carlo's bedroom door. Carlo laughed when he returned home and made the tape and "condemned" sign permanent.

Sharing a small kitchen and bathroom tested their friendship; separate bedrooms saved the friendship. David found the order he desperately sought in his room, while Carlo found primitive comfort in his bedroom furnished in early Cro-Magnon, complete with cave art depicting a hunt and the Playmate of the Month.

"David, we have got to do this. This will change your life!" Carlo said. He gave David a brochure titled "Personal Transformation" about a workshop in Big Sur that promised a new level of self-awareness and personal growth through two days of yoga, tai chi, meditation, movement, drums, dance, and Tibetan singing bowls.

David read the brochure carefully. He thought back on the exercises in his psychology class and said, "I don't know. It sounds a little over the edge. We'd be gone for three days. I've got papers and finals coming."

"You're so fucking organized. You don't have to sweat the papers. You've got one final. This is Big Sur, the most beautiful place on earth. We'll be working with masters."

"I've never heard of these so-called masters," David complained. "Besides, it costs ninety-five. I can't afford that."

"I've got us covered. If we're there early to direct people and set up chairs, Sam the Shaman can get us in free. One of the rangers reserved a free campsite at Big Sur State Park. Man, you're either growing or dying. You in?"

David stared at the ceiling and finally said, "OK."

As the fire-red horizon announced the dawn, Carlo's wood-paneled station wagon crawled toward Big Sur in Los Angeles traffic. During the stop-and-go, David looked at men in business suits, alone, driving to work. He thought of his father and then of T. S. Eliot's "The Hollow Men."

> We are the hollow men
> We are the stuffed men
> Leaning together
> Headpiece filled with straw.

David thought about how he could make a living and still be an authentic person. He considered his recent job interviews with Fortune 500 corporations. David wondered if he should go into debt to go on to graduate school. David loved to research, write, and teach. *How would I pay for grad school? How would I get the money to live? Why bother, I'll probably either be drafted or forced to leave the country. Carlo is right. This workshop will help clarify my future.*

After the tedious drive through Los Angeles, they were headed north on Highway 101, speeding to 70 miles per hour in Carlo's woodie. Buildings disappeared. The vast Pacific Ocean lapped against the highway and crashing waves caught the bright sunlight. When they reached Ventura, they stopped for a huge breakfast in a diner that overlooked the ocean. They stuffed themselves with fruit, oatmeal, four eggs, four pieces of toast, four pieces of sausage, and a large mound of home-fried potatoes.

Driving through Santa Barbara, they listened to Brazil 66, Simon and Garfunkel, and the Beatles. Carlo rolled down the windows to smell the live oak, olive trees, and endless farmland that made California the nation's leading food grower. Traveling the central coast they passed Spanish missions where simple natives had converted to Catholicism, sometimes inspired by a soldier's saber. As they passed Hearst Castle, they debated the greatness of *Citizen Kane* and discussed the symbolism of "rosebud" in the movie. They shared dreams of their future and the black cloud of uncertainty brought by Vietnam. Carlo detailed nights of hot sex and David talked of relationships that might have been.

As they reached Big Sur, wispy clouds splashed over jagged cliffs that jutted hundreds of feet into the ocean. On the green mountains, giant redwoods reached for the heavens. Reaching their state park campsite, they assembled their cots under the redwoods so that they would later sleep under the stars.

As they walked under the giant sequoias, Carlo talked about the beauty of the 300-foot trees. David paid careful attention to trail signs to ensure that they would not get lost. David reached a plaque that he read out loud, "Danger. This is the home of the mountain lion. If you encounter one, appear large and be prepared to fight." David exclaimed, "We can't camp here. They've got mountain lions!"

"Lighten up. This is a popular campground. You'll never see a mountain lion. They're afraid of people. They stay in the mountains hunting deer and squirrels."

"Then why the sign?"

"Lawyers. Everybody has lawyers. Animals have lawyers."

"OK, then why no signs about squirrels?"

"That's because squirrels never organize. They run every which way, like they're stoned. In fact, they eat so many acorns, they probably are stoned."

Mountain lions. David silently asked himself how he could pick a friend that constantly put him in danger. *When will I have normal friends? How about a normal life?*

They ascended the Loop Trail, leaving the dense forest of redwoods for a rich diversity of evergreens, manzanita, and oak. Carlo effused about the beauty of the trees, meandering creeks, and wildflowers that splashed their yellows, oranges and purples. David walked carefully, reading warning signs about staying on the trail, water rationing, first aid tips, poison ivy, and rattlesnakes. *Rattlesnakes!*

After ninety minutes of climbing to the mountain peak, they were rewarded with views of the immense ocean.

"Awesome!" David said. "It's worth the steep climb, and the risk of animal attacks to see this."

"Thanks to me, you'll have fantastic stories to tell your grandkids."

"Thanks to me, you'll live to see your next birthday."

David and Carlo perched 800 feet over the ocean at the restaurant Nepenthe. Their outdoor table provided a panoramic view of the forested hills and the sweeping blue ocean. Carlo smiled and stretched like a lion enjoying the sun. David straightened the table arrangement, putting forks and spoons in the correct order.

"Crab legs in a spicy marinara sauce. What an appetizer!" Carlo announced with excitement.

David looked at the extravagant price and winced. Since Carlo had made the trip happen and because he often paid, David was determined to pay for the lunch and be a gentleman about it. "Sounds good," David tried to sound positive.

Soon after ordering, their smiling waitress breezed back and served the plate of crab legs. "Allow me," Carlo declared. He expertly used the oversized nutcracker to break the claw. He dipped his first bite into the sauce and savored the experience. "*Molto bene*. Almost as good as my grandmother's marinara." Carlo crossed himself. "May she live to dance on her one-hundredth birthday."

David watched in amusement. "I forgot you're Catholic."

"Still," Carlo shrugged. "I've been on probation since the second grade. I think I'm too far down the Pope's list of the damned to be excommunicated." As he was reaching for his second morsel, Carlo's head turned, mesmerized with a beautiful waitress walking by. "What a fox!"

David turned, admired, and agreed, "Totally."

After lingering stares and sighs, the two looked back to their plates and were stunned to see the crab legs gone. David had not enjoyed a single bite. Two large Steller's Jays were hoping away with the stolen epicurean rarities. "Damn!" Carlo and David leaped to their feet and chased the avian thieves who split in two directions.

David's bird, holding a crab leg, struggled to fly, but its bounty was too heavy. An angry David lunged at the evil bird that stole the morsels that required two hours of pay. *Not even a bite!* David almost grabbed the bird, but the jay, reward in beak, descended to the ground below and beyond the guard railing.

There was a loud crash as Carlo, in single-minded pursuit of the avian thief, ran into the beautiful waitress. Her tray of drinks spilled. Glasses broke, scattering their fragments. A heavy fall was heard as Carlo hit the stone walkway. Carlo screamed in agony.

As a lifeguard trained in advanced first aid, David checked Carlo's bruised and swollen left arm. David probed; Carlo screamed. The elbow was bruised but not broken. A minute later, Carlo's arm was in a sling that David had cleverly crafted from Carlo's tie-dye bandana.

They returned to their table to share Portobello mushroom, grilled vegetables, and chicken. Carlo feasted as if life was to be fully enjoyed. David ate, struggling to enjoy the food, wondering if there would be a four-hundred-dollar charge for all the spilled drinks and shattered glasses. "How did you run into her?"

"Hey, that jay was better than any football running back. He had unbelievable head fakes and direction changes."

They avoided alcohol, wanting to have mental clarity for the yoga and meditation. They could not, however, resist a massive dessert entitled Death by Chocolate. David paid the bill, which mercifully included no charge for broken glass.

Carlo's shirt displayed juices, sauces, chocolate, and a couple of places where he had wiped his nose and face. David's shirt was still clean. David joked, "Dig this, your shirt looks like a Jackson Pollock. Big Sur is loaded with art galleries. I bet you could sell it."

Carlo changed shirts, wincing as he moved his arm in and out of the sling, and then walked with his food-collage t-shirt across the street to an art gallery. Five minutes later he returned to the woodie. "She wouldn't buy it, but offered to sell it on spec. I left her the shirt, my   address, and phone."

They turned off Coast Highway at the workshop yin-yang sign and followed the dirt road that wandered through the two-acre complex. The workshop venue was a massive home poised on a two-hundred-foot cliff over the ocean, surrounded with redwoods and eucalyptus. People were walking around the greenhouse, the guest yurts, and the hot tub.

Sam the Shaman welcomed the two. Carlo thanked Sam for the gig and free admission. Carlo and David started greeting arriving guests and escorting them to outdoors chairs, facing the ocean.

Guests seated, the Shaman rhapsodize about what the masters would teach during the two days. Sam introduced Master Wu Chin who would teach tai chi. Master Chin, moving like someone aged half of his eighty years, demonstrated a series of movements that looked like karate in slow motion and explained, "Tai chi brings health, flexibility, and balance. Chi is energy. Chi is breath."

Following his directions, the attendees walked onto the lawn and spread apart.

Chin said, "See beauty of ocean. Free mind of thought. Please follow."

The group followed his slow step, weight shift, and arm movement.

"Slow inhales and exhales."

The rhythm of the waves, the deep breathing, and the moving meditation calmed David, as his mind emptied of worries about money and rattlesnakes. Tai chi was followed by a break where people walked the lawns and gardens talking, admiring the landscape, and smelling the fragrances of flowers and trees.

With a vast smile, Sam held up the gong and introduced Coretta Jefferson who would facilitate the next session. Coretta stood tall with full Afro hair and a flowing African green dashiki. Coretta asked people to volunteer why they had come to the workshop. Some couples wanted better communication. A man in his forties, going through the divorce of a loveless marriage, wanted to rediscover passion. A retired couple wanted to discover what they were missing by not being hippies. Carlo wanted to be less stressed. David wanted to understand himself and decide what to do with his life.

For the next session, Sam introduced Alan Watts. David had read five of his books; *The Way of Zen* three times. David wanted to experience his oneness with the universe.

Something in the serene face of Watts showed wisdom far beyond his forty-something years, as he carefully looked at each in the room. Watts held David's stare for a few seconds. There was a connection and an understanding. Yet, something was missing. Wearing the simple brown robe of a novice monk, Watts did not match David's vague expectation of an enlightened guru wearing a white flowing robe. More disconcerting, Watts was smoking a thin cigar and carrying a can of Coca Cola.

Coca Cola? Zen master? No way. Next, we'd be seeing sponsors logos on the back of monk robes and slogans like "Taste Enlightenment with the sugar-free Satori at McDonalds."

Watts sat comfortably on the floor, but not in a half lotus. He lead a meditation where everyone took long inhales followed by exhales, emulating the sound of crashing waves. David slowly emptied of thought, only experiencing the breaking waves. He was part of the ebb and flow of life, like a wave that can be visualized as separate, yet is inseparable from the vast ocean.

An ancient gong was struck and a break announced. David

walked outside to lay on the lawn surrounded with flowers. Lying on his back, he looked at the blue sky and carefree clouds. He shut his eyes and spent a few minutes experiencing his breathing.

Something was on his nose. He opened his eyes to face a large bumblebee perched on his proboscis. As David startled, the bee stung him and flew away. The pain was piercing, his nose swelled, and tears ran down his face. The pain grew as his nose enlarged until he morphed into a Zen novice who looked like W. C. Fields.

Hearing the gong, as he walked inside, first one woman came to him then another. "Congratulations. You experienced a breakthrough! You're openly crying."

During the break for dinner, David saw her, hesitated, controlled his breathing, and then walked behind Linda in the buffet line, saying nothing. Plates full, as she turned to scan the lawn for a place to sit, they made eye contact. David said, "Hello, Linda. We met briefly in Laguna. I'm David."

Linda smiled. "Good to see you again."

"Would you like to sit together?"

"Sure."

"Far out. How about over there?" David pointed to a spot near cliff's edge with a panoramic view of the ocean. Seated, evoking Zen, David toasted, "To being one," he paused, "with dinner."

Linda laughed. In toasting, they touched their cups of water together.

David said, "I'm into this workshop. I feel more centered, calm, and aware."

"Me too. This is such a lovely escape from the intensity of

Berkeley tests, papers, rallies, and protests."

"Right. Berkeley." David remembered. "I think you and I are both graduating this June."

"Congratulations, almost, to both of us. If I remember, you're leaving UCI just as I start grad work there."

"Right. You plan to be a teacher, don't you?"

"Yeah. This summer, I'll take a couple of teaching credential courses while I work part time at a Montessori school in Laguna."

"Tell me about Montessori."

"I'll know a lot more after working there. Children are respected and given the opportunity for self-directed play and learning, instead of being seated in rows, with rigid rules and rote learning."

"I can dig it. It's great you want to work with kids. You seem to be warm and caring." David blushed.

Linda smiled. "I am. I care. I'm excited about teaching." They drifted into silence, looking at the ocean, and devouring dinner before the break would end. Linda asked, "So what's next for you?"

"I've been interviewing with big computer companies like IBM, Digital Equipment, and Burroughs. That's one reason my hair's short and my beard is gone."

Linda grew more interested and attentive. "You had a beard?"

"Yeah. I'd sit in class and wisely stroke my beard. Now it's in with the job interviews and out with the beard. Plus, I'm lifeguarding at the beach in San Clemente and they are strict about being clean shaven and having short hair."

They dined and shared reflections of their past and dreams of their future.

Linda said, "We'll be nearby, with you in San Clemente and me in Laguna."

David looked at Linda's lovely face, warm smile, and turquoise eyes. He felt nervous. David said, "Linda, I like what you're into. Could we trade phone numbers?"

Linda said, "Definitely. Do you have anything to write with?"

David pointed. "The registration desk." They walked close together, occasionally brushing against each other.

At the table, after Linda had written her name and Berkeley phone, she said, "This summer, I live with Rachel. I can also write her Laguna phone number if you make a promise."

"Sure. What is it?"

"Only you see the number. Sorry, she wouldn't want your friend to have it. He's come on too strong. Sorry." Linda shrugged.

"Agreed. Write Rachel's number and it will be our secret. Carlo's harmless. He's just enthusiastic about everything and talks before he thinks." David paused. "I'm confused. I thought her name was also Linda."

"That makes another secret we need to share." Linda held a finger up to her lips, indicating a need for silence.

David smiled, temporarily lost in looking at her. They exchanged paper scraps with names and numbers. It was difficult to reach someone in 1969, especially if you weren't sure of her name and if the phone number she gave was that of the local police department.

After a day of lectures, discussions, tai chi, yoga, chanting and meditation, everyone was surprised with two Brazilian dancers who emerged playing drums. Without introduction, without words, they played, danced, and smiled. They waved people to join. A few went forward, with Carlo being among the first to dance as the pastels of post-sunset faded in the twilight.

Carlo was attracted to the tall dark brunette who swayed with the bossa nova while watching the dancers. Carlo caught her eye; she smiled, did a subtle double take, and then looked away. Carlo walked up to the tall brunette and said, "Isn't this fantastic to be dancing while taking in the panoramic beauty of the ocean?"

"Yes," Rachel replied as she looked out to sea to avoid eye contact.

"Have we met before?" Carlo asked.

"Yes, very briefly in Laguna a couple of months ago," she replied as she turned to make eye contact.

Carlo remembered. He smiled and then laughed. "You're Linda. I had an interesting conversation with the police department."

Rachel took a deep breath. "Sorry, but you came on too strong, following me to the restroom. Sorry I brushed you off in Laguna, but I really had to pee," she said with a laugh.

"I understand, and I apologize. Linda, I'll respect your privacy at this workshop." With the hint of a chivalrous bow, Carlo smiled and started to walk away.

Disarmed, she called, "No need to leave. Please, I forgot your name."

"Carlo. Carlo Abruzzo."

"Carlo, I must make a confession. My real name is Rachel. Things happened so fast at the restaurant, I didn't want you to know my real name. There is the real Linda." Rachel nodded in the direction of her friend, who was talking with a couple.

The music stopped. The Shaman announced, "We are

finished for today. You're all invited to enjoy the hot tub outside." He paused and grinned. "Clothing is optional."

Carlo said, "The yoga earlier was so calming, so centering. It's a groovy evening. Are you going in the hot tub?"

"Goodness, no. People will be naked." She looked at the bulge in Carlo's pants and commented with a matter-of-fact tone, "Before you get in that tub naked, you may need the calming of more yoga." She walked away. Slowly the blood left Carlo's erection and filled his face with a bright red.

Minutes later, after recovering from the rejection, Carlo headed to the hot tub, removed all clothes, and then submerged into the steamy waters. David hesitated, feeling uncomfortable getting naked in front of strangers. He slowly undressed in a dark corner and then quickly got into the tub. An elderly couple started undressing. The man looked like Santa Claus with his flowing white beard and cherub face. His wife looked like Mrs. Claus.

The tub was soon packed. David was squeezed against naked Carlo on one side and naked Kris Kringle on the other. Nervous about touching naked men, David focused his mind on the day's lessons of feeling one with his breath and not being one with Santa. Just as David started to relax and enjoy the early stars in the clear night, Mr. and Mrs. Claus started joking about getting naughty and nice.

Back at their campsite, David and Carlo said good night and got into their respective sleeping bags. Carlo looked up through the majestic three-hundred-foot redwoods mesmerized with the Milky Way. David alertly watched for mountain lions and rattlesnakes. Soon, Carlo was snoring. David sought silence and threw his sleeping bag inside the back of Carlo's woodie. David pushed the omnipresent surf boards aside, stretched out in his bag, and eventually slept.

At three a.m., David bolted awake. Carlo was removing the surfboards and getting in the back of the station wagon with his sleeping bag. David whined, "What are you doing? There's not room for two in here."

"Fine, then you can get out of my wagon and sleep in the rain."

"It's raining?" David whined.

Carlo squeezed into his sleeping bag in the back of the wagon, jamming the two together. David complained. Carlo snapped. They twisted and squirmed, since one could not turn without bumping the other. Sleep quickly returned to Carlo, while David slowly returned to a fitful sleep.

The morning sun pierced through the towering redwoods as David waited nervously at the entrance of Julia Pfeiffer State Park. After a few minutes, Linda pulled up in her VW Beetle, bumper covered with flowers, peace sign, and anti-war stickers. She waved and parked. David crossed the Coast Highway to her, paused, and then awkwardly hugged her.

As they descended the makeshift trailhead, David extended his hand to help her down a steep and slippery section. Linda took his hand and welcomed his strength as they descended. As they walked toward the ocean along the 200-foot cliff, thin fog splashed against the cliff like breaking waves. Below, surf collided with massive rocks in loud percussion. Sunlight parted the remaining fog, unveiling the panorama of the endless Pacific.

"What a beautiful spot," David declared.

"So, you've never been here?" Linda asked.

"Never."

"The best is yet to come in a quarter mile."

Linda stopped at a view spot and looked at the horizon. David stopped next to her, letting their bodies touch. Linda smiled at David and then pointed across the cove. Out of the tree-covered cliff, a waterfall freely poured itself into a turquoise tide pool landscaped with rocks. The tide pool stretched into the vast Pacific illuminated with waves reflecting the sunlight.

"Amazing!" David exclaimed. Impulsively, he leaned toward Linda until their lips were inches apart. He hesitated, and then shyly backed away.

Linda gave David an inviting look. "You want to sit on that bench and take this in?"

"Cool."

After a few minutes of comfortable silence, David said, "I'd admire your plans to work with kids at Montessori. How did you get interested in teaching?"

"Good question. I've always loved kids, even when I was one. I started babysitting back in Cleveland when I was only twelve."

"Young. What was it like for you growing up in Cleveland?"

"Like right out of Ozzie and Harriet. Family, friends, picnics, ball games, school, Girl Scouts. Not in my wildest dreams was I prepared for Berkeley protests, smoking dope, and being followed by the FBI."

"Followed by the FBI?"

"Yes," Linda replied matter-of-factly. "Brad, the guy I'm seeing, is a leader with the SDS. I've gone with him to lots of anti-war protests and rallies. Nixon and Reagan have decided that we're a bunch of commies. Brad even knows the names of some of the FBI agents. It's really creepy."

"You don't look like a threat to the American way of life."

"I'm not. I'm this sweet girl from Ohio, who wants to teach kids and raise my own in a little house with a picket fence."

"Will those kids be with you and Brad?"

"No. When we graduate in June, he moves to New York for law school, and I move to Laguna. This summer, I'll be a free woman." Linda blushed and then looked over at David who was looking at the waterfall.

There was a lull in the surf and minutes of silence between the two.

Linda broke the silence by asking, "So what about your growing up and your family?"

David's entire body tensed. "I was born in San Diego. Unfortunately, when I was five, my mom died in a car accident. I barely remember her."

"I'm so sorry."

"Thanks. My dad is a career naval officer. When I was a kid, my grandparents raised me. Seventh through twelfth grades I went to military school."

"Wow." Linda tried to sound neutral. "What was that like?"

"Not as bad as it sounds. I had some great friends. It was in Carlsbad, near good surfing," David said. "In case you're wondering, I respect your protesting the war. Vietnam is a big mistake. I don't want to go."

Linda relaxed. "I'm glad to hear it. You seem like too nice a guy to get killed."

"My dad had it all lined up for me to go to the Naval Academy. He was pissed when I told him that I didn't want to be career naval. He had four-star dreams for me."

Linda reflected, "He was angry that you weren't going to live out his dreams. What are you going to do?"

"Good question. Everybody's got different advice. When my student deferment ends, I could flunk the physical, get a lawyer, enlist, wait, or go to Canada. Who knows?"

"Let's hope we can end this insane war before you have to decide," Linda said. "My brother John is over there right now, flying a helicopter. I worry about him every day. Sometimes I cry."

David looked at her wet eyes, put his arm around her, and they sat over the ocean as the sunlight struggled with returning fog.

When David and Linda reached the workshop, people mixed and talked with a new openness, benefitting from their bond of sharing feelings, yoga, meditation, dancing, and for some, being naked in a hot tub under the stars. This Wednesday, Master Chin led the group through a longer series of Tai Chi. David felt fluid.

A new teacher, Suzuki-San, explained that to be free of suffering one must be free of attachment and desire. Suzuki-San explained the Four Noble Truths of Buddhism. With stories and poetry he outlined the way of Zen. He asked, "Where is the fist when you open your hand." Language was shown to be confusing, such as "fist" implying a permanent object. "All is change." People were invited to let go of attachment.

David visualized himself not separate from life, but part of life. Looking past the cliff to the horizon, he considered himself as a wave on the ocean. Looking at the ocean, he experienced his breath while he let go of thought.

David joined Carlo in arranging the living room for the next session. This night there would be no chairs. A circle of singing bowls was created with one bowl and one wooden mallet for each person. The group was invited into the living room to be seated in front of the bowls. Suzuki-San held a twelve-inch bowl across in his left hand. The bowl was ancient, made from metal alloy, and rich with intricate inlays. Suzuki-San held a mallet in his right hand, pressed it against the bowl, and then slowly circled the mallet around the bowl's edge. A calming harmonic filled the room. Suzuki-San invited all to lift their bowls and mallets and make the bowl "sing."

David was skeptical and could produce no sound. Linda experimented and soon had her bowl singing. Suzuki-San slowly moved around the room helping participants correctly hold and move the mallet. With help, David was smiling as his bowl finally produced sonorous vibrations. Water was added to some bowls to change their sound until the room sounded like a Buddhist monastery.

A woman across the room broke with tradition and put her bowl on her head, then circled her bowl with her mallet creating a new harmonic. Carlo was inspired and turned his bowl on his head, having forgotten that his was half-full of water that showered his body as he donned the bowl. People laughed long and loud. Rachel laughed without restraint. David was doubled over with laughter until his stomach hurt and tears flowed freely.

Carlo, now the center of attention, smiled like the village idiot and started banging his bowl with the mallet. Five others, inspired by Carlo, put bowls on their heads and started banging and engaging in a modified Indian war dance. Suzuki-San looked shocked. He turned to Sam the Shaman and said, "Sometimes there is a fine line between enlightenment and insanity."

"Totally insane, man," Sam said. "Totally fucking insane."

David and Carlo returned for their final night of camping. David lit a joint and inhaled. He wanted to extend his state of grace and feeling of connection with life. Carlo took three hits and five aspirin in a desperate attempt to subdue his headache.

David braved the outdoors. Nestled in his sleeping bag, David thought of his conversation with Linda, her warmth, and how he could talk with her.

He looked up at the towering redwoods, some over two thousand years old, alive when Christ was born. He looked beyond the treetops to the Milky Way and realized that he was looking back in time at galaxies so ancient that their light had taken a billion years to reach him. Creation was a wonder without end. All is one. David slept peacefully.

4

People's Park

April was not the cruelest month. In April, from dormant roots, life flourished. From spring rain, lilacs bloomed in the dooryard. May would be Linda's cruelest month as she witnessed innocents maimed and murdered, then confronted the bitter choice of either betraying friends or facing years in prison.

In May, spiritually awake from the Big Sur workshop, Linda helped her friends create People's Park. Students looked at a barren vacant lot that occupied a city block, three streets distant from the UC Berkeley campus, and envisioned transforming the dusty eyesore lot into a park and with it a metaphor and a test-site for a bright-green future of social equity. Donations were secured for rolled turf, a medley of trees, and playground equipment. For a week, the volunteers carried and planted until their backs were sore and their arms ached, and on the seventh day they rested.

Days after completion, Linda and Alicia were strolling through the new People's Park. Both were barefoot, wearing sleeveless summer dresses, with Alicia's short dress ending twelve inches above her knees. Linda wore a headband with plastic flowers around her long dark wavy hair. Everywhere people were smiling and laughing. Students became jugglers, acrobats, and storytellers. Around a Maypole, they danced and sang, as peace signs dangled from beaded necklaces over tie-dye shirts, Indian blouses, and bare breasts. Frisbees sailed and dogs caught them in mid-air.

Linda was proud of the park she had helped to create.

Sheltered under oak and evergreens, enjoying free food, were people for whom the park was now their only home. On the vast lawn, groups of youth were in circles singing, playing guitars and other instruments. Families picnicked. Children ran freely. The aromas of Mexican food and Indian spices mixed with evergreens and gardenias.

"Would you like to know one of my secrets?" Linda asked.

Alicia turned to face Linda. "Tell me!"

"Growing up back in Cleveland Heights," Linda lightly laughed with a hint of embarrassment, "I was known as Little Miss Sunshine."

"I love it."

"In autumn, I'd roll in leaves of red and yellow," Linda said. "In winter, I'd fall backwards into the snow and make an angel. In spring, I'd skip down flowered roads like Dorothy in the Wizard of Oz. On hot summer days, I'd run through the sprinklers."

"That is so you. Happy as a Hallmark card."

"When I was a girl, I loved my collection of Little Miss illustrated books," Linda said. "Little Miss Giggles, Little Miss Tidy, Little Miss Helpful. My favorite was Sunshine. My mom would read them to me at bedtime and we'd talk about the pictures and people on each page."

"A sweet memory."

"In two months, I'll be reading books to kids and helping them learn to read."

"That's right, you've got that job lined up in Laguna."

"For sure. I'll be an aide at a Montessori school."

"So what's that about?" Alicia asked.

"I'll be working with preschoolers through second graders. The Montessori approach encourages self-directed learning, using all five senses, great learning principles."

"You're giving great vibes. I can see that you are excited about teaching."

At the anti-war rally at UC Berkeley, over two thousand were chanting, "One, two, three, four, Tricky Dick, stop the war." Brad walked to the microphone, wearing a peace sign T-shirt, bell-bottom jeans, sandals, and a frayed leather jacket. He looked at the crowd, then said, "'All men are created equal. They are endowed by their Creator with certain inalienable rights; among these are Life, Liberty, and the pursuit of Happiness.' That quotation is from the 1945 Vietnamese Declaration of Independence. It's there, man, because Ho Chi Minh revered Thomas Jefferson. The US promised to support their independence. Instead we and other colonialists divided the country in two. Like all freedom-loving people, they want their country back. They want to live in their homes in peace and raise their children. We want to burn their villages and murder their children! This war must be stopped today!"

The crowd chanted "No more war! No more war! No more war!"

Brad patiently waited for the chanting crowd to let him continue. "The president and the Congress have totally lost touch. They don't represent the people of the United States. They don't represent us. They've attacked our most fundamental liberties of freedom of speech. They have attacked our basic right to life, liberty and the pursuit of happiness." He paused as the crowd roared. "We must never forget that this nation was born of a revolution against tyranny. We must never forget our own Declaration of Independence that states 'Governments are instituted among men, deriving their just powers from the consent of the governed.... Whenever any form of government becomes destructive of these ends, it is the right of the people to alter or abolish it, and to institute new government....'"

The crowd was on its feet, inspired and empowered. Now was the time for change. Now it was their time.

In the audience, recording Brad's every word were FBI agents Albert Heller and Stephen Gottlieb. Heller said, "Did you notice that the prick even looked at us. The whole SDS is a commie front." Brad was a leader in the Students for Democratic Society (SDS), an organization with over one hundred thousand U. S. members.

"What a load of crap about no freedom," Gottlieb said. "I fought in the war so that this little chicken shit can take a mike and say whatever comes out of his mouth."

"You mean whatever comes out of his ass," Heller replied.

"I hate that son of a bitch. His day is coming. Got it all on tape. He's a second-generation pinko. His father went to prison for being a commie. We've got to keep looking for evidence that young Bradley is in a communist cell."

The FBI had talked with over forty of Brad's friends, campus activists, professors, and university administrators. The FBI coordinated with local police detectives who asked about Brad when young men and women were arrested in Berkeley and showed a willingness to cooperate in exchange for a reduced sentence.

Brad was a radical leader and therefore assumed by the FBI to be part of a communist conspiracy to overthrow the government. Berkeley had been a personal priority for FBI Director J. Edgar Hoover ever since the 1964 Free Speech Movement. The Feds suspected Brad for the bombing of the Livermore National Laboratory where nuclear research was conducted for new energy and new weapons.

Brad knew that he was innocent; he also knew from his father that innocents get thrown into prisons. Brad assured friends and family that he took no part in the bombing. When friends asked Brad if he knew who bombed the ROTC building, Brad said nothing. Not one word.

Although many parents were dismayed at their children being left-wing activists, Brad's parents were proud of him. Brad's father spent time in jail during the McCarthy era, rather than incriminate others. His dad hated Nixon for his role in coercing friends to betray friends in the Fifties.

"The old man never named names. We may have the same problem with young Bradley."

"We should squeeze his girlfriend," Heller said, referring to Linda. "Then Brad will sing."

"Good idea."

Linda Hope stumbled in the dark, as the pounding on the door grew louder. Her bare foot kicked an unseen box. She hobbled in pain and opened the door.

"The pigs have seized People's Park!" Jeff said. "They're putting up a fence. Get everyone you know to the park. We're racing the clock."

"Slow down, man. What time is it?"

"It's 4:52 in the morning."

"4:52! That doesn't count as morning. It's the middle of the night!"

"Exactly. They struck while we were sleeping. Get everyone. We've got to stop this."

Linda shook Brad out of a deep sleep. They dressed quickly, both throwing on T-shirts, jeans, and tennis shoes. Linda added a sweatshirt. She quickly discouraged of trying to comb the chaos out of her long wavy hair. She was glad that makeup was out of fashion, because she had time for none. They raced out the door. Linda stopped, went back into Brad's apartment, and grabbed two gas masks.

As they walked through their neighborhood streets, darkness gave way to pre-dawn light. Linda was starting to awaken. As they walked down Telegraph Avenue, dozens of students swelled to hundreds. Cars had trouble moving as masses of students spilled off the sidewalks and onto the wide avenue. By the time that Brad and Linda neared People's Park on that May 15, Highway Patrol, sheriffs and Berkeley police had invaded the park, chased out the street people, bulldozed away all the grass and flowers. The work of Linda and hundreds was destroyed. The police had cleared an eight-block perimeter and erected a chain-link fence around the park. All law enforcement wore helmets and pistols. Some were holding truncheons, others, rifles.

"They destroyed it!" Linda said as she looked past the police barricade, to see the tall chain-link fence erected around the former park. No Trespassing signs were posted.

"This is betrayal," Brad said. "The University administration promised more meetings with us." As SDS leaders, Brad and Jeff had been part of negotiations about the university owned lot that students had transformed into People's Park.

"It's not the university. It's not Chancellor Heyns. It's Reagan!" Jeff said.

Attacking the anti-war and anti-establishment student protests at Berkeley had helped Ronald Reagan to be elected governor. He had called Berkeley, "a haven for communist sympathizers, protesters, and sex deviants."

"Reagan thinks that the only good Red is a dead Red," Brad said.

"Let's go to Sproul Plaza. With this blockade, that's where people will be," Brad said. He, Linda, and Jeff turned and walked blocks through the crowds up Telegraph Avenue. Their determined walk gave way to hunger. Aromas from a bakery enticed. They devoured a medley of rolls accompanied with much needed caffeine.

As they walked, the sun rose over the Berkeley hills. Arrows of light hit the driving commuters, pedestrians walking purposely to work, and students drifting to campus, some in animated discussion, and others, like Linda, dispirited in their silent walking.

They joined others at Sproul Plaza, an area large enough for thousands. Sproul had long been a place of gathering, where anyone could use the open microphone to speak of civil rights and free speech, poverty and politics, philosophy and poetry.

The crowd joined in song, when a woman at the mike with a guitar poignantly sang, "Where Have All the Flowers Gone," by Pete Seeger.

Student Body President Dan Siegel spoke of freedom, of how a useless dirt lot had been transformed into a beautiful park, and about being compassionate for the street people. But when he shouted, "Let's take the park," the microphone went dead. A police officer had turned off the sound system.

The dead microphone did not stop Brad, Linda and Jeff from chanting, "We want the park!" The crowd joined the chant.

Thousands of students poured out of Sproul and marched down Telegraph Avenue chanting, "We want the park." Linda felt herself carried along with the masses. She frantically looked around. Brad and Jeff were   gone.

The student demonstration was expected. Governor Reagan, through his Chief of Staff Ed Meese, had mobilized almost eight hundred Alameda County Sheriffs, California Highway Patrol, local police and deputies.

Linda walked with the masses down Telegraph. She stared at the police, sheriffs and patrol in their full riot gear, wearing helmets with gas masks, shields, and armed with an arsenal of weapons including tear gas, pistols, and shotguns. Locked and loaded, the armed police lined both sides of Telegraph Avenue, block after block. Linda recalled 1967, when she and other protestors tried to shut down the Army Induction Center in Oakland. They were stopped with swinging clubs and fallen bodies. As she remembered the tear gas searing her eyes and lungs, she put on her gas mask. This felt worse than Oakland.

Without warning, the police on Telegraph started firing tear gas. Linda held her ground with a thousand others, while most students ran in terror. Some protesters threw rocks and bottles. Sheriffs fired shotguns. To her left, a girl was being relentlessly clubbed by a cop. Ahead was a boy on the ground, shirt red, crawling on the bloody asphalt. A woman was curled into a ball on the road, screaming.

Dozens fell wounded, dropping into pools of their own blood. Many of the eight hundred police, sheriffs, and highway patrol were Vietnam veterans. The war was not over.

There was another round of gunfire. Linda saw Jeff fall. She weaved through the thinning crowd to help her friend, bleeding but still breathing. She looked up and saw a sheriff lower his shotgun, pointing it directly at her. Like the soccer star she had been in high school, she reacted immediately, rolling sideways, turning, and running away in a weaving pattern. She escaped down a dark alley, escaping the shooting, crowds, and noise.

Walking lonely side streets, she felt sadness and helpless rage. She looked at herself. Her sweatshirt was splattered with blood. She wondered if Jeff was alive. She wondered if Brad was alive. *Where did this madness come from? Everything was peaceful yesterday. The park was beautiful.* In her mind, she could hear Paul McCartney singing "Yesterday."

When Linda reached her apartment, she realized that her purse and keys were at Brad's. She knocked on the door. No answer. She crawled through an open window and into her place. She phoned Brad, but no one answered. She searched and found Jeff's number. No answer.

Her heart was still racing. She was soaked with perspiration. Mouth dry, she went to the kitchen to pour a glass of water. Her skin was clammy. *I think I'm going into shock!*

Linda gulped the water, warily walked to her room, crawled under a blanket and collapsed.

Hours later, Linda awakened to the sound of the apartment door being unlocked. Brad walked into her room and asked, "Are you all right?"

Linda slowly straightened to sit on the edge of the bed.

"Wow. You look pale," Brad said.

"I'm not feeling great. Could you get me a glass of water?"

Brad returned with the water and watched her quickly empty the glass. He brought another.

"Thanks, sweetheart," Linda said. "You OK?"

"Yeah, I'm fine. I didn't see you anywhere, especially after the tear gas. With the shotguns blasting, I split and went back to Sproul through backstreets. Someone told me that Jeff's in the hospital."

"The pigs got him with a shotgun. I tried to go to him, then saw a cop point the shotgun at me. I'm amazed I'm alive."

"What happened?"

"Our training and time at Oakland Induction paid off," Linda said. "I rolled and weaved through the crowd. Cops beating people everywhere. Thought the pigs had me trapped. Finally, I spotted an opening to an alley. I got out. I'm alive. I think."

For a long time, Brad and Linda held each other.

"I'm glad you're OK," Linda said. "When I got here, my pulse was so fast and my throat so dry, I worried about going into shock. I must have slept hours."

"I'm going to look for Jeff and then to an organizing meeting. We can't let them stop the Park. Want to go with me?" Brad asked.

"I think I'm too freaked to hit the streets until class tomorrow. I need to cleanup and get it together. Take her," Linda said as she handed Brad her Raggedy-Ann doll. "Right now, she's got more energy than me and looks better."

Brad gave Linda a weary smile.

"Call me if you find Jeff."

After Brad left, Linda showered and put on fresh clothes. Spot remover failed to eradicate the blood on her sweatshirt. She felt on the edge of an emotional meltdown. She had a bowl of chicken soup.

She could not stop thinking about the clubbing, the chaos, the shootings, how surreal it looked through the dirty lens of a war-surplus gas mask, and how she had felt like an animal trapped for slaughter. She felt guilty about not helping Jeff and not leaving with Brad to search for him.

Normally comfortable with chaos, she could not tolerate the disarray of the room. She vacuumed her apartment, undoing the mess of her roommates. She scrubbed the kitchen and bathroom until her home was antiseptically clean. Everything was in its place - furniture bought at the Goodwill store, stacks of books, and wildflowers brought back from hikes. Posters of Jim Morrison, the Beatles, and Jimi Hendrix mixed with Botticelli, Monet and Renoir.

She sipped a cup of chamomile tea and looked out the window to the world of Berkeley. Past the iconic Campanile, fluffy white clouds floated in the clear blue sky. Linda thought of civil rights marches and Martin Luther King now lying dead. She thought of endless anti-war rallies and the thousands dead in Vietnam. *Was it doing any good?*

For the first time, she did not feel remorse about leaving Berkeley in a few weeks. She wanted to graduate, say the inevitable goodbye to Brad, see her folks in Ohio, and move to Southern California. She was ready for teaching and field trips to tide pools and decorating for the holidays. She put on Simon and Garfunkel's *Bookends* album.

Linda finally settled in for a couple of hours of study, as shadows of the late afternoon stretched across the floor. Midterms were coming, and she took comfort that she would now have little time for marches and rallies.

As darkness descended, Linda turned on the small black-and-white TV. Berkeley had made the national news, with the police riot labeled Bloody Thursday. One hundred and twenty students were reported as seriously injured. A few were sequestered in hospitals in critical condition from shotgun wounds. Actual injuries were much higher; most injured students were afraid that if they sought medical attention it would lead to their arrest. After commercials about families excited about their new cars and women their new clothes and men finally achieving sought after approval by drinking beer, the news continued with the war count of over 40,000 U. S. soldiers who had died in Vietnam, over 300,000 injured, and over 500,000 Vietnamese killed or burned with napalm. Linda screamed at the TV and unplugged it.

She walked to the mailbox and returned with a letter in her shaking hand. It was from an army hospital in Tokyo. The letter from her younger brother, read:

> Dear Linda,
> Looks like I'll be home in Ohio before you. I'm already a little closer as I write from my hospital bed in Tokyo. The good news is that I'm alive after my chopper was shot down. The bad news is that I lost both my legs.
> I've been wearing my stubbies for a while. Sorry, I waited so many weeks to write, but I didn't want to upset you. I've been visiting different places - an ICU in Tuy Hoa, a real hospital in Saigon, and now Tokyo. I'll continue to get care at the VA in Cleveland. I'm already the best guy in a wheelchair on the basketball court.
> I should have never left school, but I'm going back with help from the GI Bill. I want to learn how to build prosthetics. In future years, I hope to wear them.
> Whoopee. I'm getting a Bronze Star. I'm a big hero.
> I know you'll worry, but don't. Now I've got to write Mom and Dad. Mom will freak.
> Love ya,
> John

Slowly, Linda dropped the letter to the ground. She turned off the lights, curled up with her teddy bear, and thought of growing up with her younger brother. *John, remember how your friends were always at our place with their cars in our front drive? You'd turbocharge, fix flywheels, and lower the front. You were the expert, John, the car guy. I guess sometimes the boys came by to stare at my girlfriends, and me but it was really you. Dad was so proud when you rebuilt the family car engine. He took you to work and bragged about you. The army promised to make you a master mechanic. They lied. They wanted a body to fly a chopper for as long as he had a body. John, remember how you were nervous before school dance. I taught you the swing. You learned fast. You were a good dancer. You asked me how to talk with girls.* Linda stroked teddy's head. Her eyes were red and swollen. *I'm sorry that I picked on you when you were little. How we fought over the one bathroom sink. I'm so sorry for that time I beat you at one-on-one soccer and then called you a spaz. I called you a spaz! I'm so, so, so, so sorry!*

The next morning, Linda heard Brad's distinctive knocking on her front door. As she let him in, he looked at the dark circles under her eyes.

Brad asked, "How you doing?"

"Last night, I got a letter from my brother John. His chopper was shot down. He lost both legs. He was an athlete; now he's in a wheelchair. I taught him to dance. Who will date him now? How's he going to raise kids?"

"We've got to stop this insane war. Instead of ending it, they've expanded it to Cambodia and Laos," Brad said. "Now we've got over five hundred thousand like your brother over there. Over forty thousand dead. Three times that many wounded."

"Stop!" Linda shouted. "I wanted your sympathy, not your statistics. I'm hurting. I want you to care!"

"Sorry."

"I can't walk to campus with you this morning," Linda said. "I'm having trouble getting it together."

"I'm really sorry about your brother. I know you love him."

"I should've loved him better," Linda said. "But now I will!"

"Jeff's in intensive care. Cops at the hospital took one look at my beard and wouldn't let me in. I'll try again."

"I'll try, too. Sorry about my blow-up, Brad. I'm sorry about everything."

"I brought you something to cheer you up." Brad smiled as he gave her a box of chocolate-mint Girl Scout cookies.

After Brad left, Linda thought of their passion when they became lovers. It was months before she realized that he cared more about politics than her. Now, they were weeks from finals and saying goodbye. She played the Beatles' *Rubber Soul*.

On May 21, Brad and Linda joined thousands for a midday memorial for James Rector, who had been killed with a shotgun by one of the sheriffs. Unarmed, James had been watching the protest from a rooftop. James Rector was a student. Now he was dead.

After Bloody Thursday, after all the press about unarmed students being shot, and after the funeral of James Rector, Governor Reagan escalated the conflict by activating over 2,000 National Guard. Carrying loaded rifles with bayonets, they stood in army-green uniform, guarding the university buildings, the streets of Berkeley, and the fenced lot that had once been People's Park. Some of the guardsmen were also Cal students who had taken place in protests, before being ordered to report for duty. Many had joined the Guard in hopes of staying out of the war in Vietnam, only to now be at war with their friends.

For days, the streets of Berkeley were barricaded as National Guard helicopters sprayed tear gas whenever there were new attempts to gather in protest. Berkeley was under siege.

Reagan declared, "If there has to be a bloodbath, then let's get it over with." He banned public assemblies; to protect the United States Constitution, he banned Constitutional rights.

The next morning, Linda dressed in a gauzy Indian blouse, tiered cotton skirt, beaded headband, and put on her peace-sign necklace. She was deliberately looking at the world through her rose-colored hexagonal glasses. After a week of being depressed, she was determined to have her life back to normal. "All you need is love" was her new mantra.

Arms folded, she stared at the box of Girl Scout cookies. *Brad, you know I'm trying to lose seven pounds. Why did you give me these stupid cookies?* The last time that she had told Brad of her weight reduction goal, he said that only a strict ballet choreographer would want her to lose a pound. Staring at the cookies, she suddenly smiled with her flash of insight. She gift wrapped them, tied a ribbon, and attached a note. The gift would be a peace offering.

Barefoot and singing, she walked to campus.

To deliver her peace offering, she detoured before going to her sociology course. She walked into the National Guard Building with her present, a gift-wrapped box of cookies and a the note "Make Love Not War." The building signage showed that Colonel James Walker was in charge. At the front desk was a middle-aged woman, wearing a modest full-length dress.

Linda walked up to the woman who startled. Linda smiled. "Hello. This is for Colonel Walker."

The woman looked suspiciously at Linda, barefoot in her hippie attire. "May I give Colonel Walker your name?"

"No need. It's a peace offering." Linda smiled, placed the gift-wrapped package on the desk, turned and exited the building.

Linda walked less than two blocks before being seized by a policeman from behind. A squad car braked to a halt in front of her. Two more policemen were soon running toward her with hands on guns. Behind Linda the National Guard Building was quickly being emptied of all occupants. The police turned Linda against a parked car, slammed her body on the car and forced her legs to spread eagle. She was frisked, groped, and handcuffed. She was read her rights as one officer locked her in the back of the police car. Her crying was ignored. She was being taken to the police headquarters.

"We have the bomb suspect in custody and we are en route to the station," the officer announced through the radio.

Linda was shocked. This could not be happening to her. Shaking, she asked, "What are you guys talking about? I'm not involved with any bomb. I can barely light a candle."

The second officer turned to her with a hard stare, "You were positively identified as the woman who left the gift-wrapped bomb at the National Guard Office. You were identified as giving a woman a package and announcing that it was a bomb for Colonel Walker."

Linda could not believe the insanity of this. "It was Girl Scout cookies. I'll open the package and show you. I'll eat all of them and gain weight if you want."

The officer cut Linda's explanation short. "You stated that it was a bomb. You are being held while the bomb squad and FBI investigate."

FBI! Linda could not believe that giving away a box of Girl Scout cookies was ruining her life. She did not want them in the first place.

Linda heard herself demand, "I'm entitled to a phone call. I want to call the Girl Scouts."

Linda was put into a small dark room in the police station basement. In the clammy room that had not been ventilated in years, Linda turned an ashen gray. She shook.

She was interrogated about the package. She was grilled about what she said. With icy stares of disbelief, the investigator repeated his questions for over an hour. She repeated her answers.

When the police interrogation ended, it only got worse for Linda. FBI Agents Heller and Gottlieb entered the room. Linda recognized them. They had been stalking Brad for months. Albert Heller's face was sharp angles; his motion, mechanical. Linda had never seen eyes that cold. She tried to imagine that he had once been a small boy, but when she peered into his eyes, her imagination was of no help.

Gottlieb stared at Linda. His military stance and unsmiling face revealed nothing. Methodically, they interrogated Linda about what she said and did at the National Guard Office. She gave the same answers. They looked with the same disbelief.

Heller, with a voice that was flat and hard, asked, "Where did you get the bomb?"

"There's no bomb. Just open the box of cookies," Linda pleaded.

"Sure, and get blown up. You'd like that, wouldn't you, sweetheart?" Heller tore into her like a pit bull. "What about the bombing of the National Lab last year?"

"I don't know anything about that."

Gottlieb bared his teeth like a jackal. "You must know. Your boyfriend knows everything about it."

Linda looked at the jackal. She wanted to sound calm, but her voice quivered. She felt her body shaking. "I'm innocent. Brad's innocent."

"We've got all we need on him," Heller said. "You might as well keep yourself out of prison. We could arrange a suspended sentence for you in return for information about the bombing."

Linda was stunned. She knew they could see her shaking. She was nauseous from the stale, moldy air. She fought for control. She felt helplessness, then rage, and then screamed, "You assholes! You know those are cookies! That's why you're offering a deal. This is blackmail. You have no legal right to hold me. Release me now!"

The jackal leaned forward. His eyes narrowed as he stared into Linda. The pit bull leaned back, looking at Linda with a cruel smirk. Finally Heller stated, "You know, even if the package does contain cookies, I've got witnesses that will testify that you said it was a bomb. You could still go to prison."

5

Like Father, Unlike Son

David read the front-page article in the *New York Times*, "Raids in Cambodia by U. S. Unprotested." In secret, the war that Nixon promised to end had expanded into Cambodia and Laos. Strategic Air Command B-52s were being used in the secret bombing raids.

David thought of the B-52 in the movie *Dr. Strangelove* where the B-52 was carrying nuclear bombs. *Dad, what are you in the middle of?*

David caught her as she walked across campus. "Patricia, it's good to see you."

"Oh, David, you surprised me."

"I saw you walking and wanted to say hello."

"Hello."

David took a deep breath and continued, "I enjoyed seeing *Funny Girl* with you."

"Yes, Barbra deserved the Oscar. She has an incredible voice. It was sad at the end."

"Yeah, she deserved the Oscar." They walked the next fifty yards in silence. "*Romeo and Juliet* is playing at the Port. It's getting terrific reviews. Would you like to join me?"

Patricia looked at David and touched his arm. "Actually, I'd like to sit and talk for a minute."

"OK." They sat on a bench that overlooked the central park

of UCI.

"I think we should just be friends," Patricia said. "I know lots of people are into casual dating, but I'm looking for a relationship. You told me that you've never had one. Sorry."

David looked stunned. "I suppose you're right. I appreciate your honesty."

"You're a sweet guy. I'll see you in class. Thanks for being understanding."

"Sure."

Patricia started to stand, then hesitated and asked, "David, can I ask you a personal question?"

David felt threatened. "OK."

"You keep asking me to movies about love. Do you know what love is?"

David's face turned red. He looked at Patricia and shrugged. She slowly stood, touched his shoulder, and walked away.

Long after Patricia was gone and after the sun set behind the layers of choking smog and hours after the moon refused to show itself, the question was still echoing in David's mind. *Do you know what love is?*

No. I want to know, but I don't have a clue. I've got more ways to avoid opening up than a clam. David curled into the fetal position. What really hurts is that I've never known what it feels like to be loved.

David sank into a dark hole of sadness. That dark hole had been there since his mother died. He could only vaguely remember ghostlike images of her. He remembered an empty childhood, with his father always absent.

You need to learn about love. Years ago, you couldn't swim; now you've got a box full of medals. In 1964, you'd never seen a computer; now you're close to graduating with honors with a degree in computer science. It's time to learn about love.

Psychiatrist Dr. Grace opened the door to her office and invited him in.

"Should I sit or lie down?" David asked Dr. Grace.

"Why don't you sit here?" Dr. Grace motioned to a comfortable chair that faced her, with an uncluttered desk between the two.

David faced her. "You were recommended by UCI Student Health Services."

He detected a Mona Lisa smile and an inquisitive look. He felt that she wanted to hear whatever he had to say.

David was silent until finally saying, "I guess that I am here for several reasons. I am almost ready to graduate from UCI and I'm not sure what I want to do with my life." She continued to listen. More silence. "After I graduate in June, I will lifeguard one last summer in San Clemente. If I guard six days a week and pick up overtime, I can make more money than the fulltime jobs I've interviewed for." Silence. "After the summer, I'm not sure what to do. Part of me wants to become a professor. I might financially scrape through grad school by being a teaching assistant, working computer labs, getting a scholarship, and lifeguarding. Some companies are interested in my joining their management training programs. Selling computers sounds intriguing and probably brings in the most money."

"It sounds like you're weighing several alternatives," Dr. Grace reflected.

"Yeah, but there's so much uncertainty. I don't know who will give me a job offer, if anyone. IBM said they were interested in my being a system engineer, but they have a freeze on hiring. I think some other companies are leery of hiring a guy, spending months training me and then losing me to the draft. I'm close to broke, so grad school looks unlikely. At any moment I could get drafted for Vietnam. Maybe I should join the coast guard and get the whole thing over with."

"No money, no job offers, and the draft would make anyone anxious," Dr. Grace said.

"It's hard with Vietnam hanging over my head, so I guess I need a plan to stay out of the war, and then get on with my life.

"How would you stay out of Vietnam?" Dr. Grace asked.

"We spend hours talking about that when I guard. There's a phone in each tower, so we can talk for hours. One guard had joined the army reserves, but his unit got called up. His was in a medic unit. Big mistake. They're the first to get called up. Another was in the National Guards and got called up. Some people say to join the navy, but thousands of seamen have been killed and tons are injured for life. The coast guard sounds safe, and maybe I'll join them, but they patrol rivers in Vietnam and get in shoot-outs with drug smugglers."

"It sounds like you have been doing research," Dr. Grace said.

"I have. I graduate in a few weeks and lose my student deferment. Then they can nail me."

"How do you feel about that?"

"Frustrated. Angry. Nixon got elected promising to end the war. Instead he's using secret bombing to expand the war into Cambodia and Laos," David said with anger. He thought about his father and the secret bombing, but decided to keep the conversation focused on career options.

Dr. Grace looked at David as he lapsed into silence while nervously shifting positions in his chair.

"You've seen the killings on TV. Innocent farmers and children screaming as they burn from napalm."

Dr. Grace listened without comment.

"My friends have a hundred ideas about how to stay out of Vietnam. But The Man keeps changing the rules and then ignoring the new rules. Used to be you could get a deferment as a grad student. Gone. Deferment if married. Gone. Deferment if you had kids. Gone."

"You don't trust The Man?"

"No way. If the army honored their medical criteria, they'd reject me for flat feet, but I know they would give me a pass in the physical. Per army regs, I could be rejected for having an obscene tattoo."

"Do you have a tattoo?"

"No, but I'd get one if it would keep me out."

"What would the tattoo look like?" Dr. Grace asked.

"It would say Fuck War."

"But you think that the army would ignore that?"

"Yes, but my fellow soldiers wouldn't after I was drafted and they saw it and beat me up."

"So what are your plans?"

"I've started a written plan. I'll try to flunk the physical. If I passed the physical, which I would, then fight for time by appealing at the local, state, then national board. Then start over with conscientious objector."

"It sounds like a good plan."

"Sounds like it, but they could just ignore my appeal, arrest me, and ship me to basic training. So I'd need to be ready to flee to Canada at least two days before any deadline."

"How do you feel about being treated this way?"

"It's totally unfair. Meanwhile, I guess I'd better graduate and get a job."

"What's your top career choice?"

"I'm not excited about these big corporate management-training programs. They sound uptight. My dad used to complain about navy bureaucracy and paper pushing."

"Your father was in the navy?"

"He's in the navy. He's a rear admiral at Pacific headquarters based in Hawaii."

"How does he feel about your not wanting to serve in the military?"

"He wants to disown me. We had a big blow-up last Christmas."

"You feel that your father wants to disown you. And how about your mother?"

"She died when I was five."

"Just you and your father all these years?"

"It's just been me all these years. After she died, he sent me to Alabama to live with Grandpa and Grandma Bess. Three years later he moved me to North Carolina to live with Granddad and Grandma June."

"So much of your childhood was with your grandparents in North Carolina?" Dr. Grace asked.

"No, when I turned twelve, Dad boarded me at the Army and Navy Academy in Carlsbad, California."

6

The Trip

David's long journey to university graduation was close to completion, requiring only the discipline of writing papers and studying for finals. Yet, like Odysseus and the Sirens song, David was totally distracted by sylphs in mini-skirts that ascended twelve inches above the knee. Women required gymnastic agility to sit down without revealing everything. What little that was not exposed could easily be imagined.

It was under this burden of over-stimulated hormones that David struggled to the end of university life. *Don't look up. Keep your head down, study and pass the finals!*

David hoped to graduate on time, in four years, from the University of California at Irvine (UCI). Graduating on schedule was impressive considering that in the first two years David had changed his major from pre-medicine to English literature to philosophy to eastern religion to psychology to social ecology and finally to computer science. David was saved by several factors: he had a natural curiosity that caused him to take extra classes in diverse fields; once he settled on computer science, he was totally organized with a plan to graduate on time; most importantly, David had no choice. He was broke, paying for the fourth year with his own money.

During the week of Finals, everywhere David walked, students looked like the living dead. They studied late into the night finishing papers and preparing for finals. Some were up all night. Many all-nighters took "uppers," "speed" and other pills from the pharmacological family of amphetamines.

David's hard study and organization paid off. He completed

a well-received paper based on his computer model of urban transportation. He excelled in his last finals. Outside of waiting for the official university paperwork, he had graduated.

As Carlo and David drove past the live oak and towering eucalyptus trees that lined Ortega Highway, the sun rose over the mountain. Bright orange and yellow vectors refracted through the clouds. The two continued on the highway, leaving civilization behind.

After a long winding drive, they found Sam and Electra's home and parked. As he and Carlo got out, they heard a howling animal and almost jumped back in the car. Then they heard the moans of a second creature. These moans almost sounded human. In fact, they were. The howling was accompanied by a primitive rhythm of a bed pounding against the wooden timbers of this rural shack.

"It must be Sam and Electra," Carlo speculated and grinned. Carlo walked into the woods to take a pee.

David read Alan Watts' *The Joyous Cosmology*. They waited. Finally, after all the animal cries had echoed against nearby hills, ensuing the primitive Latin percussions of a bed pounding against the wall, and after cries of ecstasy that caused winged creatures to take flight, there was silence. Carlo waited a couple of minutes, then knocked on the door.

Sam and Electra lived on a half-acre farm on the Ortega Highway, inland from the beach communities. They had lived together for a few years. They possessed no marriage license, a legal document that they saw as a city hall middle-class bourgeois trap. He introduced her as his "old lady." Depending on her mood, she introduced him as her "old man" or as her "magic man." This morning, Sam had been one hundred percent magic.

They grew organic vegetables, pot, and peyote, and local ranchers hired Sam to find water. He could walk a property holding a bent rod in each hand. When standing over an underground stream, or a well, the rods would invariably cross as if by magic. If you needed to find water, he was your water witch. Sam, in his late forties, had an energy level that even Carlo could not match.

Sam had a reputation of being eccentric. For example, whenever a car backfired, Sam dove flat on the sidewalk, a habit from serving in the Korean War. In sympathy, Electra usually hit the ground with him while shouting "incoming." No one knew if Electra was also somehow shell shocked, or if she simply thought that she was being supportive of her magic man.

"Far fucking out! Good to see you!" Sam exclaimed. He and Electra wore Cheshire-cat smiles.

"Sam, Electra, great seeing you," Carlo said as he gave each a hug. They were sweaty hugs.

"David. Haven't seen you since Big Sur," said the Shaman. "Electra, this is Carlo's roommate, David."

"Electra," David said as they awkwardly engaged in sweaty hugs.

"Totally," Electra said.

"This LSD is pure Orange Sunshine from the Brotherhood. Can you dig it, man?" Sam spoke with reverence. "This used to be legal, but the narcs shut that down last year. It's made in Switzerland just like all the world's best medicine and chocolate."

Electra laughed with delight. Her laugh contained the echo of the recently heard carnal greeting of the sunrise.

"One for you and one for you," Sam announced as he

handed Carlo and David each one tablet of pure LSD, which Carlo eagerly gulped; having never taken LSD, David cautiously swallowed. It would be twenty minutes before David and Carlo would feel any effects. Electra and Sam had dropped their acid an hour before.

On foot, the four started their journey. As they followed the yellow dirt road to a hilltop, Carlo started singing from the *Wizard of Oz*. Soon they were all singing as they danced arm-in-arm on their dusty adventure. They agreed on who would be Dorothy, the Tin Man, the Scarecrow, and the Cowardly Lion. As the LSD increased its pharmacological effects, roles were traded. David let go of being the Cowardly Lion. Carlo discarded his role as the Tin Man and scampered merrily along as Toto. Unlike the movie, this Toto stopped at a large cactus to lift his leg and pee.

With the day's newborn sun to their back, their shadows stretched up the hillside. Literature, science, philosophy, and religion wove a rich tapestry in David's mind. He discussed Plato's Allegory of the Cave with the parallel realities of beings and their shadows. Sam and Electra listened, absorbed, and reflected. Toto peed on another cactus.

The acid switched off the left-brain's analytical filtering; the right brain experienced with new vividness. The arid hillside's sparse vegetation was witnessed as a botanical garden. Smells became a rich banquet. David savored the air's sweet mist as if he were at a wine tasting. Colors intensified. Shadows became cubist masterpieces as if Picasso had swept his brush across the landscape. A delicate lupine became a swirling purple black hole transporting each to a parallel universe.

A creosote bush transmogrified into a living sculpture. A manzanita stripped its red bark to reveal a delicate skin. As they walked past trees, the perspective changed, as the trees seemed to slowly pirouette. Life was a choreographed ballet. Life was reaching, dancing and naked.

They sat on the hilltop. David looked up to the clouds floating in slow motion. Above, a cumulus puppy dog chased a dove. The dog raced and skid to catch its flight, and then stopped, ears cocked, crouched tight. It wrestled its tail and chased the wind.

A pond became a fiery reflection of the golden orb above. Distant hills were covered with tangerine orchards. Looking to the east, David saw vast apple groves on another hill. Forbidden fruit beaconed. David walked toward the distant orchards, leaving his friends behind.

As the road wound and curved, feelings of fear mixed with awe and wonder. Did his feet reach for the ground, or did the ground rise to his steps? He had lost control. He had lost the meaning of control. There was movement, light, and experience. The one-time philosophy major asked, *Where is David? Who is David? Is there really a David?*

The dusty road met the feet of the wandering pilgrim. He walked the valley floor until he could no longer see his friends, nor view the rich orchards. Against the shades of dust, the creosote bush stood with its woven blue-green branches and subtle leaves.

David heard a warning rattle! Inches to his left crawled a brown rattlesnake six feet in length. Not being coiled, it warned instead of striking. David felt a jolt of fear mixed with a curious wonder. The two shared the Earth and shared this trail. Both wanted to live in peace. *Perhaps I should make peace with this snake.*

David was then seized with dread. *Get control! You're on acid. One snakebite and you're dead.* David froze as the deadly snake serpentined away. After long standing, David continued his journey to the tree of knowledge.

David recalled his past readings about evolutionary biology. Every strand of the DNA in his body had survived a thousand generations. His was the DNA of primitive apes that avoided being swallowed by the giant snakes of earlier times. As he walked the road that curved, undulated, and rose under his feet, he felt as though he were riding a giant serpent goddess. The experience felt not like a visual hallucination; rather, an acute perception. Although not seeing a serpent goddess, he sensed her being. In his head, he heard The Doors singing about riding a snake. The windy road, the serpent goddess, carried him to the apple grove where he tasted the forbidden fruit.

David felt watched. *Am I being followed? I must avoid others. I must not be found.* Afraid, he hid in a cluster of rocks. As the hot sun burned, he removed clothes to get cooler. David felt himself dying as he disappeared into the rocks. Minutes passed ever more slowly, until time stopped.

Carlo found David an hour later. "Where'd you go, man? We were worried about you."

"You rescued me." David smiled. "This trip, man, like blows my mind." He was rescued from the snake; freed from the serpent goddess. The road did not slither. David felt free of the acid-induced paranoia. Carlo guided him back to the yellow road.

"This stuff is incredible," Carlo enthused. "We want to go to the beach."

"Sounds great."

Carlo looked at David and smiled. "You must be tripping. I'm not used to seeing you walking around naked."

Upon hearing this, David realized that he was naked and unafraid. He found his jeans and tennis shoes, and then put them on and joined the others.

The VW bus drove them to South Laguna. David held the

wheel, but did not experience being the driver.

"The thing, man, is this lifts the veil, if you can dig where that's at." Sam was sharing his personal enlightenment. "We're taught not to be creative. They, like, did this study and asked first graders 'Who is an artist?' Like every hand went up. Then they like asked these sixth graders, and only two hands went up. We're brainwashed, man. Picasso, total genius, said 'we should stop teaching kids art. Instead, we should learn from them.'"

The others nodded their heads in acknowledgement. Sam continued, "I freak, therefore I am. But The Man doesn't want us to freak. The Man wants us to be cogs perfectly fitting together in their military-industrial-complex machine. Acid lifts the veil. It frees our inner artist. We are free to do our own freak." The other three listened intently to this enlightened man, Sam the Shaman.

When they descended the final hill, the ocean and sky stretched to infinity. The magic bus took them past the glowing yellow cottages with green trim and evergreen shrubs; past white abodes embraced with rose-colored rhododendron generously overflowing. Spanish haciendas displayed hanging ivy and cypress that coexisted with palm trees.

The bus parked itself. The bus rocked and wiggled and chortled as each person inside changed into bathing suits. The four descended the rickety stairs embedded in the cliff that surrounded the lagoon. Electra put a pink azalea in her hair. Carlo and David raced across the sand and jumped into the water. They put on their swim fins as they dove under the incoming waves.

Almost feeling detached and out of body, David watched himself swim and catch a wave that lifted and carried him, as he bodysurfed in slow motion. He watched the sunlight reflect on the wave's face; he witnessed the white foam slowly cascade down onto the aqua shoulder of the breaking wave. David was one with the wave that carried him, bodysurfed him, and pirouetted him on the wave's face. When the wave crashed, David flipped under it and popped out behind.

He swam in slow motion to Carlo, who pointed and whispered, "Dolphins." In the water, no more than 30 feet away, four dolphins were slowly making a carefree journey northward. Carlo and David dove under the water, imitating their new friends by putting their arms to their sides and making powerful dolphin kicks. Carlo and David surfaced, gulped air and again descended, swimming near the majestic creatures. A dolphin swam close and looked at David. Smiles greeted smiles. The dolphin gave a powerful flick of the tail and moved on.

"Totally far out!" Carlo exclaimed as the dolphins journeyed away.

"Groovy," David replied. "What a stoke when we made eye contact."

"I swear he smiled."

"Definitely."

Life was perfect. After an hour of rides, David walked to shore. At the edge of the cove, he wandered into a tiny forest of cypress, ferns, and flowers. A small waterfall poured into a delicate stream that flowed to the ocean. Orchids fell from the sheltering trees in their own waterfall of white, mauve and violet.

Colors of gardenias merged with shapes when he looked inside the teardrop petals patterned with saffron ridges. He touched the fabric of a petal. The sweet fragrance penetrated and lifted. Sweet tastes of honey, vanilla, and nutmeg lingered on his tongue.

From the chaotic sounds of crashing waves, a theme

emerged, Beethoven's *Ninth Symphony*. The final movement sounded as vivid as if played in a concert hall, as themes were tested and rejected, until the Ode to Joy was heard, first from the cellos and basses, then a soloist, and then the entire orchestra and choir. The sunlight cascaded through cloud canyons in the sky, terracotta with the late afternoon's refraction of the aged and allegorized sun. The beauty of God's creation was fully experienced as an ode to joy.

7

Party Animals

"Yesterday I dropped acid," David began his session with Dr. Grace. "It was an incredible trip."

Dr. Grace showed a flicker of startle and then asked, "How often do you use drugs?"

"About once a week I smoke dope. I have the occasional drink, which I consider a stronger drug than grass. This was my first acid trip. That's the extent of me and drugs."

"You said that it was an incredible trip."

"There was a dark point in the middle of the trip. I was sitting on rocks alone, when I realized that I'm a caricature of my father. I avoid being close to people...to women. I'm avoiding the whole marriage-responsibility-money-wife-and-kids scenario."

"You do not want to be like your father, so you avoid getting involved with women?"

"I never get anywhere with girls. I'm going to be a virgin for the rest of my life." Silence. "It's all so hopeless. I never develop a relationship. I never have sex. In this free-love generation, the only thing free is masturbation after an expensive date and making out."

"Do you masturbate in front of your date?"

"No! I don't masturbate in front of anyone!" David replied with embarrassment. "I like to make out; I just rarely let my hands wander, or try to take any clothes off. When I do, I get rejected."

"You have a Unitarian mind, but a Catholic penis," Dr. Grace commented.

David turned his gaze from the window to her. At first, he was stunned and then his laughter swelled into a release, similar to a good cry. He failed to think of a clever reply, so he asked, "What do you mean?"

"You've told me that you've taken psychology courses. You are familiar with the unconscious. You consciously speak of wanting to have sex, yet your behavior indicates otherwise. You came to me saying that you were practicing abstinence. You could be a candidate for priesthood. What do you think is behind your behavior?"

"Well for starters, I'm not Catholic. When I changed majors several times at UCI, I actually majored in comparative religion. I probably relate more to Zen Buddhism."

"A recurring theme for you in therapy is that you're uncomfortable about being a virgin. When I ask you about sex, you change the subject. What are you afraid of?"

David sat frozen in his chair, staring into space. Finally, he said, "When I was five, me and some other kids gathered in a tool shed. Lorraine suggested that we all get undressed. She must have been eight, the oldest; we tended to follow her lead. She wanted us undressed; I said I didn't want to. Rob, a little bully, challenged me, 'Hey, little Davey, what are you afraid of?' We started to undress."

David's voice was pained. "There must have been six of us. I was the last to undress. We were looking at our naked bodies. I looked at Lorraine. I looked at Rob's penis." David stopped and looked for a reaction from Dr. Grace. Finding none, he continued, "I looked at the one small window on the side door of the garage. I saw Grandma Bess looking in. She was very angry. I was afraid. She opened the door and said, 'All of you get dressed, go home, and don't ever do this again!'"

"How did you feel?"

"Afraid, embarrassed, guilty. A couple of weeks later, Dad came to visit and confronted me. I was crying. I was shaking with guilt. I said that Rob made me undress. Dad replied angrily, 'Your mother would have been ashamed of you, if she'd lived to see this.' I sobbed and promised never to do it again. I felt perverted."

Dr. Grace said, "That would have been frightening for a young child. Did this happen soon after your mother's death?"

"Yes. She had died recently. I don't remember exactly. It had been a matter of weeks."

"You must have felt terribly alone," said Dr. Grace.

"I must have." David tried to remember feelings long buried deep inside him. "I was. I felt terribly alone."

"You said that you felt perverted."

"From Grandma Bess and Dad's anger, I knew I'd been bad."

"What did you fear most about exposing yourself?"

David's face turned red. Sitting alone in therapy, he was too embarrassed to say anything.

Over the next few minutes, Dr. Grace helped David talk about childhood fears and shames, from fear of losing others to the shame of having a penis.

Dr. Grace summarized, "You were a little boy. Only five years old. Alone. You'd lost your mother. Your father was angry. It is completely understandable to fear loss. Now, you have an adult perspective. Look at it as a frightened and grieving five-year old. Can you empathize with that little boy?"

After a long Sunday with overtime and dinner out, David

returned home to see motorcycles parked in front of his house.

"Cool place," grunted a Hell's Angel as he revved his Harley and then roared off. Four more left David's home, got on their bikes, smirked at David, and then blasted off.

David walked into his house, stepping over an obstacle course of trash. His neat, organized, vacuumed home had been hit by a tornado. Seat cushions were everywhere. Food and beer cans were piled in corners. Carlo, without David's knowledge, without his permission, had thrown a party. David was furious. Carlo would be hunted down and made to clean the place.

In looking for Carlo, David did not need to search far. Carlo was passed out in David's bed, lying face down, and naked. Before David could yell at him, the bathroom door opened and a gorgeous girl walked out. "I'm Debbie." She smiled, scanned David's body, and then gave an alluring glance. "You know Carlo?"

David was speechless. Looking at Debbie, the blood emptied from David's brain and rushed below his beltline. Debbie's blue eyes again looked deep into David's. Her contoured lips hypnotized. Her breasts revealed their luscious roundness through the T-shirt three sizes too small. Her mini skirt revealed the path to paradise.

Debbie said, "Carlo could have had me, but he passed out from all the Tequila. Too bad. I was in the mood for some loving." She looked directly at David and waited. Hearing no response, she asked, "Could you give me a ride back to the campground?"

"Sure," David's replied as he stood in a trance staring at Debbie.

As they started to leave, she looked back sweetly at Carlo, still out cold, and said "Thanks for the party." She looked at David with a carefree smile.

David drove her to the campground. He faced a ranger who pointed a flashlight at David and then at Debbie. David took her to campsite 87 and started to say goodbye. Debbie kissed David. While lost in a passionate kiss, she unzipped David and started to stroke him. When the two finally came up for air, she said, "Let's go back to your place."

David U-turned and drove off with Debbie. They were barely past the ranger's station when Debbie started sucking on him. In less than five minutes, he transitioned from shock to pleasure to wild excitement to having an orgasm. He kept the bus on the road and only missed one stop sign as the windows fogged.

Back home, with Carlo still passed out in David's room, he took Debbie into Carlo's room. They lay on the bed and started kissing. David removed her T-shirt and his own. They embraced. He was lost in the passion of their kisses as they pressed together. As his lips and tongue pleasured her breasts, his fingers pleasured her clitoris through her panties. Her every moan and "oh yes" encouraged David to do more. Finally, he removed the rest of her clothes.

He ran back in his room and searched the dresser drawer for his Trojan prophylactic, found it and ran back to Debbie. Seeing his limp penis, Debbie pulled David on top of her for more kissing. After a few minutes lost in pleasure, David gained an eager erection. Debbie put the rubber on him. David awkwardly entered her. He felt his penis inside her vagina. *Amazing! Now I'm not a virgin!*

Debbie responded to David's every stroke inside her. She yelled, she arched, and then she completely relaxed. David went deeper and slower, lost in her beauty, with passion building. He exploded in another orgasm. They lay together and almost drifted to sleep as their naked bodies pressed together.

Minutes passed before they dressed. As David again drove

Debbie back to her campsite, she said, "Don't worry about Dad. He doesn't carry a gun when he's off duty, and I won't tell Killer about you."

"Killer?"

"That's what the other Hell's Angels call my boyfriend. Funny, huh. Anyway, I won't tell." Debbie continued as David listened in stunned muteness, "I'm tired of him leaving me without a ride. Next month, I get my driver's license so I can start driving myself."

"No driver's license until next month? You told me that you went to Long Beach State!"

"Silly. I said I like to hang out at Long Beach State." She leaned over and gave David a goodbye kiss, then jumped out.

She's got a cop for a father and a Hell's Angel boyfriend named Killer! Under age, her dad could have me arrested for statutory rape of a minor. Sex, dope, war. It's getting where a guy can't cross a street without committing a felony, going to prison, or getting killed.

"I had sex. I'm no longer a virgin." David announced at the beginning of his next therapy session. "Now I've got some idea of what I have been missing." He looked at Dr. Grace for a major reaction.

There was none. "Tell me about it."

David flushed with embarrassment. *I can't talk with a woman about sex! It would help if she congratulated me. I guess she's trained to be neutral.* Dr. Grace was a medical doctor; he was there to get better. He took a deep breath and described Debbie's beauty, her surprising aggressiveness, his excitement of being sucked on, his rapture with her body, and the delight of stroking his penis in and out of her.

David worried about her age and Debbie's father, the cop

with a gun, and Killer. Dr. Grace probed for feelings. David talked about anger, nervousness, passion, and fear. David was definitely becoming more open about his feelings.

Dr. Grace revisited the session and where David talked about exposing himself to other children when he was five. David slowly revealed that he felt that he had lost the love of his parents. As a child, he had blamed himself for the loss. "I felt that there must be something terribly wrong with me not to be loved by my parents. I felt perverted. I felt perverted because I had a penis. I sound crazy."

"You are not crazy. David, you are twenty-one with beliefs that you developed as a young child. You're still holding on to the feelings of a boy. The feelings can make sense to a five-year old. Now they're interfering with enjoying your life."

He desperately wanted to let go of the neurotic beliefs that he had learned so long ago. He needed to unlearn.

8

Guns and Flowers

Linda cowered in a jail cell with 58 other women. She was overpowered by the stench of sour milk mixed with urine. With no showers and a primitive toilet, the women were filthy, and the blankets dirty from being used by others. She was frightened. Her life was reduced to a narrow cot, 36 rules, and a cell full of threatening people.

Linda climbed onto her cot, and turned to face the wall with its peeling lead paint. She tried to think of walking in a beautiful park, but the room overwhelmed the fantasy. The coldness of fear penetrated to her bones. She curled into a ball.

With an arrest record, I can never get a teaching credential. My career is ruined for giving away Girl Scout cookies. Doing her best to hide it from the others, she cried.

She thought of her paraplegic brother. *We'll dance again, John. You'll get your prosthetics. We'll dance again. Brad, you need to do everything in your power to end this war. I'll never tell them anything. They can't keep me in jail for a box of cookies. Can they?*

After 34 sleepless hours in the jail cell, with bread and evaporated milk her only food, Linda was released on bail posted by Brad's father. Linda rushed to Brad's arms and cried for a long time.

Marvin Friedman, Brad's father, was an entertainment lawyer in Los Angeles. Linda had always admired Marvin, who, in the McCarthy era, had gone to jail rather than name-names. Like Brad, he was committed to ending the war. He promised to personally be her lawyer and he wouldn't take a dime. Marvin was politically well connected. Thanks to those connections, he was reinstated to the bar after his time in prison. Marvin was also well connected with the media and knew how to use it.

The next day, Linda met with an award-winning journalist who was a friend of the Friedman's. Linda gave an interview about the hours of interrogation with the police and FBI agents. "Jailed for Giving Girl Scout Cookies" was the title of the syndicated article that was published in 187 papers, with a few papers placing it on the front page. The article described Linda's efforts as kindhearted and that in her youth Linda had been a Girl Scout. The bomb squad was ridiculed with a satirical description of how to dismantle a chocolate mint cookie. Linda was becoming famous.

The National Guard's receptionist could not recall that Linda ever said the word "bomb." The receptionist could not recall Linda saying anything threatening. The article caricatured the FBI who had deployed eight agents and a bomb squad over a box of cookies.

Articles ran in papers and magazines for days. Letters poured in from supportive Girl Scouts. Letters and more articles were published. In one, the reporter estimated that the box of cookies had cost the taxpayers $347,000 and recommended that Linda be given an honorary merit badge for dispensing the world's most expensive cookies. Soon concerned citizens, students, and a number of Girl Scout families were writing letters to their congressional leaders and to the White House.

The FBI stubbornly told Linda and attorney Marvin Friedman that she would go on trial for making a bomb threat, unless she cooperated in naming names. Linda refused. She worked with Brad's father in preparation for her trial.

After a stressful week of trial preparation, studying for finals, and trying to sleep, Linda answered the phone. Marvin

Friedman said, "Wonderful news. The Attorney General has decided not to charge you. They've dropped the case."

Linda won.

The days were a whirlwind for Linda. On campus, both friends and strangers smiled and gave her the peace sign. Students applauded when she walked into class. After giving more interviews, she saw herself on television. But nothing was better than one phone call.

"I talked with John Lennon today!" she told Brad.

"No way!"

"I swear. He's been calling Max everyday since Bloody Thursday. I guess he sees Berkeley as important to stopping the war. He and Yoko are in Montreal doing another bed-in for peace. He'd read about my cookie story!" Linda continued, "I'm with Max and others at the Center. All of a sudden, Max hands me the phone and I'm talking with John Lennon!"

"What did he say?"

"First he ordered a box of Girl Scout cookies. I was asking him what flavor. Can you believe I'm joking about Girl Scout cookies with John Lennon?"

"That's it?"

"No, he talked about nonviolence and Gandhi. We must be peaceful to have peace. If we keep talking about peace, then we can have peace."

"I'm just amazed that you were talking with John Lennon!"

"He emphasized a couple of times that we don't want to give The Man any reason for violence at the big rally, like not getting hassled by the pigs and not playing their games. I was shocked. I don't remember everything. He said, 'Give peace a chance.'"

"You're famous!" Brad hugged Linda, lifted her off her feet, and spun her around.

"Graveyard Train" blasted from the speaker as Linda warily moved with the masses down Telegraph Avenue listening to Creedence Clearwater. She found small comfort in being surrounded as she looked at cops holding shotguns, National Guards with loaded rifles, and sharp shooters positioned on roofs. Thousands and thousands moved in careful cadence down the broad street of Berkeley approaching the confrontation in People's Park on this Memorial Day, a Friday in 1969.

Onlookers applauded the moving masses. Linda heard accolades from those lining the streets and those leaning out windows smoking joints. Smiles and shout-outs were heard from locals that she had never met, "You took down The Man!" "Right on!" "Power to the people!" It was a celebration. Stoners smoked dope without a care. She relaxed, waved, and breathed deeply, tasting lavender and skunkweed laced with sage. She was in a parade.

The sun scorched. Linda was slightly embarrassed by her sweaty underarms and nervous about soon taking the stage. Guys took off shirts. Locals holding hoses in the air sprayed water to keep the crowd cool.

As the parade neared People's Park, Creedence was singing "Proud Mary." Linda was light, engaged, and almost dancing. Holding her fingers in a "V," she flashed peace signs to others.

Brad took the stage, and leaned into the microphone. "Thank you for being here on this Memorial Day. You created People's Park with compassion for those who have no other home. You showed courage in being here to promote peace. We expected five thousand. There are thirty thousand of you, man. Thirty thousand!" There was a massive applause.

"Two weeks ago on Bloody Thursday, one of our fellow students was innocently watching our protest when he was shot and killed. I'd like you to bow your heads in a silent prayer for James Rector." Brad bowed his head and no sound was heard as the seconds ticked slowly by during the silent prayer. "It was compassion that inspired so many of you to transform a dirt lot into a beautiful park for families, children, those from local homes, and those who have no homes." Brad stopped for the applause.

"For those who remember World War II, this Memorial Day is a day to honor the living and dead who stopped the world from falling to Nazism. I respect their position. For many of us, it is a reminder that we could be drafted to die for a war against a people arbitrarily divided into two countries; divided against themselves by colonialists. The Vietnamese want to be one people living in peace." Applause.

"Our nation is not threatened by the Vietnamese who want to reunite in peace and live under a democracy. We are threatened when our own democracy is subverted in the name of military dominance. President Eisenhower warned us in his farewell address, 'We must guard against the acquisition of unwarranted influence, whether sought or unsought, by the military-industrial complex. The potential for the disastrous rise of misplaced power exists and will persist.'

"This Memorial Day also reminds us of the millions who were victims of war. My uncle Julius was a victim. When he was only seventeen, he was marched into a gas chamber in Germany and exterminated with hydrogen cyanide. My mother survived the horrors of the Holocaust." Brad's voice broke, and he fought tears. "She taught me to speak up for those who deserve compassion, courage, and peace." The handclapping had a solemn cadence.

"Now, the searing heat and choking gas from napalm is killing thousands and crippling millions of children and civilians in Vietnam. The gas dropped from U. S. helicopters violates everything that we honor in America on Memorial Day." The applause was long.

"Who is getting rich on these millions of gallons of napalm and Agent Orange? Dow Chemical. To save innocent children, to save their families, and to save our own soldiers, we must dump Dow."

"Seventy percent of U. S. citizens want us out of Vietnam," Brad continued. "Our mothers want us out. Our fathers want us out. We want out." Brad paused for the thunderous applause. "It's time to listen to the people." He paused. "The people want to end this war today!" He paused for effect. He let his eyes scan the throng. "In a democracy, people should be heard, not silenced with guns. We are drafted against our will to kill and to die, supposedly to bring freedom. Instead The Man denies the most basic freedoms of U. S. citizens. The majority in the senate and congress want the war to end. Does our president not hear them? Our people want freedom. President Nixon, hear us. You are elected to represent the people. Your people cry to end this insane war. There is an easy way to end the war in Vietnam. Just end it, man. You are the Commander in Chief. End it today. Bring our people home alive. Bring peace today. Peace now. Peace now. Peace now." The crowd joined Brad in chanting for "peace now."

"Compassion, courage, and peace," Brad continued. "Linda Hope is the embodiment of all these qualities. She was interrogated and jailed for delivering a peace offering, a box of Girl Scout cookies for the National Guard." The crowd cheered Linda, who was standing on the stage nearby, blushing. "Everyone who meets Linda is touched by her warmth, her caring, and her wholehearted desire for peace. There was a time in this nation when you were allowed to make a simple gesture of goodwill. What could be more American than a box of Girl

Scout cookies?" The crowd roared. "Linda suffered hours of police and FBI interrogation for delivering a box of cookies. She did not know that chocolate mint was a felony!" There were waves of laughter. "She didn't know she would be labeled a terrorist for cooperating with the latest group of so-called communist subversives – the Girl Scouts." There was laughter and applause. "Please welcome a courageous and caring hero, Linda Hope."

Linda looked nervous as she took the stage. Brad could seem the tremor in her hands. The park was filled and overflowing. Surrounding the crowd of thirty thousand were almost three thousand National Guards with bayoneted rifles and tear gas guns.

Linda took a deep breath, stepped to the microphone, and said with an unwavering voice, "Today we are gathered in peace." After one sentence, the crowd was applauding. "I'm amazed at being here, at all the attention, at being in the papers. All I wanted to do is make a simple peace offering and give them a box of cookies." There was more laughter and applause.

"To our friends in the National Guard," she paused, "And I truly mean friends. We are of the same age, the same hearts, and many of you are fellow students. Be assured that we are gathered in this beautiful park, this People's Park, seeking only peace and love." The cheering was long. "I promise my fellow National Guard, police, and FBI, that I did not bring any more cookies." There followed more laughter, cheering, and applause.

The demonstration, speeches and march had been thoughtfully planned. Linda, Brad, Alicia, and others had worked with the American Friends in hopes of making the day non-violent. After the murder of James, it had not been easy to convince SDS leaders, Black Panthers, and other activists, that the day must be peaceful. There had been meetings, scenarios, plans, and training.

At one meeting, Alicia had suggested that everyone bring flowers and share them with the Guard. The idea was embraced. From her vantage point on stage, Linda saw the "peace monitors" walking among the National Guard and heavily armed police. Alicia was one of the "peace monitors" giving flowers to them. With several, she could not resist flirting. Linda saw the hope of peace. She was encouraged to see no helicopters and no raised guns.

Linda continued her speech. "I promise that I will never again touch chocolate mint." The crowd laughed. Many National Guard laughed. "It is time to show that we are a nation of compassion, hope, and freedom. Please, let's open the heavy locks, let's open the iron bars, and, all over the world, free these poor Girl Scouts." At this point, everyone was laughing and applauding, even some of the police. Guardsmen, all with pre-approval to use tear gas, were muttering that they could not use the choking gas. They could not hurt these people.

"On a serious note, thank you for being here to free our brothers, now dying in the jungles of Vietnam. This is very personal for me. My brother, John, just returned from serving, but returned without his legs." Linda started crying.

Composing herself, Linda continued, "It is a joy to see your smiling faces in the warm sun, to see peace signs and flowers. Hold peace close to your hearts, and share your love like flowers." The applause was long and loud.

"As part of my temporary fame, I got a call from John Lennon," Linda continued. "He asked me to convey this personal message to you: 'Give peace a chance.'" Applause. "We have a new president and a new Congress. They were elected with the promise that they would end the draft, and that we would have a swift peace in Vietnam. We were promised that our brave soldiers, many drafted against their will, would come home alive." Linda again thought of her brother and almost cried. She unfolded a paper to read a quotation, "A great man and fallen hero, Dr. Martin Luther King, said, 'We are now faced with the fact, my friends, that tomorrow is today. We are confronted with the fierce urgency of now. In this unfolding conundrum of life and history, there is such a thing as being too late.' We cannot wait. Peace must start today." Linda received a long applause as she left the stage.

The next day, Linda was again in national papers. Some articles included photographs of her on stage and quotations from her speech. There were photos of National Guard in friendly conversation with protesters; a few holding their fingers in a "V" to give the peace sign. There was even a photo of a daisy blossoming from the barrel of a soldier's rifle. It was a day of peace. No shots were fired, no tear gas used, and no crowds dispersed. On the far edge of the crowd, a brave and enterprising troop of Girl Scouts was selling cookies. In 1969, that troop achieved the national sales record.

9

A Funeral

As the hearse slowly ascended the final hill of the Point Loma cemetery, David stood apart from the family, and the crying women. He wore his one dark suit, with white shirt and tie.

This military cemetery was once a battlefield after the Bear Flag Revolt of 1846 spilled south and men fought to free the California territory from Mexican rule. Now it was a place to honor the dead. David looked across the green hills decorated with monuments, memorials, and obelisks for the fallen soldiers, sailors, and marines of the Spanish American War, World War I, World War II, Korea and Vietnam. *Heroes. They were always heroes and the wars were always just.*

Would David someday bury his father here, next to his mother? His dad had taken him here when he was a boy. They had looked at the deep sea fishing boats motoring to Baja and naval ships traveling to distant shores. *Would I be expected to build a monument for my father? Hero of World War II, the good war. Silver Star for heroism. Admiral. Father who abandoned his only child.* David felt bitter and angry as he looked at the gray ocean under the flat light.

The hearse arrived. Marines in dress uniform carried the remains of John Eastman, Marine Second Lieutenant, age 22, to the gravesite. The blue jackets, red trim, and white caps framed Eastman's coffin with patriotic dignity. Sabers, guns, and rifles were prominent, as if to protect the fallen dead.

David thought of John as his coffin was lowered. Words were spoken in John's honor. The gun salute put every frightened bird in flight and started a chorus of howling dogs.

Then David was lost in memories of the years he shared with John at the Army and Navy Academy. He remembered the two of them being among the few boarding cadets who rarely went home for the holidays. He recalled classes, morning inspections, marching, being yelled at, and goofing off. He and John were stars on the water polo team. On a few occasions, the two escaped to the nearby beach for meeting girls and flirting. He recalled double dating at Disneyland when John got his car.

David remembered taking long shoulder rides with John in big winter swells. He remembered saving John, when his friend had been knocked unconscious in a massive wipe out. David was given a medal for saving John's life. A lot of good it did. Killed in a jungle in Vietnam, aged 22, John Eastman was dead.

"I've been thinking more about careers. I want to help people," David said. "I like my gig in the computer lab where I get paid to help students debug their programs. When I guard, I feel great when I rescue someone."

"Helping people feels great," Dr. Grace said.

"Right. In the computer lab, I get compliments about explaining things. I've thought about being a professor." David lapsed into silence while Dr. Grace looked at him.

"A couple of days ago, I went to John Eastman's funeral. He's my age," David said. "He was my age and now he's dead. We were pretty good friends at the Army and Navy Academy. We surfed, goofed-off, met girls."

"I'm sorry that you lost a friend."

"I'm good at losing friends. I started to make friends in Alabama, after everyone stopped laughing at my California accent. Then Dad moved me to North Carolina. I started to settle in and make friends, then he moved me back to California where everyone laughed at   my Southern accent."

"You sound angry about losing friends."

"I am. John was a friend for four years. Now Carlo is a friend of almost four years. My time will be up soon. Four years seems the limit."

"It must be hard to get close to people if you feel that inevitably you will lose them," Dr. Grace said.

Words choked in David's throat. He wiped his eyes. "Killed in a foreign jungle. Only twenty-two. John was a great guy. Funny. Model cadet. Marine officer. Got a medal. His parents must be so proud of their dead son."

"Would your father be proud of you if you were killed in Vietnam?"

"Probably, especially if I got a Silver Star like he did in World War II." David clenched his fists. "He loved to have me come on board a ship for Christmas dinner wearing my cadet dress uniform with him in his dress uniform. Him getting all the sharp salutes, 'yes, sir,' 'yes, Commodore Eliot,' 'aye aye, Admiral Eliot.' He liked to show me off and look like a great dad. Yeah, he would be proud if I died a hero."

"You sound bitter about him being gone most of the time and then showing you off."

"When I was little, I was in awe of him. I loved going on those ships. I tried to always say the right thing. As I grew older, though, I grew to resent it, especially him parading me around at Christmas."

"How did you feel about your father being away so much of the time?"

"It was lonely without him around and no mom. Dad's priorities were the navy, deep-sea fishing, and golf. After my mom died, he moved me from San Diego to Mobile, Alabama, to live with Grandpa and Grandma Bess, my dad's folks. I only saw Dad a few times in Mobile."

"How did that feel?"

"Like he wanted nothing to do with me. I was just interfering with his life."

Dr. Grace looked at David, waiting to hear more.

"In a couple of years, Dad got promoted to the Pentagon and moved me in with Granddad and Grandma June, my mom's folks, in Raleigh, North Carolina. Then he'd come down from Washington a few times a year, and my grand folks would take me up to see him. Then he'd get sea duty, and I wouldn't see him for months."

David found the box of old photographs. He looked at childhood photos of his grandparents, his early friends, military school, and holding surfboards with John Eastman. He looked at himself on a podium wearing swimming medals. He stared at himself standing stiffly in dress uniform. In the photos he never smiled.

He studied the photo of him and his dad on a fishing boat. In the photo, David smiled, holding a large Bonito that he had caught. Then he studied a photo of himself at age four, dressed for Easter Sunday holding his mother's hand.

Underneath the photos was a turquoise pendant suspended on a necklace of rough turquoise nuggets. It was his mother's. The egg shaped pendant, two inches long and embraced in a silver setting, contained an intricate pattern that covered part of the polished stone. Lost in fascination, David held the pendant. A card described how the pendant was from a holy place in Tibet. Tentatively, David put the necklace around his neck and looked in the mirror. He saw a boy trying to smile before his vision was blurred with tears.

10

Busted

The apartment door flew into the room, kicked in by the FBI agents. Stunned, Brad looked into the gun pointed at his head.

"Bradley Friedman, we have a warrant to search you and this apartment. I want you facedown on the ground. Now! Move! Spread eagle!" As Brad carefully kneeled to the floor, he was kicked flat to the ground and then searched by FBI agent Gottlieb, while Heller held the pistol pointed at his head.

Then Brad could hear his home being torn apart and shouted, "What the fuck are you doing?" Gottlieb replied with a boot kick to his rib. At first, Brad could not breathe. When he did, he felt searing pain in his rib and wondered if it was cracked by the kick.

"Found it!" exclaimed Heller. "Must be half a kilo. Too much for you to smoke. Who are you selling this to, Friedman?"

Brad was outraged. He had been drug-free since the FBI had started investigating him and other SDS leaders months ago. His apartment was clean and he knew it. "You pigs. You planted that. This is totally illegal. I demand to call my attorney." Brad's speech abruptly ended as a club hit the back of his head, leaving him unconscious.

After a miserable and sleepless stay in the crowded jail cell, Brad was released when his father posted bail. When he walked into the police lobby, his dad looked shocked at Brad's appearance.

As Marvin Friedman hugged his son, Brad released a

muffled scream, finally got his breath, and said, "That hug hurt. I think I've got cracked ribs from being kicked by the FBI."

"Sorry. I didn't know," Marvin Friedman said. "We'll get you to a doctor."

"It's OK. Not nearly as bad as the time you had to take me from the football game to the emergency room. Don't worry about me, I'm indestructible."

"Your mom's worried sick. We'll go to a doctor today. Plus, an x-ray of a fractured rib will help in court, if this goes that far." He walked Brad to Marvin's rental car and drove away.

"They kicked me, knocked me unconscious, and framed me because I'm in SDS and make speeches for peace." Brad's voice was full of anger. "The drug bust is total bullshit. I've made sure that our place has been drug-free for months."

They drove in silence for a few minutes.

"You turned the wrong way, Dad."

"I want to go up this hill. I found a place where we can talk. Your room may be bugged, and no car can follow us here without being obvious." After a few minutes of hill climbing on the narrow road, Marvin parked the car, and walked to a park bench. They sat and looked across the bay at San Francisco. They admired the Golden Gate Bridge, a gateway to Asia or the start of a long drive to Canada.

"Brad, I know that you're framed. You tell me you've been clean and I believe you, but a jury may believe a book full of government evidence against you. I went to jail rather than name names during the McCarthy hearings. I know how these guys work. You're facing up to ten years in prison for felony possession of marijuana with intent to sell, and life in prison if they make a case for conspiracy to blow up a national lab. I'm a lawyer. I've read the charges."

"That's complete bullshit. I had nothing to do with bombing

the Lawrence Livermore lab."

"I know. I've retained a good friend and top criminal lawyer, John Wasserman. He started researching the case while I flew up here. He's started negotiating with the FBI and with Judge Ellsworth. John's briefed me on the situation and alternatives." Brad listened in pain, shifted uneasily on the bench, suffering from the shooting pain of cracked ribs. Marvin continued, "I hired John because he is a highly competent criminal attorney. I think the best deal that he can achieve is for you to either choose two years of prison or two years of military service."

"What!" Brad shouted. "Dad, this is totally unfair. I didn't do anything except exercise freedom of speech. The FBI planted that grass. They've got no evidence connecting me with a bombing because there is no evidence. The judge should throw those FBI assholes in prison, not me."

Marvin was pained as he heard his son speak the simple truth. "Yes, this is totally unfair. We could fight this in court and maybe win, but the federal government will go after you on many counts, including the bombing of a national lab. I know you're innocent, but you must get real! This isn't about what's fair. This isn't about justice. Deals will be made. Former friends will try to keep themselves out of jail by testifying that in the past you sold them drugs."

"My friends would never sell me out," Brad said firmly.

"That's what I said about my friends during the House of Un-American Activities witch-hunt, but a few of my supposed friends did name me, and I went to prison. Did you ever give any grass to a friend?"

Brad shrugged.

Father and son sat in silence, staring across the distant bay. Marvin continued, "The FBI will present mountains of evidence. They will show pictures of you with Weather

Underground suspects in the national lab explosion. This isn't about the FBI evidence being the truth. Anything can happen in that courtroom. John feels that the FBI is likely to win in court and then you would face ten years in prison minimum. When I was young, I refused to compromise. I'll never forget facing that monster Joe McCarthy when he paralyzed Hollywood with his witch-hunt. I refused to answer his questions at the House hearing. That son-of-a-bitch Nixon couldn't get anything out of me. I refused to name names. I'll go to my grave knowing that Marvin Friedman never betrayed a friend. And I know you, son. You won't betray your friends." Marvin's speech faltered, and his eyes welled with tears. "You won't squeal. And because you won't, your prison sentence will be harsh."

In silence, they watched cargo ships coming into the bay and navy ships going out to sea. Marvin pressed on, "Brad, Son, ten years in prison would destroy you. If the system didn't destroy you, other prisoners would. You don't want to spend ten years with murderers and sex offenders." While the words "sex offenders" hovered over Brad, Marvin almost said more, but he couldn't.

For minutes, Brad sat deep in silence. His dad respected the need to think.

Brad said, "If I get in my car and start driving to Canada, the FBI would be watching and likely intercept me. If I snuck over the border, I'd be caught by Canadian authorities and turned over to the FBI."

"I think you've made an accurate assessment of trying to escape to Canada," Marvin said. "This isn't like kids going to Canada to avoid the draft. The FBI would charge you with unlawful flight to avoid prosecution, and Canada would cooperate with arrest and extradition."

"If I jumped bail and went into hiding, I'd be hunted, and life would be miserable for you and mom."

"As you've said, the FBI is watching, and you'd be caught."

Brad slammed his fist on the table, then immediately held his pained rib. His voice was a mix of pain, anger, and defeat as he said, "I'm trapped!"

"Son, this is the time to compromise. How bad would it be to spend two years in the coast guard?"

"Dad! The coast guard patrols the rivers in Vietnam. They're sitting ducks! A compromise could be a death sentence. Joining the military is a total sell-out. It violates everything I stand for. Even if I didn't get killed, I would be morally responsible for killing others. The military is a killing machine and that includes coast guard river patrols."

"There are risks in the coast guard and navy, but prison, Brad, prison."

"The FBI case is such bullshit. Last year I sold a little grass to friends at cost. At least, I thought that they were friends. The stuff in my apartment was an FBI plant. We're talking years in prison because I speak out against the war."

"For Ruth, prison is the unspeakable horrors she lived in Auschwitz – the starving masses, the tortured, the death of her brother. Seeing you in prison would break her heart." Marvin started crying. "Brad, we both love you."

Brad tried to choke back his own tears when he saw his father cry.

Linda ran and hugged Brad; he immediately yelped in pain. "Sorry," Brad said. "Fractured ribs from being kicked by the FBI."

"They're horrid! They kick you, frame you, and jail you on false charges. They bust me for giving away Girl Scout cookies. Meanwhile, Reagan throws away our Constitutional rights and uses us for target practice. Nixon secretly bombs Laos and Cambodia. The FBI is after the wrong people."

"Totally surreal," Brad said with a sigh.

"I've missed you," Linda said as she held his hands, unable to hug him. "Your dad's wonderful being here with you. So what are you two planning?"

Brad reached to hold her hands with his shaking hands and said, "Canada is now out. I should have gone last year. Now the FBI would follow me and probably nail me. Even if I got to Canada, the FBI would charge me with unlawful flight to avoid prosecution, and Canada would cooperate with arrest and extradition."

"You sound like a guy on the way to Columbia Law School," Linda said.

"Dad's hired a top criminal lawyer who feels that the FBI will present enough evidence to put me in prison for ten years, even though most of it is complete bullshit. I'm trying to come to terms with not expecting justice."

Linda sat intently listening as she pulled her hands into her lap. Her face and hands were sweating.

"Linda, I have been searching for a way out of this. My dad and my lawyer have negotiated a way to avoid prison by my joining the military for two years. I think I've lined-up a gig where I can serve at the VA Hospital in San Francisco. Yeah, I'll have to join the army, but I'll stay away from Vietnam and live in San Francisco."

"Wow. How did you engineer this?"

"I met with Jared Sandberg over at the VA Hospital. He's a surgeon and army major. He's in for a few years because they paid for his medical school. I grew up with Jared's younger brother. Sandberg will request me after I enlist."

Linda stared at Brad in disbelief. "Honey, I think that you are so desperate, you're ready to grab hold of a rainbow. Look, my brother was promised training to be a master mechanic when the army recruited him. Next thing we know, he's flying helicopters in the jungle. Now he's lucky to be alive if you call it lucky when you've lost both legs. A major is nothing. You join the army and you'll end up in Vietnam."

"Jared is confident about this."

"You're being delusional! Don't you remember all the workshops we attended, where vets told their stories about being lied to by the army?"

"This is my best shot. Maybe, my only hope. If ten years in prison wouldn't kill me, it would kill my mom."

Linda was shocked. "Brad, the army violates your core values. Everything you've fought for. Don't do it. Prison is not your only choice. Fight them."

"Please, hear me out. Yeah, the FBI planted the grass. Who's the judge going to believe? They've got sworn testimony from people that bought drugs from me in sixty-seven. I can get ten years as a drug dealer. Ten years, Linda."

"This is total bullshit. You sold grass at cost to friends. Everybody does that. Fight them, Brad. I fought them and won."

"Possession of marijuana is a felony. Sale is a felony on multiple counts."

"Right, but fight them."

"Remember Steve getting three years in prison for possession of one joint?" Brad asked.

"I remember."

"He was out in eighteen months for good behavior. Couple of months later, he hitched back east to see family and friends.

But in leaving the area he broke parole. Now, he's back in maximum-security prison for years. One joint!"

"Insane."

"I'm proud of you for fighting and winning, Linda. My dad was incredibly proud that you refused to give the FBI any names or say a word about me," Brad said.

"I never would."

"But you hadn't broken the law. They got you for Girl Scout cookies. The FBI's got a whole book on me. They showed it to my attorney." Linda looked at Brad's blurred image through her tears. Brad said, "I've cut a great deal."

"This blows my mind. You're going to join the army?" Linda said in shock.

"I've cut a deal where I won't go to Vietnam."

"The army's going to train you to be a killer, just like they did to my brother. Flew a chopper. Killed before he got killed. He even wrote my dad, begging to be sent a Colt 45, since army rifles kept jamming. This is my brother who promised me that he would avoid fighting and would never kill anyone!"

"That won't happen to me."

"I've heard it all before. I thought I knew you. I thought I loved you. You've sold your soul. I don't know who you are." Linda was angry and crying.

"Linda, you got a thirty-four-hour taste of jail, but you don't know what prison would mean. My dad went to prison when he was innocent. My mother was in Auschwitz. She has numbers tattooed on her arm. My going to prison would break her heart. It could kill her."

Linda very gently placed her arms around Brad, avoiding his fractured ribs, and sobbed. As the minutes wore on, she attempted to talk, but could not. She finally was able to say,

"Months ago, we agreed that in June you would move to New York and I would move to Laguna. Now it's June. We've been friends, we've loved each other, but we knew it was ending. I'm sorry. I hope they don't destroy you like they destroyed my brother." She continued while sobbing, "You're in a horrible dilemma, and you've got to do what's best. I hope this works out for you, Brad. Please be safe."

11

Collateral Damage

Days after saying goodbye to Brad, and after graduating from U.C. Berkeley, Linda was flying home to Ohio. She replayed her breakup with Brad over and over. As the flight descended, she was comforted by the views of Lake Erie, old neighborhoods, and even the Cleveland cityscape.

After her father drove her home from the airport, she stepped out from the car and into her mother's long embrace. Linda took in the lush greeting of trees and flowers, grateful beneficiaries of her mom's green thumb. Her gaze swept the two-story pale-blue Colonial home, white trimmed, with its sun porch lined with rocking chairs facing the street.

Her brother opened a side door and maneuvered down a makeshift plank in his wheelchair. Linda tried to hide the shock of seeing John with no legs as he skillfully descended the ramp. She ran to him and hugged him for a long time while she cried.

Later in the afternoon, after the unpacking, hearing family news and local gossip, Linda and John sat alone on the porch, she in her favorite rocking chair and he in his wheelchair. From high in the great tree she heard the loud whistles of a Northern cardinal defending his territory.

Linda looked at John and realized how much his eyes had changed. They were still hazel, but the brightness had been replaced with a distant stare. Unlike the past, he did not look at her or her parents when they talked; he stared into the distance, aware, alert, on guard.

Linda decided that he had heard too many questions from others and that she would talk. "I feel so relieved to have graduated. No papers, no finals. I'm looking forward to teaching. I'll be at a Montessori school with the most darling little kids."

John interrupted, "Just for the record, I can still have kids. Someday, you can be Aunt Linda." He didn't know if he startled her. He did not look. "Don't know if I will. Maybe I'll do some coaching for kids missing a limb or two."

"I wasn't sure you wanted to talk about it," Linda said.

"Don't mind," John replied. "I should've stayed in college like you, but I didn't know what I wanted to do, so I dropped school and got a mechanics job at the GM dealer. You know how I've always loved working on cars and trucks?"

"Yes, I remember you scraping together all your savings to buy that old '56 Chevy. Then you begged Dad to lend you the money to rebuild the engine. When you were done with the two-tone painting, your dream car made you the king of Cuyahoga County."

John smiled and looked down the street lined with trees and familiar homes and then said, "Yeah, I never had trouble getting dates after that baby. When I went to 'Nam, I made good money selling that Chevy."

"What was it like in the army?"

"The recruiters talked up how the army would train me to be a master mechanic. I was excited about fixing helicopters." John quickly looked left when he saw a car turn on to the street. He stared for a while. "I learned to fix choppers, but it wasn't long before they had me flying them. In the beginning, I shuttled officers around from Saigon to their battalion headquarters or out to where their command was scattered. They'd rotate in some colonel who'd never been in on-the-ground jungle combat and I'd fly him around while he dished out orders. Some poor grunt on two hours sleep would set up a whole perimeter, digging foxholes, and then this colonel would radio the guy's officer and tell them to move the perimeter six inches to the left. More hours of useless work and no sleep, just to prove the colonel had the biggest dick."

Linda was unnerved by the lack of emotion in John's narration and how he would hear a noise and startle. "It sounds disorganized."

"For the brass it's by the book and CYA. It's the guys in the jungle who know how to fight." John again stared down the street and into the trees. "And then, when you finally get an officer who knows what he's doing, the army reassigns him, or rotates him back stateside. You'd be surprised at how many in the army are clueless."

"Wow."

"I wish I could have just shuttled the brass, because it really got hairy when I started flying the big choppers into battle and then evacuating the dead and wounded. It was kind of funny when I stopped wearing my helmet on my head and started sitting on it so the Cong wouldn't shoot bullets up my ass." John paused, looked at the trees lining the street, stared at faces a thousand yards away, and then continued with a flat voice, "Then it happened. Last month I flew a company into a Cong-controlled area for search and destroy. Rockets were everywhere. All you could see was fire and smoke. The noise was deafening. Our chopper exploded and went down and the next thing you know I woke up in an ICU looking like this."

"You're lucky to be alive."

John's voice was thick with irony. "Yeah, a lucky man. But, hey, I got a Bronze Star and a discharge." John looked at Linda and saw her crying. "Hey, don't cry, Sis. I got the GI Bill. The army's going to pay for me to go to college. I'm applying to

Purdue. I'm going to get a degree in medical engineering. I want to make prosthetics."

Hours after John went to bed, and hours after Linda finally found sleep, she bolted awake to the sound of a gun blast. She heard her father shout and her mother scream. Looking out the window and seeing nothing, she ran downstairs, looked out the back window and shrieked.

She ran into the backyard, evaded her father's attempt to grab her, and ran to what was left of her brother in his wheelchair fallen backwards to the ground, holding a shotgun in his mouth, with the remains of his face lying in a pool of blood. Dead.

Hours later, Linda found all the army bottles of prescription drugs. She slowly read John's medical file detailing his leg pain, back pain, hearing loss, and severe depression. Looking in the wastebasket, she found crumpled note: *Nothing left but pain. I cannot be a burden. The only end is the end.*

In the days that followed, she mechanically helped with funeral arrangements, the memorial service, and calling friends. Honoring her parents' request, she did her best to keep the press away. Her father refused the army offer to participate in the funeral service.

There was only sadness during her week in Cleveland. At the funeral, well wishes from friends did not make her well. At the memorial service, words of comfort did not comfort.

April was not the cruelest month. No longer was it May. June was a malevolent monster.

12

Father's Day

It was Father's Day and some families were in San Clemente for a day at the beach, a picnic, or the start of a summer vacation. The windblown ocean was a choppy froth that discouraged most from going in the water. There would be no action for the lifeguards.

David looked out at the ocean, and thought of the Father's Day when he was nine and he went fishing with his dad. David had been eager to do everything right. His father praised him for catching four mackerel. He remembered reveling in the rare praise.

David struggled to feel at peace with his father. He feared that he would become a man too much like his father. His mind drifted on the hot afternoon. The outside phone line rang in the headquarters tower and David answered.

"David, I'm glad I reached you, Son."

David took a deep breath. "Dad. Happy Father's Day." After their big fight, they had not talked. David had not sent him a Father's Day card.

"Thanks, Son. I'm not too far away. Over here at Camp Pendleton. I thought we might have dinner. Is your calendar open?"

"Yes. Where do you want to eat? I'm off at six, so I could meet you at the restaurant at seven. At nineteen hundred hours." David did not want his dad to stop by his house; it would fail inspection.

"Nineteen hundred hours it is. How about at the Seafood Grill?"

"Yes, sir." David knew the protocol for a phone conversation with his father. Be brief and to the point.

At 1900 hours exactly, David walked through the front door of the Seafood Grill. David had gone home to shower and change. He was wearing a white button-down dress shirt, pressed pants, and dress shoes, all normally reserved for job interviews.

As David scanned the crowded waiting area, his dad walked up, extended a handshake, and said, "Hello, Son. Good to see you. Look at you. You're dressed up, and I'm in my civvies." Dex, age fifty, was wearing a golf shirt, khaki pressed pants, loafers, and a checkered sports coat.

The two shook hands and then stood at ease until their name was called. David then followed his father to their table.

"It's been a long day that started at zero six hundred with some heavy brass, but finished with golf. The Commandant of the Marine Corps ran the breakfast meeting," Dex said.

"I'm impressed, Dad. You're hanging out with members of the Joint Chiefs of Staff."

Dex smiled. "Well, don't get the wrong impression. I don't spend much time with the four-stars. When I do, it's mainly to listen and say 'yes, sir' and 'aye aye, sir,' but I have to be well prepared for any questions. General Chapman was holding a powwow at Camp Pendleton, where he used to serve as commanding officer. Likes to get back here. We had to do some long-range logistics planning for Vietnam."

David queried, "Long range? I thought Westmoreland and Nixon said that this would be over soon." His father paused, looking out as if formulating an answer. *I shouldn't have started with such a direct question. I just reacted. Be nice. This is Father's Day.*

Dex said, "Well, Son, don't believe everything you read in the papers. We've developed plans for different scenarios."

David listened, half expecting his dad to elaborate. This should lead to an interesting therapy session. Am I angry? Afraid? Trying to provoke? Being myself? Will there be a blow-up?

Silence settled in like the evening fog. *How am I? Thanks for asking for the first time in my life. Great. Lots of insights in therapy. My acid trip was amazing. I experienced my oneness with the universe and I got laid.*

David ended the silence. "Happy Father's Day." David handed his dad a gift bought minutes earlier at a bookstore.

Dex unwrapped the book *Great Golf Courses of the World*. Dex looked at the photography of favorite golf courses. "Look at that Green Monster. I played Doral. Tried to break ninety that day, but found too many water hazards. Just like my career in the navy, too many water hazards." Dex chuckled to himself and then looked at David. "Thank you, Son. Thoughtful of you."

"Sure, Dad."

"It's a great game and never-ending challenge. You should take it up."

Right, Dad! I'm broke because of you, and you want me to spend a ton of money on a rich man's game. David was angry but tried not to show it. On the drive over, he had vowed to give this guy a chance and be more accepting. "Maybe someday."

Dex noticed David's quick flash of anger and said, "I've got an extra set of clubs I could give you." Dex waited for a reply from David, but only heard silence. "Golf is a good way to advance your career whether you're in the military or in business. It gives you uninterrupted hours to talk with the others in the foursome."

"Maybe someday." Then as an afterthought David added, "Thanks."

"You're a college graduate now, aren't you?"

"Yes, sir. I've got my degree in computer science with honors."

"I'm proud of you, Son. I always knew you were smart. Wish I understood computers. Under my command, I've got an information technology team. Every time I ask for something, they ask for more money. It's a challenge for me to get the missions right, and answer to my commanding officers. This old navy dog needs to learn some new tricks." Dex paused and then asked, "So what's next for you?"

He's getting down to business. Should I tell him how I finally got laid, even though you never had the guts to have "the talk" with me and kept me locked up in that all-boys military academy? No, be cool. "After guarding this summer, I hope to start selling computers in the fall. Got my next round of interviews with Burroughs, Hewlett-Packard, and Digital Equipment. IBM says they're interested, but have a freeze on hiring."

"All good companies. We're buying from all of them. I'm surprised they'd hire guys who could be drafted after they spend a bunch of money training them. I guess they figure it's better than hiring a gal who'll get pregnant and quit on them."

David opened the menu, but didn't focus on the choices.

"Have you gentlemen decided what you like?" The waitress asked.

"Well now, Sally, I believe that I like you." Dex drawled and smiled.

Sally stared at her order pad. "What would you like for dinner?"

"I'll have the surf and turf," Dex said. "Make my steak well done."

"I'll have the salmon medium rare with a baked potato," David said.

"Would either of you like to order a drink?"

"Jack Daniels on the rocks," Dex said.

"A bottle of Coors," David said.

"I apologize, but I'll need to see your ID." David let her look at his driver's license, and Sally was gone.

Sitting at the corner table, both devoured their meals, beers, and Jack Daniels. David looked through the picture window at running lights of boats tossed in the lonely swells.

Dex said, "I guess your graduation exercises are coming soon."

"Yeah, about three weeks."

"That will be a proud day for you."

David knew where the conversation was going and said, "I'm proud, but I won't be at the graduation exercise. All guards are on duty every weekend."

"I'm surprised you're not going to such a milestone in your life. Especially, since you're graduating with honors."

"You just don't get it, Dad. I'm broke. Graduation with cap and gown is thirty-five bucks. Losing a day of work is another thirty-five bucks. I've spent my last dollar on school, textbooks, car, gas, and food. It all adds up." There was intensity and anger in the final sentence.

Dex offered, "Understood. I could cover the money. I'd like to see your graduation."

"You can't buy me off, Dad! You cut me off last year. In fact, you cut me off when I was five years old."

13

Secret Service

As July 4 unfolded, every inch of sand was covered with people, their umbrellas, beach towels, food, toys, and large radios and cassette music players.

David and Carlo drove the Scout that day. The two guards slowly cruised the beach, hearing music of every genre and every continent – classical, jazz, Latin, blues, rock, folk, and movie themes. Parents listened to Sousa marches, while their stoned teenagers listened to Jimi Hendrix. Couples nestled under blankets, serenaded by baritones from Frank Sinatra to Jim Morrison.

The two administered first aid through the day. They helped panicked mothers find lost kids. David and Carlo earned overtime by driving the Scout from 6 p.m. to 9 p.m. on that July 4. David had told no one that this was his birthday.

Fireworks were illegal on San Clemente Beach. From the cliff, Martinez in Headquarters could see the Scout's location. There was a blackout section from 30 yards in front of the guard vehicle to 30 yards behind. The rest of the beach looked like a battlefield with fireworks and rockets of every color. Explosions were loud enough to leave everyone deaf for days.

On Monday, Carson Johnson, with the Secret Service, called David. "You're in. If you still want to lifeguard at the Summer White House, there's a party this Friday. Budget is fifty each, for two lifeguards.

Friday, Carlo and David got off work at 5 p.m. and drove

directly to the president's Summer White House, one mile away at Cotton's Point. They rode in Carlo's woodie station wagon because it looked slightly more respectable than David's VW bus. Carlo had even taken it to a car wash. Their hair was normally short, as required of all lifeguards, but after their Wednesday haircuts, they looked as clean cut as the Secret Service.

Carlo said, "Outta sight. This is for real, right? The Secret Service is paying us to meet the most powerful people in the world."

"This is totally happening. Fifty each."

"What will you say if you meet the president?"

David said, "Now that I've graduated, lost my student deferment, and been reclassified 1-A, I'm going to recommend that lifeguards be exempt from the draft."

"I can see I've gone too far with you. I tried to pull you out of your introverted intellectual shell, and I've created a Frankenstein monster. This is not the place to campaign for anything. The place will be crawling with Secret Service."

"You're right, let's get stoned now," David dared. "It will be too dangerous to do it at Nixon's home."

"Christ, you didn't bring a joint! What if they search us?" For once, Carlo was being cautious.

"Ever since that Big Sur weekend, my mind has flowed like a river. Those Tibetan Bowls did it for me."

Carlo turned his focus from driving to study David, then announced, "You're fucking with me. You're not going to smoke anything and you're going to behave at the Summer White House."

"Of course I am. The Secret Service invited us after they spent time with me in headquarters doing their beach surveillance. Even though I was pissed off about being classified 1-A, I was respectful and cooperative. It was only in my mind that I was thinking one, two, three, four, we don't want your fucking war."

Carlo was playing the theme song to James Bond's Goldfinger at full volume. As they approached the Cotton's Point security gate, he turned off the music and spoke to the guard, "We're going to the president's estate."

The guard was calm and formal, "Your names?"

"Carlo Abruzzo and David Eliot."

The guard checked his list, and then looked at Carlo and David, clean-cut and in lifeguard jackets with state emblems. They were motioned to drive into the estate.

Carson Johnson greeted the two. David was assigned to lifeguard the swimming pool; Carlo was assigned the beach. David stood by the pool wearing his red lifeguard trunks, lifeguard jacket, both with California insignias, and holding an orange rescue buoy. At the party, over 40 people were in the pool area, talking and politicking; no one was swimming. This started looking like an easy and welcome fifty dollars to David.

David looked around Nixon's summer estate, named La Casa Pacifica, which is Spanish for The House of Peace. The mansion, other buildings on the estate, and large gazebo, all were painted white with orange tiled roofs. David marveled at the size of the estate, rich with trees, flowered gardens, and magnificent views of the ocean.

Soon, six men in sport coats and slacks were walking toward him. The man in the center was recognizable with slick hair, pointed nose, and affected smile. "Hello, young man, I understand that you are the lifeguard who has been helping my Secret Service." Richard Nixon, president of the United States, greeted him.

David got past his shock and replied, "Yes, sir. It's an honor to be here."

The president smiled and said, "Well with the lifeguards on one side of Casa Pacifica and the marines on the other, I guess I'm protected, especially if I try that surfboard that my daughters gave me." The suits surrounding the president laughed as if he had told some great joke. The entourage moved on.

The president! That was quick. Damn. I forgot to ask him to stop dropping napalm on women and children.

On the beach, Carlo was watching a dozen of the White House party playing volleyball. Carlo was impressed with Kissinger's serve and with his deep gravel-voiced banter. Carlo sang "Foxy Lady" softly to himself, while mesmerized with a tall brunette, playing in her white tennis outfit.

After the game, she walked slowly past Carlo.

Carlo smiled and said, "You made some great plays out there. Enjoying yourself?"

Jessica replied, "Yes, life's too short not to have fun."

"I'm Carlo. I lifeguard at the state beach. I usually only get to this beach if the surf is good."

Jessica smiled and said, "You surf? I'd love to learn how."

The next evening, Jessica and Joyce waited for Carlo to close and lock his tower. The three walked to a secluded spot on the Riviera district beach. Carlo laid his 10-foot Dewey Weber surfboard on the sand and demonstrated how to catch a wave. "You see a wave coming that hasn't broken, but is close to breaking." Lying on the board he continued, "You take a few hard strokes like this, then push up to standing in the middle of the board with one foot forward." He demonstrated as he talked, then pointed out to surfers in the ocean. "Watch. See how he paddled, got up, and is riding at a diagonal in front of the break."

Carlo had Jessica then Joyce each practice several times on the board in the sand. "Excellent." He encouraged as each, in their revealing bikinis, practiced lying on the board and then standing. Carlo viewed their progress from several angles, until David arrived carrying his 9-foot, 6-inch, Hobie. David smiled at all. Carlo had already claimed Jessica as his surfing partner. David was delighted to be with Joyce. The four walked to the water and waded in until waist deep.

David told Joyce, "OK, lie on the board facing the front, and I'll lie on the back."

Joyce lay face down on the board that David was holding to keep it steady. Water splashed and Joyce squealed, "It's cold."

David said, "OK. An awkward request, but you'll need to spread your legs so that I can fit on the board." Without showing concern, she spread her legs, and David mounted the board face down with his chest resting on Joyce's buttocks, partially covered with a small bikini bottom. "OK, let's paddle." They both paddled through the incoming wave, as David flattened over Joyce, held the board upright as the wave splashed over them, then continued to paddle.

Soon both couples reached a good spot to catch waves. The surf was small, and they were able to keep the boards upright.

Carlo said, "Let's show them how to catch a wave."

David replied, "Right. Joyce, swim over to Carlo and Jessica. You and Jessica can sit on Carlo's board and watch. David demonstrated how to wait for the right wave. He stroked, stood, rode the wave 50 yards, and then kicked out. He made it look easy. As he paddled back to them, the women applauded.

David said, "OK, Joyce, sit on my board, and I'll tell you

when to start paddling for the right wave." David helped lift her on to the board. She smiled at David.

Jessica and Joyce sat on their respective boards. When the right wave approached, Carlo and David starting shouting instructions to lie down and paddle. The women paddled frantically. Jessica, with a modicum of fear, pulled out just before she could have captured the wave.

Joyce caught the wave, started standing, and then fell off. She reminded David of Sandra Dee in the Gidget movies, but Gidget never wore a pale-blue wet bikini that revealed as much.

Joyce and Jessica were laughing, paddling, sometimes catching a wave, and always falling within a few yards. As the lesson continued, David and Carlo repeatedly swam after the boards with all the enthusiasm of dogs chasing sticks. Like dogs, they hoped to be rewarded with treats.

Then Joyce caught a wave, stood, and actually rode it halfway to shore. Everyone was cheering and excited. Within five minutes, Jessica caught and rode a wave. She was ecstatic. Two novices were officially declared surfers and given As in the class.

Walking to shore, while still waist deep in water, Carlo congratulated Jessica and spontaneously kissed her lips. Seeing this, Joyce gave David a sidelong look, but failed to catch his eye. She leaned her wet body against David and said, "Thanks for the lesson. I can't wait to tell my friends back home that I surfed." She moved her lips inches from David; he pulled her close and kissed her. Her body felt wonderful, and he started getting an erection and tried to pull away. Joyce firmly pulled David closer for a lingering kiss.

After the surfing, Joyce and Jessica drove their rental car back to the San Clemente Inn, so that they could change for dinner. For some reason, the women did not want Carlo and David to see them at the inn. They agreed to meet for dinner at 7:30 p.m.

Carlo and David had secured a table overlooking the ocean. They were given the best view in the place, thanks to Carlo recently delivering premium marijuana to the manager. Twenty minutes later, Joyce and Jessica walked in wearing stunning silk dresses that stopped far short of the knees, as was the fashion. David stood up, hugged Joyce and held her chair. Carlo raised his glass to Jessica, but did not stand, presumably to avoid displaying his enthusiasm. Jessica smiled warmly as she seated herself.

In anticipation of ordering seafood, and being Italian, Carlo ordered a bottle of Pinot Grigio. The four enjoyed the wine from their table on the cliff over the Pacific. The sun slowly disappeared at the edge of the cobalt blue ocean, as distant clouds became pink, then fuchsia, and then fire red. Fresh seafood was ordered and devoured, as evening became night.

Jessica shared her story of becoming part of the White House staff. She had always loved writing. She had graduated with honors in journalism from the University of Southern California. Working for Bob Haldeman at J. Walter Thompson, she had performed brilliantly on the election campaign that was key to Nixon's winning the presidency. Now she was a liaison in foreign press relations, being fluent in French, Spanish and Portuguese. Carlo listened like an awe struck teenager.

Joyce described growing-up in Maryland with both her parents working for the State Department. Washington D.C. had always been her home, from birth through her law school at Georgetown to the present. Joyce explained that she was in the Justice Department. She was in California until Thursday handling a "West Coast situation."

Joyce gazed at David and thanked him for the surfing and wonderful evening. With a touch of sadness, she said that she was having a difficult time going through a divorce. No one noticed Jessica's incredulity.

Jessica paid for the dinner as she described the generous travel and meal budget for White House press relations. Carlo suggested brandy and music at his and David's home. The women readily agreed.

Through the streets of Dana Point and San Clemente, Joyce successfully followed Carlo's woodie while driving her rental car and said, "I like my David. He is interesting, sensitive, and handsome."

"Agreed. I like Carlo's looks, body, and passion. When he looks at me, I feel undressed!"

"Yes, his interest in you has been quite visible."

Jessica laughed. "Yes, the poor boy, I need to help him with that. I almost did on his surfboard, feeling his wet body on top of me."

"Oh my god. I know. Feeling David's strong body between my legs was driving me wild." She paused and smiled dreamily. "We're officially California surfers! Isn't this great. A romantic evening, hot young guys, beautiful sunset."

Jessica agreed, "Young and yummy. This is such a welcome relief from meetings, memorandums, briefs, and dealing with rooms full of egos." A minute lapsed before Jessica said, "I noticed that you were quite vague about the West Coast situation. How bad is the nuclear incident?"

"Sorry, I wish I could say something, but I can't," Joyce said.

"I also noticed you talk about going through a divorce. Is there something I don't know?"

"Don't say anything. Please! Lately, Sheldon has been a prick. I work as hard as he does, yet I carry the heavy load with the house and kids. I deserve this. I just wished I felt a little more relaxed about having a brief affair."

"It's too bad these lifeguards are so straight arrow and clean cut. It would be fun to smoke some grass."

"Their jobs may require the look. You never know."

"These two are flawless. Foxy ladies!" Carlos said, "On a scale of one to ten, each gets a twenty."

"Agreed. I'm hot for Joyce. It's surreal. Like, I'm out of my league."

"Hang in there. Her whole body language shows that you turn her on. I'm definitely in heat over Jessica. Paddling out, laying between her legs, on her stoned-fox wet body. When she pulled me close for that second kiss in the water, I could have made love to her right then and there." Carlo paused. "Don't do anything stupid back at our place. None of your long philosophical discourse. No discussion of politics. Nothing heavy. Just music and dancing in the dark. You got that Socrates?"

David grinned and said, "Yes, coach. Got it. Hey, you've got to admit, I was cool at dinner."

"Right on. You were! And funny. You've really loosened up since you got laid."

David said, "Yes, the transformative effects of sex, acid, and therapy."

"After Joyce gets through with you, you'll have a lot to discuss at your next session!" They laughed, and Carlo continued, "It's too bad they're with the White House. Some dope would enhance the romantic mood."

"Not a good idea. Joyce is a U. S. Attorney."

"Don't they work with the Narcs?"

"I think she works on White House issues. Not sure. Still, you'd better make sure there is no odor from the stash."

"We're covered. It's in the coffee beans. It's outrageous that smoking grass is a felony. Remember Ken Booth going to prison for possession of a joint?"

"Get a law-and-order judge and your life is ruined."

The two cars arrived and parked in front of David and Carlo's place. Carlo opened the door for Jessica, and David for Joyce. Each movement was like steps in a tango.

As she approached the house with David's arm around her, Joyce said, "The sky is beautiful." They both looked up to a sky filled with millions of stars. David pulled her closer. They fused into a kiss that brought them and their lingering passions together.

Minutes later, when David and Joyce finally walked through the front door, Carlo and Jessica were not in the living room. Through the door to Carlo's room, they could hear Jessica screaming "yes" in at least four languages.

Joyce and David looked at each other and laughed. David offered, "I could pour us some brandy while you're selecting some music to drown out the jungle sounds."

Blushing, she said, "Excellent idea." She flipped through the 33-RPM record albums: Beatles, Moody Blues, Carole King, Simon and Garfunkel, Doors, Stan Getz, Mozart, Bach, Beethoven, Debussy, and Stravinsky. She selected Rachmaninoff and put the vinyl record on the player, and then dropped the needle. The Russian's piano music filled the room with dark passion.

David sat next to her on the sofa. The brandy warmed in their hands. Joyce drank the elixir. David said, "A toast to an intriguing intellect, a beautiful woman, and a promising surfer." Joyce's eyes glistened. Glasses clinked in a toast, and they drank. David said, "Intoxicating."

"Yes, it's a delicious brandy."

David, slightly blushing, said, "What I was trying to say is that you're intoxicating."

While Rachmaninoff wove together complex themes into a rhapsody, Joyce and David were lost in fusing kisses. While Rachmaninoff explored themes by Paganini, David could not resist letting his hands explore her delicious body and she could not resist his hands. With piano and strings rising and falling together, they were naked in David's bedroom. Their lovemaking was beautiful. After their orgasms, they lay together for a long time.

David floated through the next few days as easily as the white cumulus floated in the sky above. *So this is why they call it love making!* The next night, he took Joyce to the Laguna Art Festival, strolling the grounds on the hot July night, discussing art, history, and civilizations. The night was long with lovemaking.

The following evening, he took her to Tortilla Flats. He talked about the lingering influence of California once being ruled by Spain and then Mexico. She talked about growing up in Washington D.C. with politics at the center of everything. David talked about being an admiral's son. When he asked about her work, she always deftly changed the subject.

The conversation shifted to romance. They left without finishing the main course and with every intention of creating their own dessert.

After another night of making love, and after they both dressed, Joyce sat on the sofa with David and said, "These past days have been wonderful. I'll never forget you."

David replied, "You're a beautiful and passionate woman. Will you be back here this summer?"

"Probably not."

"Maybe I'll get to Washington in the months ahead. My dad's already had two tours of duty in the Pentagon. How about giving me your address and phone number?"

Joyce looked startled and blushed, then stammered, "You know things are crazy for me right now. I may be moving. I've got your number, and I'll definitely call when I'm back out here."

"Please do." David pulled her close, and they kissed for a long time.

Joyce stood. There were tears in her eyes. "Bye." She walked to her rental car and drove off.

Two days later, after Joyce was gone and after David finally recovered from sleep deprivation, he returned home from a day of guarding to see Carlo sitting on the sofa with a Cheshire-Cat smile. Carlo said dreamily, "I dig this Maui Waui. Amazing." Both breathed the pungent aroma from their favorite marijuana. "And you've got to have it with this primo Anejo Tequila."

David took a deep hit, held it in his lungs until he coughed. Carlo laughed. David laughed, and then took another hit, this time keeping it all in his lungs. Then another hit. Then another.

Carlo poured him a shot of Tequila. "Haven't seen much of you lately."

"Nor you. But I've heard all these wild animal sounds in the middle of the night from your room. Jessica sure can scream 'yes' in lots of languages."

"I noticed the wall adjoining your room was rocking like an earthquake." Carlo took another shot of Tequila. "Jessica is amazing. She's drop-dead gorgeous. Totally uninhibited. She took me on more rides than Disneyland; every one an E-ticket." Carlo paused, flushed, then said, "You know what she wants? She wants to have a threesome. She said that you're hot and that she wants to suck you and fuck you."

David blushed, squirmed, and crossed his legs. "Wow. I've never been in a threesome."

"You've barely been laid. Live, man!"

"Yeah. But a threesome just feels too weird. Sorry, man, I can't do it."

Carlo enthused, "Do it, man. Jessica is a stone fox. Can you imagine her naked, sucking on you while I'm fucking her? She will blow your mind. Live life! When you're lying in some jungle in Vietnam slowly bleeding to death, going through your list of regrets, you'll regret no threesome with Jessica. Or soon, you'll be old and married with screaming kids, wishing you'd lived out your fantasies. Do it, man!"

David blushed. He slowly took another long hit of grass and then another shot of Tequila. Feeling a little dizzy, he stared at the blank wall. Finally he said, "Sorry man, I just can't do it. Plus, I'm eight miles high over Joyce. I might be falling in love."

"Sorry to tell you, but you need to forget Joyce. She's already flown back to Washington. Jessica told me that the divorce story is a lie. Joyce is totally married with kids, just looking for some adventure."

"She lied to me? I thought she really cared." David sulked, then stared at the picture on the far wall, and then remembered how she wouldn't give her address and phone. "Lying about her marriage. Wild threesomes. Don't these women have any morals?"

"Of course not. They work for the White House!"

14

Laguna Beach

Is that Linda? Looking through kinetic art shape-shifting with the ocean breeze, David stared at the woman in the distance. By now, Linda should have moved from Berkeley. He had left two messages with her new roommate, Rachel, but never received a call.

People strolled through this outdoor Laguna art show looking at watercolors of Italian streets, acrylics of women with smiles as cryptic as the Mona Lisa, and carvings that gave shape to gnarled wood. David weaved through the crowd toward the woman, passing booths of framed photographs, watercolors, and carvings. He looked at the woman in the plain cotton dress, black gypsy shawl, and long wavy hair blowing in the wind. As he approached, he grew confident that it was Linda. He felt nervous.

"Linda, welcome to Laguna," David said. "I haven't seen you since Big Sur."

Not seeing David approach, she startled. "What a surprise." She failed to smile, embrace, or even extend her hand. She wore no makeup or jewelry.

"I can see that you didn't expect to run into David Eliot."

"No, ah, David."

Amid the meandering crowd, David stood face-to-face with Linda. In Big Sur, she had often smiled at him and listened with lively attention. Now she seemed distant and unsmiling with sad eyes. He felt discouraged, but decided to continue. "We are both graduates."

Finally she gave the hint of a smile. "Yes, I've said goodbye to Berkeley. How do you feel about graduating?"

"Great," said David. "I was stoked to get my diploma. I celebrated for twenty-four hours before getting a letter from Uncle Sam reclassifying me 1-A. No more student deferment. They couldn't even give me a week to celebrate. Just one day."

"That's horrible," Linda said. "What are you going to do?"

"Stay out of Vietnam."

"I've heard that one before. Tough to do, unless you move to Canada."

"That's step eighty-five in my plan."

Linda laughed, "Step eighty-five?"

"I'd love to tell you and catch up for a few minutes. Do you want to sit?" He motioned to the bench.

"Okay," Linda said as they moved and sat down.

"I went to the American Friends and they gave some wonderful coaching. Have you heard of them?"

"Yes. Good people. I've got to hear about these eighty-five steps."

"The basic idea is to find a number of different issues that can be appealed at the local board, then state, then national - medical, religious, denial of due process. On medical, I've got x-rays of my flat feet. For due process, I went to my local board then sent them a long thank-you letter documenting what they said, including their several errors. I'm preparing for conscientious objector, I sent fifteen dollars to the Universal Life Church and I'm now a minister."

"Funny," Linda said and then covered her mouth with both hands. "I mean, ah, are you real religious?"

"No. I'm more into the kind of spiritual teachings we

experienced at the Big Sur workshop."

"Groovy."

"I could show you the eighty-five steps sometimes," David said and noticed Linda biting her lip and looking away. "I mean, anyway, I haven't seen you in three months. What's the latest with you?"

For the next 15 minutes, Linda told of the creation of People's Park, Reagan's destruction of it, her staring into a loaded shotgun, being interrogated and jailed for giving Girl Scout cookies, her temporary fame in national press, and speaking to thirty-thousand. David listened in amazement.

"What a mind blower! Interrogated by the FBI and jailed over a box of Girl Scout cookies!"

"Unbelievable. I used to be a sweet little Girl Scout who marched in our Fourth of July parade in Cleveland Heights," she said. "Then I marched in Oakland for civil rights and for ending the war. Now I'm afraid to get within a hundred yards of a cop."

David became self-conscious of his short hair and clean shave. He was glad that she hadn't seen him in his headquarters uniform. He said, "I've got to start reading the papers, sorry I missed you on the front page."

Linda looked at the expanse of the Pacific Ocean.

David broke the silence. "What a mind-blower that you talked to John Lennon."

Linda's face brightened with a full smile. "At first I was amazed. Then I felt like I was being unfaithful to Paul."

For a second, David looked puzzled. Then he burst into laughter.

"Give peace a chance," Linda quoted Lennon.

They silently sat on the bench, people watching.

"It sounds like Brad and his dad really came through for you."

"Yes, he and his dad were great after the arrest. Two weeks later, the FBI busted him. Because he was an SDS leader, the FBI planted a kilo of dope on him. Brad chickened out of a legal battle, cut a deal with the judge and agreed to join the army. Brad and I have split."

"Joined the army?"

"That's right, after years of leading the fight against Vietnam, he joined the army."

David was disturbed by the bitterness in her voice. He was also relieved that she wasn't dating Brad.

"While you've got a chance, go to Canada. The Man won't play by the rules," she said.

"I remember in Big Sur, you talked about student teaching. I can see you being good with kids and finding it fulfilling."

"Thanks. I've started being an aide at the local Montessori school. These little ones can be so sweet, at least when they're not running in five directions."

As they both stared out at the ocean, David felt that it was a now-or-never moment. Either she would go out with him, or he might not see her again. "Linda, I like you and I'm not saying that because you're famous." Linda looked at David and smiled. He continued, "Would you like to go out for dinner next Friday? Then we could go somewhere and listen to music."

She looked stunned and then said, "Thanks for asking, David. Maybe later in the summer. I'm a total mess right now."

"You look fine." David tried to say it as a joke and hide his disappointment at being rejected.

Linda slowly went on, "A couple of weeks ago, I went home to Cleveland. It was a shock to see my only brother, John, home from Vietnam after losing both legs in this horrible war. He was so distant and depressed. We were close. I love him. I, I, I loved him. He killed himself."

David reached and took Linda's hand in his. "I am so sorry. That's horrible. "

"Horrible." Linda started crying. "He could fix anything. Wanted to be a master mechanic. Wanted to get an engineering degree at Purdue. My big brother always protected me...." She held herself tightly. Her stream of tears became a river. Her sobs, crashing waves.

David pulled his chair next to her and held her. She returned his hold. The river flowed. The waves crashed.

Rachel sailed the borrowed catamaran along the jetty that protects boats from rough surf. She expertly tacked into the wind, keeping the sail trimmed, as she and Linda tacked toward the mouth of Newport Harbor that opened to the Pacific Ocean. From shore, modern cliff dwellers overlooked the boats, beaches with sunbathers, and the vast ocean of ever changing blues and greens.

"Coming about!" Rachel shouted as she and Linda ducked under the swinging boom, and then continued to tack into the unpredictable wind. As they approached the next beach, Pirate's Cove, they could hear the children screaming with delight as they raced into the cold water, and then laughing and daring their friends to follow their example. Others were engaged in games limited only by a child's imagination as they ran from cave to cave. Girls built sand castles. Boys leaped from rock to rock in mock sword fights. Pirates.

"So, you're going to dinner with David?" Rachel said.

"He's sweet. I've never had a guy just listen to me like that. He was that way in Big Sur. I told him this would be platonic.

After Brad and John, I'm too messed up for anything heavy."

"I hope he respects your wish. I have platonic friends in GOO."

"Goo?" Linda asked.

"Get Oil Out. GOO." Rachel clarified. "I've also had a guy slide his hand between my legs after agreeing to be platonic."

"David won't have a chance to do that. Besides, I would just end it."

"I hope you don't get involved before you're ready. Look at what you've been through. I miss going out with Wes, but I'm not ready to see anyone." Rachel said. "Coming about!" Both shifted sides and worked the sheets to fill the sail.

"At least you know what you want. All I know is what I've lost. I've lost John, lost Brad, lost Berkeley. My mom wants me to move back to Ohio. I never want to see Cleveland again. I was an anti-war hero. I tried going to the rally in LA, but I freaked. I suffocated in the crowd. Freaked. I'm done with rallies."

They sailed in silence. Progress was slow as they tacked, sailing into the wind.

After hearing screams of delight from the children playing on shore, Rachel said, "Someday I'd like children, I think, but first my PhD and saving all the beautiful creatures of the sea."

"Just saving the whales will take years. Sounds like a late marriage."

"No hurry," Rachel said. "I'll live to be one hundred. Time for everything."

"I guess I'm in no hurry, since John married Yoko, and Paul married Linda."

"I still can't believe that you talked with John Lennon."

"My Girl Scout cookie fame."

"Coming about!" The women slid across the canopy that connected the two pontoons of their catamaran as the boom swung across, almost brushing their hair. Rachel navigated the sailboat around the large yacht motoring out to sea. Some from the deck waved. Two guys whistled.

Their boat was now on a broad reach as they returned to the harbor rather than testing the 14-foot Hobie Cat in the big swells of the open ocean. Rachel next maneuvered around a fishing boat, passing close enough to smell the Bonito, Mackerel and Sardines mixed with the sharp aroma of diesel fumes. The fishermen were happily sharing a beer as they bragged about the big one that got away. Pirates.

Rachel returned to topics debated in women's groups - marriage and last names. "If I ever marry, I will not give up my last name, but perhaps I will add my husband's surname somewhere in the middle of all my other Latin names. Possibly I will also include the names of some favorite boyfriends."

"What's with all the Latin names?"

"Honor. We must honor our mother's family, our father's, cities, history, and tradition. *Familia*. With all our names, everyday is *El Día de los Muertos*." Rachel was amused with herself. "Now that you're personal friends with John Lennon, tell me what's going on with the Beatles?"

"They've split for real. It's the end of music!" Linda said. "It's terrible. The same day that Paul and this other Linda get married, George and his wife Pattie get busted for possession of hash. It blows my mind. They're in their own home minding their own business, and dragged off to jail, just like Brad."

"The world is upside down. A president can draft a million guys to fight an illegal war. No problem. An oil company can break the rules and cover 800 miles of beaches with tar that kills all the birds and fish. No problem. But light up a joint and you go to prison."

"Exactly! It's insane."

"Coming about!" With increased expertise, the two shifted weight and then hung over the pontoon rising into the air, using their weight to counter the lift. The wind was stronger in the middle of the harbor.

Linda was still thinking of the Beatles. "Then only eight days after Paul's marriage and George's bust, John goes off to Gibraltar and marries Yoko. It's like some chain reaction. And only after marrying Yoko, does John call me. He calls me from bed just to rub it in."

"If only John had met you first," said Rachel.

"So, what do you think of John and Yoko posing nude for their *Two Virgins* album?"

"They were naked and unafraid. She tempted him with an apple and he won her with Apple Records."

Linda rolled her eyes. "I heard that the others were so upset with Yoko being in the recording studio, that Ringo quit the band in the middle of recording the *White Album*. Paul had to do drums for some of the numbers." She leaned out as the boat lifted in the stronger wind. "January 30 was their last public performance. Can you believe that the cops busted them for singing from the rooftop!"

"The police, and everybody over thirty, are afraid that a revolution is coming," Rachel replied. "Paranoia runs deep."

Linda was still thinking of her favorite rock stars. "The Beatles have split. It's sad. *Two Virgins* is nothing compared with *Sergeant Pepper's*. What do you think is the greatest album in music history?"

"*Beethoven's Ninth*," Rachel replied. "It captures every emotion. In his time, Beethoven set music free, just as the

Beatles have in our time."

Their journey complete, she sailed the boat on to the sand. Linda and Rachel dragged the cat to the storage area and then they sat, spending a few quiet minutes watching boats and people.

Linda asked, "What makes you so committed to the environment?"

"One day in the Venezuelan jungles with my father changed me. I was ten. No eleven. He's a brilliant geologist for a major oil company, a vice president. He was a hero to me, flying to distant countries, braving hardships and dangers. We drove deep into the rainforest to an area of producing wells. The locals wanted to sell their crafts. When my father waved a woman away, she pleaded for him to buy something. She cried that her daughter was dying of cancer from the oil that polluted all their streams. They drank the water then got fevers and cancer. The oil company had dug pits, poured chemical waste into it, and then covered it with dirt. Peasants came and built and farmed on the covered toxic pit. The peasants didn't know; there were no warning signs."

"No signs. That's incredible. That would never happen in America."

"You'd be surprised. The power of the oil industry. They're one reason we're in Vietnam. The oil companies love the war. Their biggest customer is the United States Department of Defense."

"Wow."

"I listened to this poor mother who had lost a son to cancer and now was losing her baby. I started crying. She had tried to raise chickens for money, but the chickens died. The village was dying from my father's oil." Rachel stopped to regain her voice and wipe her eyes. "My father said that the woman should not be living there, that the government had sold the land, that his company obeyed all laws, never bribed, and protected the environment. But I listened to that poor mother and saw destruction everywhere. My father was once everything to me, now a man I cannot trust. I walked into the jungle a happy girl. I walked out a woman with a destiny. I will stop the destruction."

"No wonder you're fighting Union Oil over the Santa Barbara oil spill."

"I have seen such destruction much of my life. Millions die so that a few get rich. *Me ayudan.*"

They were silent. Linda was lost in thoughts she wished would vanish.

After minutes of silence, Rachel said, "*Yesterday* is my favorite song."

Linda lamented that all the Beatles were married. There were no more perfect men. The band had split apart; this was the end of an era.

Twice during the week, David and Linda got together. They dined at Tortilla Flats, where they had first met. They talked about their four years of university life. She described herself leaving Cleveland looking like a debutante, and a few months later, being a flower child in Berkeley. Although English literature had been her first love, her decision to work with children drew her to psychology.

She talked about her love of music and of the Beatles evolution from hard-driving get-up-and-dance rock and roll to a masterfully orchestrated psychedelic fusion of the East and the West. When her brother went to Vietnam, she became active in antiwar protest, active in the Movement. David listened to her life at Berkeley and felt her commitment to bring change. She described rallies and being in civil rights marches. She had journeyed a long way from Cleveland Heights.

They discussed friends and roommates. David assured her that he was different than Carlo. Linda said that her friend Alicia would be a perfect match for Carlo.

There was a connection between David and Linda. Each listened, supported, and showed genuine interest in the other's future. David felt good when he brought a sparkle to her sad eyes.

Linda talked briefly about her anger with Brad's decision to enlist rather than fight the FBI. She shared some of the heartbreak of losing her brother. David listened without asking her to go deeper into the darkness of her loss.

Once when a waitress brought chips and red salsa, David saw revulsion on Linda's face as she ran outside and threw-up. In the future, he made sure that neither salsa or ketchup reached their table.

They talked of future dreams. She brightened when talking about teaching. She described the young children at the Montessori school and invited David to come on his next day off to be a guest reader.

As promised, David drove Linda home early, gave her a good night hug, and resisted the impulse to kiss her.

15

Call of Duty

Carlo slowly opened the letter from the United States Army. While reading, his jaw dropped and all color left his face. He shouted, "No way. No fucking way. I joined the Reserves to stay out of this war. I'm going to die. I'm going to die." He handed the letter to David. It stated that Carlo's Army Reserve Unit had been activated. In 14 days, Carlo was ordered to report to Fort Ord for combat training. The letter was dated four days earlier. Carlo had ten days to make a desperate attempt to avoid fighting in Vietnam.

The next day, Carlo followed his father into the den, so that they could talk alone. Carlo looked at the wall displaying his father's golf trophies, awards, plaques and photographs. One photo showed his father, Giovanni Abruzzo, seated next to Senator Alan Cranston; another with him shaking hands with Governor Ronald Reagan. His father's proudest possession was framed and centered, the Bronze Star, for his father's heroism in the United States Army during World War II.

"How is the lifeguarding?" Giovanni asked his son.

"A few rescues and lots of first aids. I'm enjoying my last months on the beach."

"The joys of youth. Carlo, you would be good in my business. Someday you could run Abruzzo Construction."

"Someday, Papa. First I want to make my own

million."

"I like your spirit."

Carlo squirmed in his seat and began his semi-rehearsed speech, "Papa, my army reserve unit has been called up. In nine days, I am scheduled to start combat training at Fort Ord. A few weeks after that, fighting in Vietnam."

Giovanni winced at hearing the fate of his eldest son. "Does your mama know?"

"I am telling you first."

"Let me tell your mama. This will be hard for her. Very hard."

Carlo felt hopeful that his father would help him. His father had the political connections, having helped raise funds to get Nixon, Reagan, Cranston, and others elected. Carlo was trying to proceed carefully with his very Republican father. "President Nixon is in serious negotiations to get the U. S. out of Vietnam."

"Nixon is a tough communist fighter. He is looking for a way out that will not allow communism to spread. But Carlo, what does this have to do with you? What are you trying to tell me?"

"Papa, I don't want to get killed in Vietnam. They may end this war in a few months. I don't want to die for nothing."

Giovanni stared out the window, past the roofs of houses lower on the hill. He looked to the distant ocean. He felt torn. For two minutes he stared, saying nothing. Carlo was silent as he waited apprehensively. "Carlo, you know that in World War II, I went on missions where I was told I would not come back. In Burma, I carried deadly explosives. One bump and I would have been dead. I served my country. Japan bombed and invaded our country. Hitler wanted to rule the world. I did what I had to do."

Carlo's father had always been a hero to him. After listening carefully, Carlo spoke from his heart, "Papa I admired what you did in World War II. The fate of democracy was a stake. You were a hero. I would have served in World War II. Vietnam is different. You've been watching the TV broadcasts of the ceaseless killings that don't seem to be getting us anywhere. President Nixon wants us out. It would be senseless for me to die there."

Giovanni said, "We've seen so much on television: burning villages, killing of women and children. There is sickness in what we do in Vietnam." He looked at the ocean. "Yes, they say that I'm a war hero. When I went behind an enemy and slit his throat, I did my duty, but I don't feel like a hero. No, Carlo, I don't wish you such nightmares. I'll see if I can help you."

Carlo walked to his father and hugged him, "Thank you, Papa."

"Carlo, if I help you out, I need you to make me a promise."

"What is it?"

"You will complete your education. I went into the army the day after I graduated from high school. I never had the chance for a fine university education like you. Promise me that you will graduate from the university."

Carlo winced. "Yes, I promise."

"I need the facts," Giovanni said. "You have a copy of a letter from the army?"

"Yes. Here is the copy." Carlo removed the copy from his shirt pocket and handed it to his father.

"I barely know Nixon. I contributed to Reagan's campaign, but he won't help. Alan Cranston and I go back a long way. He has been campaigning to get us out of Vietnam. And there's Jack Jennings. He's on the Armed Forces Committee in Congress. In the past, he and I made a lot of money together.

Let me see what I can do." Giovanni stared out the window, thinking. "What about your history of asthma? How did you get in the reserves with that?"

"They're taking anyone. If you can fog a mirror, you're in."

Giovanni chuckled, "I'll call Jack and Alan. I'll see what I can do. Don't say anything to Mama. No need to depress her now. She loves you Carlo. We love you."

"And I love you both. Your help means so much to me."

"Don't thank me, yet. This is a tough one. Nine days. You're mama has been in the kitchen all afternoon. We're in for a big Italian dinner."

"I have this recurring fantasy about Nixon trying his surfboard, getting hit trying to catch a wave, and me rescuing him as I ask for a presidential pardon from going to Vietnam," David said.

"Great idea, man! But I'm the one who needs to do the rescue. I'm nervous about the call-up of my reserve unit."

"Total bummer. How did it go with your old man?"

Carlo let out a deep sigh. "Papa was surprisingly cool. We talked and he said he would help. He knows Senator Cranston and made a big donation to his campaign. Surprising, since Papa is such a hard-core Republican and Cranston's a Democrat, but Papa is a smart businessman. Lot's of heavy connections."

A week later, David banged on his roommate's bedroom door and said, "Carlo, phone call for you. Some army major or general. Sounds serious."

Carlo tried to shake himself awake. "What time is

it?"

"After seven. He's waiting on the phone."

Carlo staggered into the bathroom, struggling with the early morning hour, threw water on his face, and then stumbled his way to the phone. "Yes, sir."

The deep voice was full of authority, "Carlo Abruzzo?"

"Yes, this is Carlo Abruzzo."

"This is Major General Anderson, United States Army. What's this letter about you not intending to report for duty?"

At first, Carlo could not speak, and then said, "I'll get the letter and be right back, sir."

Carlo ran to his bedroom, found the letter, and walking back to the phone, whispered to David, "Major General...failure to report for duty. I'm a dead man. Dead."

Carlo opened the letter that his father's attorney sent to General Anderson with copies to the Abruzzo's senator and congressman. It requested a medical discharge. Carlo lifted the phone and said, "I have the letter."

"Are you going to answer my question?" General Anderson asked with impatience. "You're in the United States Army Reserves. Are you reporting for duty, or refusing?"

Carlo sat paralyzed with fear. Finally he was able to speak, "I'm sorry, sir. I have severe asthma attacks. I must use medicine. I don't meet army regulations."

"In other words, you could serve as a hospital orderly," the General stated.

Carlo could not continue the chess game. It sounded like checkmate. "That's certainly your decision. I have severe asthma." Carlo made no mention of lifeguarding, surfing and skiing.

After a long silence, General Anderson gave an icy reply, "I'm giving you a 30-day stay while we investigate you."

"Thank you, sir."

"Don't ever try this again." Anderson's voice was ominous. The phone went dead.

Carlo was shaking. He needed both hands to get the phone back in the cradle.

At Linda's Montessori school, David proved to be an entertaining reader. He held most of the children spellbound and didn't mind when one boy ran around the room yelling while he was trying to read to the group. Linda smiled at the way that he related to the children. After school, the two took a long walk on the beach, enjoying time together.

Linda was rediscovering how to smile. Like fresh shoots of flowers emerging after spring rains, she blossomed for a few minutes playing with children, walking the beach with David, matching wits with Rachel. She could sometimes smile in these sunlit moments, but in the darkness of night, alone, looking at her brother's photo next to a flickering candle, she could only listen to Joni Mitchell and cry.

On the beach the next day, a woman frantically ran to Carlo, "There's a man exposing himself."

"Where?" She pointed to a man standing on the other side of the railroad tracks. He was wearing a hotel robe, open and blown back by the breeze, naked underneath. The man was perfectly located to flash people in passing trains.

Carlo lifted the phone to talk with David, "There's a man behind my tower who is exhibiting himself. A woman's complaining. How do we handle this?"

David choked his laughter and finally said, "Make a citizen's arrest. I'll call the San Clemente police."

As required whenever a lifeguard leaves his tower, Carlo grabbed his rescue buoy. He jumped to the ground and then turned to run through the tunnel under the train tracks that provided the exit from the beach. The exhibitionist saw Carlo approaching and started to run away. Carlo pursued the man for several hundred yards, but Carlo was barefoot; the exhibitionist wore tennis shoes. Carlo followed on the winding dirt trail connecting the beach to the campgrounds. The man disappeared around a bend in the trail. Carlo never saw him again. Dejectedly, he walked back to his tower.

The police arrived at the headquarters tower. David was dressed in his headquarters uniform of khaki jacket and trousers, and polished black shoes. David looked as clean-cut and official as the police. David commented, "Lieutenant Rich Gonzalez. I'm surprised that you personally took this call."

"I try to spend a few hours a month with each patrol officer," Gonzalez said. "How's the surf?"

"Three-to-four foot, but blown out." David and Rich were both surfers. Sometimes they would find each other surfing the same spot at the same time.

"So what's this call about an exhibitionist?"

"It was reported by a woman to Carlo, who went in pursuit of the guy, but the exhibitionist escaped his grip."

Gonzalez and the other patrol officer laughed loud and long. Gonzalez finally stated, "And that's exactly how I am writing it in my report." In the historical archives of the San Clemente Police and the State of California are copies of a report that states: "Lifeguard Carlo Abruzzo ran in pursuit of an exhibitionist, but the man escaped his grip."

Carlo's stomach knotted and he started shivering when he saw the unopened letter from Major General Anderson, U. S. Command Headquarters. He opened the letter as slowly as a man would place his head under a guillotine.

As Carlo read the letter he grew taller, his smile beamed and the guillotine vanished. Freedom! He was light, floating, ecstatic.

David heard Carlo's loud rebel yell and ran into the living room. "What happened?"

Carlo shouted, "I'm free! I'm out! No Vietnam! Free at last! Free at last! Free at last!"

While Carlo was jumping on the sofa as if it were a trampoline, David read the letter that stated that Carlo was honorably discharged from the Armed Services for medical reasons.

That evening, David was driving north on Pacific Coast Highway through South Laguna. Gray clouds hid the sunset. The VW's 40-horsepower engine whined as he climbed a hill. Distracted by countless commercials, he turned off the car radio, wishing that he could afford a cassette player.

Finally he arrived in Laguna Beach, renowned for artists cloistered in galleries over dramatic ocean cliffs, recognized for its annual Art Festival, and lately famous for busting Timothy Leary for possessing two joints of grass that resulted in a ten-year prison sentence.

David took a right on Agate Street and found parking near Linda and Rachel's rented yellow cottage. As David stepped out of the car and walked to the front door, he could faintly hear crashing waves.

Linda opened the door and smiled at David. She wore a

blouse that revealed her peace sign necklace. She wore her favorite white Levi's and sandals. Her gypsy shawl was a laced pattern of black and blue.

He paused at the doorway, drawn to her turquoise eyes accented by robin-egg-blue cut-glass earrings. She asked, "Would you like to come in?"

"Sure. Good to see you." David viewed the mix of local art, posters of favorite music groups, brown sofa, lamps, piles of books, record collection, and stereo. Staring at him were her posters of John Lennon, Bob Dylan, and Jim Morrison and Rachel's posters of whales, rainforests, and an earthrise photo taken from Apollo 8. In the background, Simon and Garfunkel sang.

"So, *The Graduate* sounds good?" David asked.

"Sure, I love the story and I haven't seen it in a while."

Progress was unexpectedly slow in the snarled traffic. Blocks ahead, David saw flashing red lights. He turned right to take side streets. "Looks like an accident. Let's see if we can get to the theater on time. You OK walking a few blocks?"

"Sure."

David parked, and they started walking through the crowds. He started to reach to take her hand, but pulled back. "How's it going?"

"OK. I've started my two teaching credential courses. October, I start my grad courses in early childhood development. I'm waiting to hear if I'll student teach in the fall." There was no response from David. Linda broke the silence, "So what are your plans now that you've graduated? Plastics?"

They both laughed at their reference to *The Graduate*. David replied, "I love that line from the movie. Nobody asked Dustin

Hoffman what he wanted."

"Seriously, I admire your plans to get into computers," she said. "You must be smart."

"Huh?" David tried to joke by sounding dumb. Linda laughed. He realized that she was laughing more than in their recent times together. Something felt different. With each laugh, he found himself relaxing a bit more. David continued, "I'm astonished that I graduated in four years, after all the times I changed majors."

"I knew lots at Berkeley who may never graduate."

"Tune in, turn on, drop out."

Almost like an improvised tango, the two moved through the crowds that overwhelmed the sidewalk. Reaching the theater, David bought their tickets but didn't offer to get the expensive popcorn and drinks.

Two hours later, when they left the theater, the two were smiling, and then like the couple in the movie, their expressions became enigmatic. David asked, "Would you like to walk along the ocean?"

"Groovy."

Reaching the beach, both took off their shoes and walked barefoot in the sand. David took Linda's hand, which she warmly squeezed as she leaned closer. The moonlight reflected on the waves. She said, "I love these classic tales of overcoming the expectations of one's parents to become your own person."

"Do you think they'll stay together?" David asked.

"We'll have to wait for the sequel."

"I guess in Hoffman's new movie, *Midnight Cowboy*, he takes a completely different role."

"I'd like to see that," Linda said. They walked close to the water's edge, tasting the salty air and feeling the sand with their bare feet. A wave crashed near shore and they stepped back. "What a line," Linda continued. ""Mrs. Robinson, you're trying to seduce me. Aren't you?"

"Getting naked was a pretty big clue."

"At that point, I think that he was supposed to be a virgin. What do you think?"

David's face flushed, unseen in the dark. He couldn't think of anything to say.

They walked for a minute in silence and then Linda asked, "Your graduation ceremony is almost here isn't it?"

"Yeah, but I won't be there," David said. "It's on a Saturday. They need every guard on weekends. It's impossible to get off."

"You must be disappointed."

"Not really. Why conform? And there's the money. They want 35 dollars for the cap and gown and I'd lose another 35 in pay. I paid for everything this year - tuition, textbooks, the VW, food, everything. Hate to admit it, but I've got to watch every dollar."

"You paid for the works. Like, wow, my folks covered everything. I bet your dad's disappointed to not see you graduate."

"I told him on Father's Day. He wasn't happy."

Lying together in the sand, Linda leaned into David and rested her hand on his heart. David turned and saw her looking at him with a kind of sad wonder.

David said, "Things have been very tense between me and Dad since I saw him last year. He freaked at my wearing a beard and beads. I told him I wouldn't fight in Vietnam and I wouldn't go in the military. He was furious, kicked me out of his home and off base. My dad's an admiral."

"High up in the navy?"

"Yeah. His rank is the same as an army general. He's used to giving orders, not getting back talk from his son. America, love it or leave it. Might makes right."

"I admire you for standing up to your father. This horrible war killed my brother."

They walked along a rocky cove. From an Asian storm, big waves that had traveled thousands of miles crashed against the rocks with a violent thunder.

School was out and summer vacations were in. Families reinvented themselves as nomads, caravanning in cars and trucks pulling trailers and RVs to traverse the land and see American. The San Clemente State Beach campground was full.

The beach was overflowing with families, many bringing elaborate picnic settings and large umbrellas. Delighted children ran in all directions. They jumped in the ocean with inflated mattresses and quickly lost them. Parents lost children and frantically begged the lifeguards to find them. Marines were on the beach, enjoying a day off from nearby Camp Pendleton. The guards were busy with rescues and first aids.

Working full time, David was slowly escaping poverty.

On Sundays, David was free from being in the headquarters tower; instead he drove the patrol vehicle on the beach. It was a challenge to weave through the crowds. On Sundays, David felt a sense of freedom, wearing only his red lifeguard trunks, instead of his police-like headquarters uniform.

Three days later, Linda opened the door and smiled at David

who threw his arms open, stepped forward and gave Linda a hug. Then both awkwardly stepped back. David wanted to kiss Linda, but he just stood three feet away and warmly gazed at her. "It's going to be a beautiful sunset," David said.

"Let's go."

David drove them to Cliff Drive. He took her hand and they walked to a white gazebo, embedded on a rock outcropping on the cliff over the ocean, surrounded with hydrangea, tall, reaching, with massive flower heads of purple, pink, and blue lilac. They entered the gazebo, stepping under the wisteria that covered the gazebo like a purple waterfall. The flower fragrances mixed with the salt spray. Linda and David, bodies touching, leaned out the ocean-facing side, and viewed the distant fluffy clouds painted pink and lavender by a sun now below the horizon.

"How was your day?" David asked.

"I slept and slept and slept, then spent the entire morning in my robe and fluffy slippers. I fixed myself French toast and a mimosa, then I curled up and read a book."

They left the gazebo to walk along the dramatic cliffs over the ocean. As David took Linda's hand she smiled at him and walked with a carefree sway. David said, "Right on. I slept halfway into the morning. Felt great. Carlo and I had a massive late breakfast at Denny's, then we enjoyed a couple of hours of surfing."

"I've never surfed. Everyone asks me about it in Ohio."

"I'd be glad to teach you," David said. In the dark, she could not see his blush in the twilight mist.

"Groovy. My friends would be jealous that I was taught by a handsome California lifeguard." They walked on looking at the scattered people in the park, some beneath eucalyptus and palm trees. David felt conflicted with part of him wanting to stay focused on Linda, and part of him feeling a lifeguard's compulsion to warn people that from palm trees, coconuts can fall on heads. He took Linda's hand and they walked until reaching a fork in the pathway, with one choice staying above the cliffs and the other descending to a deserted beach.

"Beautiful cove. Tempted?" David asked.

Linda shrugged, smiled, and then wrapped both her hands around his arm. They descended. David and Linda removed their shoes and walked barefoot on the beach in the evening mist. They looked up in search of stars but only saw a cloudy light show of pastel. Linda asked, "What color do you see?

"Purple."

"Green."

"Emerald." They laughed at the simplicity of their dialog.

"Agate, marbled with red and pink, and the penetrating turquoise of your eyes," said David.

"I'm in the arms of a poet," Linda said as she squeezed David's arm, muscled from swimming and surfing.

David reached around Linda's waist and pulled her close. In the evening mist, the rest of the world disappeared. From the cliffs above, they heard music. Their lips came together and never parted as one haunting song fused into another. The Youngbloods were singing, "Get Together."

The two paused from their passion, and then Linda fell on top of him as they returned to their timeless kissing. David loved the touch of Linda's breasts and the weight of her body. Their kissing continued with a deepening passion as he lifted his leg between hers.

Eventually, the distant music stopped. David rolled over. He gently brushed sand from Linda's face and was tempted to brush her legs and derriere. He looked at Linda and said,

"Kissing you is wonderful."

"Dreamy," Linda whispered.

Both sat, listening to waves barely visible in the growing darkness. Linda said, "I think we've moved past platonic."

David laughed and then asked, "How do you feel about that?"

"It feels a little surreal and a little wonderful."

16

Peeing Envy

"You are hereby directed to present yourself for the Armed Forces Physical Examination by reporting at...." David read the Order to Report. This was the first step toward shipping him to Vietnam. It was not a request; it was an order. He was not yet in uniform and they were commanding him.

He made a phone call, "Mike, this is David. I've got to go through the pre-induction physical."

"They're closing in on you. Get ready to be humiliated," Mike said.

"What was it like?"

"I got my notice after I wrote my local board asking to be designated a conscientious objector, Mike explained. "I included my minister's certificate, papers I'd written about my beliefs and talks I'd given. The Board replied by sending me the Order to Report."

"Wow. I was thinking of trying the conscientious objector route," David said.

"Go for it; just don't write the Board a letter. Wait until they draft you, and then have a lawyer insist on a Board hearing. He'll include your certificate that you're a minister in the Universal Life Church."

"Got that thanks to you. So what was the physical like?"

"For three hours the army checked my eyes, ears, nose, and throat," Mike said. "Soldiers looked at my urine and looked up my ass. They'll grab your balls while you cough. They'll make you fill out forms and take quizzes."

David was angry. Uncle Sam had him by the balls. "There's got to be a way to beat this."

"Don't bother. They don't give a shit. They'll pass you. They need bodies. They passed me. I can be drafted anytime, but I'm ready. I can fit everything I need in a 30-pound backpack, and be out of the country in hours. My passport's ready. I won't kill."

"You're an inspiration."

"We've talked about some of this before. Didn't you tell me you had an 45-step plan to stay out of the war?"

"Yep, of course it's all theoretical. Now I need a real plan that works."

"I can dig where you're at. Hang on for a minute." Mike walked to a file box, looking for his folder titled Draft Resistance. "O.K. I found my list. You can try to fail the physical. Army regulations prohibit drafting homosexuals, drug users, men with irregular spines, poor eyesight, and problems that prevent marching 20 miles per day. The regulations are written to screen out anyone who'd slow the movement of troops."

David cringed as he heard Mike read the list and especially at hearing the word "homosexual." He considered his options and then said, "I could tell them I use drugs."

Mike laughed. "They'll just laugh and pass you. I've heard of all kinds of stuff. Guys spike their blood pressure by taking amphetamines and staying up all night. On this short notice, there is no way that you can get your weight over 256 or starve to less than 107. You could try putting chemicals in your urine sample. The problem with all this is that you'll get a 1-Y deferment for only three months, and then you've got to come back and repeat the ordeal."

"But I could bring a disqualifying urine sample?"

"No, you've got to walk around in your underwear and urinate in front of them," Mike said.

"I've got to pee in front of a hundred guys?" David whimpered.

"Cheek to cheek. Get ready to be totally humiliated, man."

Three days later, David was driving in the Los Angeles gridlock traffic as he inched to the required U. S. Army pre-induction physical. The countless clutching and shifting in stop-and-go traffic added to his frustration and anxiety. If he passed the exam, he could be drafted immediately.

David had heard the expression, "Life is cheap." This was the first time that he felt it right down to his quivering muscles. His life was so cheap that for a few bucks Uncle Sam could buy his time and throw him into the jungles to see if he would kill or be killed.

David clung to a hope that he would fail the physical because his flat feet failed army regulations. He brought x-rays as proof.

David exited the freeway and crawled through the rough neighborhoods of L.A. Anxiety and anger gave way to merriment as he joined Country Joe and the Fish in singing the anti-war "I-Feel-Like-I'm-Fixin'-to-Die Rag."

He parked, entered the prison-like federal building, and then took the stairs one at a time like a kid in trouble on his way to see the vice principal. As he opened the door labeled Army Physical, he smelled a semi-toxic mix of body odor, piss, and cleaning ammonia. He presented his letter and took the clipboard with forms. The corporal told David to undress and get in line.

Wearing only his boxer shorts as he stood in a long line to

take the first test, David decided to flunk the test for color blindness. A sergeant showed each young man a book with colored dots and asked, "What numbers do you see?" Each person ahead of David correctly answered "4, 27, 8."

When David reached the front of the line, he was asked what numbers he saw and answered nervously, "I'm sorry I don't see any numbers. Just dots."

The sergeant stared at David, "Didn't you hear the other guys? 4, 27, 8." He waved David on to the next station. David had passed the color-blind test.

David then attempted to fail the hearing test. He politely asked the tester to repeat instructions and talk louder. David looked strained as he tried to listen. At the machine, he tried making enough wrong answers to be determined partially deaf. One corporal said to another, "This guy would be good in artillery. Those guys all go deaf anyway."

The other corporal joking replied, "Yeah, but it's too bad they can't hear the incoming shells." The army decided David could hear.

At the eye chart, David squinted as he tried to read the letters below the big "E." The army captain warned, "I can put cheaters on the bus to Vietnam right now. You want to try a little harder!" David almost wet his pants. He read out loud every line including the microscopic last line, "M-A-D-E-I-N-U-S-A."

David was now too frightened and discouraged to try failing more tests. The intelligence test had one hundred multiple-choice answers; get 20 right out of 100 and you passed. A monkey making random marks would score 25 and be qualified to be an army private. If David scored below 20, they would accuse him of cheating and put him on the bus. He was trapped. He scored a 97.

David was trudging along, enduring the humiliating ordeal.

A sergeant gave him a cup and told him to fill it with pee. David waited for an opening at the 20-foot trough of a urinal, so crowded that the naked guys were pressed together, butt cheek touching butt cheek, as they looked into their cups and peed. David was silently trying to talk his penis into peeing into the plastic cup. Guys in line behind him were waiting impatiently. David had frantic conversations in his mind, *The guy next to me, who is touching me, can't be a fag or he would have opted out of this whole process. But what if he is volunteering and trying to hide his homosexuality. What if he is touching me on purpose?* No pee.

He tried a new train of thought; I just drank a gallon of water. There is water everywhere. I'm desperate to pee. I'm looking at a waterfall. No pee. It was his reluctant penis versus the U. S. Army. What if the army drops me into the jungle for refusing to pee? He regretted not drinking more water before he arrived. He was a lifeguard trained to sit in a tower for hours without a bathroom break. David felt like everyone was watching. He had peeing envy.

Red in the face from trying, a few yellow drops trickled into the cup. After three minutes that seemed like 30, the crowd thinned. David was no longer being touched. After repeated visualizations of waterfalls, David finally had enough urine in the cup.

David and fifty other guys were ordered into a room. The sergeant ordered, "Stand on the red line and face the south wall. Hey, you. Yes, you. The other south wall. Pull down your pants, bend over, spread your cheeks." David did as instructed and was embarrassed as he spread his feet and touched the guys next to him.

An army physician worked with way down the line with a flashlight. He stopped behind the boy to David's left. The physician said, "All right comedian. Spread your buttocks, not the checks on your face." The dull-minded boy turned bright red, finally understood, and did as instructed. The room filled with laughter.

Forty minutes later, the ordeal of the physical ended. David got dressed and waited in the room with the others. Finally his name was called. His X-rays of flat feet were returned. He was given a new form boldly stamped with the word "Passed." In the end, if someone fogged a mirror, they were approved for military service. The army needed millions of bodies in the jungles.

His hearing test, color blindness test, and flat feet all failed army regulations, but they passed him. David's trust in the U. S. government was gone. As he crawled home on the smoggy freeway, David was determined to get control of his life, resolve his problems through therapy, get a good job, and stay out of Vietnam.

David took a deep breath and said, "Three days ago, I walked around naked with hundreds of guys." There was no reaction from his psychiatrist. David was amazed at his inability to get Dr. Grace to react. "I drove to LA for the whole ordeal of the pre-induction physical. I tried to flunk the color-blind test, the hearing test, the eye chart, but they were approving everyone. I passed the army physical and can be drafted at anytime."

"It does sound like an ordeal," said Dr. Grace.

"The most difficult part was standing at this long urinal with a bunch of naked guys. My butt was pressed against the butts of the guys on either side as I tried to pee."

"How did it feel to touch naked guys?"

"Like I was a fag. I've always felt weird getting naked in front of other guys. Changing for swim team or showering together at the end of a workout."

"You said you felt like a homosexual. Did you find

showering together arousing? Touching naked men arousing?"

"Arousing?" David replied. "Like I don't get a boner. No, it's not arousing. I cringe."

"Are you curious about what the other men look like naked?"

David blushed and was slow to answer. "Yeah, I guess."

"That doesn't make you homosexual," Dr. Grace said. "It makes you curious. Did you often see your father naked?"

"Never."

"Do you dream of being naked with men? Having sex with them?"

David tried to remember. In therapy, he struggled to remember dreams. "No, I don't remember any. I once dreamed of being carried into a jungle by Amazon women."

"It doesn't sound like you are homosexual."

"I was so uptight that I couldn't even pee in that cup. Other guys could. I've got peeing envy." David waited for a laugh but got no response from Dr. Grace. "I could not even control my own penis."

"In an earlier session, you described being caught with other kids, looking at each others naked body. Your father was very angry when he heard about that."

"Yeah, talking about that with you was kind of a breakthrough. After that session I lost my virginity and then had that week of far out sex with Joyce."

"When you were caught naked with other kids, you were embarrassed," said Dr. Grace. "When is the first time that you felt embarrassed being naked?"

David stared at the wall, trying to remember. "I have this vague memory of maybe being age three. My mom was having a garden party in the backyard. I ran out naked, holding my penis." David looked at Dr. Grace for a reaction, but she just continued to listen. "Her friends laughed. My mom laughed."

"How did she laugh?"

"Oh, like she was embarrassed and trying to not make a big deal of it," David said. "They laughed at me. They laughed at my penis. My long march from self-esteem to self-doubt had begun."

While David drove, Linda turned from looking at the cottages in Corona del Mar to look at David and said, "I had no idea that folk dancing could be so groovy. I'd never done it before."

"I love it," David said. "I've done it a few times at that UCI folk dance club. Which were your favorites?"

"There were so many. I like the Greek dancing because it was simple and exhilarating. I like the Hungarian dancing where I would spin off from you to the next guy and then the next. Your favorites?"

"I was proud I could do the Russian line dancing getting down in the full squat and then kicking. I dug the Scottish country dancing, even though I went in the wrong direction a couple of times."

"I know, I know!" Linda was laughing.

David continued, "I like best one-on-one dancing with you."

When they arrived at her cottage, David looked at Linda. Her smile was as ambiguous as the Mona Lisa. As they gazed, seconds seemed like minutes.

Finally, with a warm yet cautious smile, Linda asked, "Would you like to come inside?"

Dehydrated from the vigorous dancing, she poured two

glasses of ice water. As she served the water, she asked, "Would you like some wine?"

"For sure."

Linda poured two glasses then peaked into Rachel's room, and saw that Rachel was not there. Linda went into the bathroom that she shared with Rachel. When Linda saw her blouse soaked with perspiration, she scurried into her bedroom, and got a new blouse. Back in the bathroom, Linda removed her blouse and bra. With soap and a damp washcloth she freshened herself everywhere. She added perfume to the nape of her neck, stared at the mirror, and then perfumed the inside of her thighs. She put on the new blouse with no bra underneath. Back straight, she again starred in the mirror, smiled, and returned to the living room.

David was seated next to the record player. He looked at Linda, approvingly smiled and said, "I like your record collection."

"Put on an album."

David removed from its sleeve the Moody Blues' *Days of Future Past* and put the vinyl on the player.

"Would you like to smoke some Acapulco gold?" she asked.

"Yes."

Linda turned-off the lights and turned David on. Their first kiss lingered. Their next kiss stretched from one song to the next. They stretched the length of the sofa, wrapped together. David's hand eagerly explored Linda's back, then breasts, and then legs. As the album progressed, with each song they wore fewer clothes as Linda removed David's shirt and he her blouse. His leg slid between her legs and they were lost in passion.

Linda moaned as her hips rhythmically raised and lowered while David's tongue circled the areola of her breast.

Suddenly, the front door opened.

"Rachel?" Linda said.

"It's me," Rachel replied.

"Please wait outside for a minute."

The door closed. In the dark David and Linda scrambled to dress and turn-off the Moody Blues before "Nights in White Satin" would reach its climax.

Rachel shifted the phone to her other hand as she continued talking to a friend.

"Yesterday was most interesting," Rachel said. "I had been at an all-day workshop about mating behavior. I had to present the behavior of California pinnipeds. I was nervous because it included key professors. I wasn't trying to be funny, but when I described the mating behavior of sea elephants, I started getting laughs. At first I was embarrassed, then I went with it and delivered some pretty good one-liners. At the cocktail reception and dinner overlooking Newport Harbor, a few grad students and a couple of professors were flirting with me in ways that reminded me of tropical bird mating dances."

"Yes, yes, I know. I held my tongue. No caustic remarks," Rachel continued, shifting the phone. "I would like to get a PhD in four years, not seven."

"I get home around midnight, exhausted," Rachel continued. "As I approach the front door, I hear the Moody Blues playing loudly. I try to look through the windows, but the drapes are closed. I open the door and Linda, my new roommate, frantically asks me to wait outside."

Rachel held the phone listening to her friend.

"No, I didn't see her. I just heard her voice from the sofa. I honor her request, close the door, wait outside, and spend the next two minutes wondering if I'll get new material about primate mating behavior."

Rachel listened to her friend on the phone and then continued. "You would like Linda. We met in a behavioral biology class at Berkeley. Now she's working on her masters and teaching credential at UCI, while she lives with me. We were friends at Berkeley. Then we went to a wonderful workshop in Big Sur, had long talks, and now we're close. We're still learning how to coordinate our time when one of us has a guy over, like last night."

Rachel listened and then continued, "I'm outside, assuming she and some guy need to get dressed. So I waited a couple of minutes, heard footsteps inside, no more Moody Blues, and then entered my home. I smelled grass and saw two wine glasses on the coffee table. Linda, whose hair is completely disheveled, is with this guy David, that we met at Big Sur. He seems like a nice guy, but his roommate is a turn-off, very aggressive."

Rachel shifted the phone and continued, "David would be your type of guy, clean-cut lifeguard and surfer. So, Linda says she'll be walking David to his car. About to leave, he looked at my earthrise poster and said that it has given him a new perspective about our planet. He asked me if it had been photographed during Apollo 8. I said 'yes' and now I'm impressed that he knows something about the Apollo program, since I am crazy about it. He asked me about my work. He sincerely appreciates my saving animals. I can see that he's bright and caring, and I decide that he could be good for Linda, but I think she's moving too fast. She just broke up with Brad at the same time I ended seeing Wes. Worse, Linda just lost her brother. He returned from Vietnam a depressed paraplegic, and then killed himself while she was visiting."

Rachel listened for a while and then said, "Absolutely. She needs time to grieve her losses."

"How was your date with Linda?" Carlo asked.

"Awesome," David replied. "We went folk dancing at UCI," David said. "Dances from all over the world, mainly Europe. There were a number of foxy ladies there. There were these cool dances where you spin off from one girl and onto the next. We should go sometime."

"Forget the dancing. What happened later?" Carlo asked with a gleam in his eye.

"We ended up at Linda's place. I knew that things were promising when she went into the bathroom wearing one sweaty blouse and came out wearing a new blouse, no bra underneath, and offered me wine and dope."

"All right!"

"I've never enjoyed kissing anyone more than Linda. We totally lost in it, on top of each other, listening to the Moody Blues. I told Linda I was self-conscious of my sweaty shirt. So she removes my shirt."

"Out of sight."

"She was so responsive when I slid my hand under her blouse and touched her breasts. Soon I had her blouse off and we were really lost in each other. I was almost ready to slide my hand down her panties, when roommate Rachel opens the door and it was time to go home."

"Time to go home!" Carlo exclaimed. "You two should've just gone into Linda's bedroom!"

"I'm trying to be tuned into how far she wants to go."

"Sounds like all the way."

"But she's been depressed about breaking up with a guy in Berkeley and with her brother committing suicide. I'm worried that if we go too fast, she'll freak."

"I dig. You want to treat her with respect, but she wants you. The dancing, the wine, the dope, Moody Blues, you're almost naked, the passion. Next time, you have to make love."

Carlo walked into his bedroom and returned wearing a Tibetan bowl on his head and holding a ceremonial wood mallet. Sitting in a half-lotus, he hit the bowl with the mallet while shutting his eyes to experience the sonorous reverberations, and then appeared to enter a trance.

David thought, *Maybe he's trying to get into a Zen state; like in Big Sur. Perhaps he's having a séance with an ancient god. He's channeling Bacchus. No doubt, tripping on some past orgy.*

"Visualize your next date with Linda," Carlo said slowly as if talking from a trance. "You arrive at her home when the sun is low on the horizon and the clouds are soft shades of red. You bring her a simple bouquet and compliment her dress, her jewelry, and her eyes." Carlo continued, deeper in the trance. "You take her to the Seafood Grill."

David interrupted. "That's expensive."

"Do you want to make love with Linda, or not?"

"Yes."

Carlo opened his eyes and stared at David, "Then don't be such a fucking tightwad! For once in your life, spend a little money. Show her that she's important. The Seafood Grill has great food, a panoramic view of the ocean, and it's nearer your place than hers. After dinner, you'll be all alone at our place and I'll clear out and spend the night with my folks. This way you don't have to worry about Rachel."

"Thanks," David said. "You're a good friend." David looked at the living room and kitchen and then said, "I'll need to spend hours cleaning the place."

Carlo gave a Cheshire-Cat smile. He hit the Tibet bowl with the mallet and returned to his trance as the chime filled the room. "At the restaurant, you're buying her a bottle of Pinot Grigio to go with the sea food."

"A whole bottle?"

"Yes. Not a glass of house wine. Not two bucks for a half-gallon jug of gut rot. A nice bottle of wine," Carlo spoke with authority. "Now stop pulling me out of my trance. Center yourself."

David sat in a half-lotus, resting hands on knees with each thumb touching index finger.

"You're seated with a view of the ocean, as you requested when you made the reservation," Carlo said. "You look at the ocean and at Linda. You talk and laugh and drink and dine. After dinner you walk on the beach under the stars. You kiss, first gently, then intensely. You want each other. *Amore!* Now you're at our place. You offer her a glass of Italian liqueur. Amaretto. You smoke our best Maui Waui. For music, you have the album ready. Moody Blues was a good choice last time, except you have to come before the end of Nights in White Satin where Justin Hayward starts reciting the poem."

David corrected, "Mike Pinder recited the poem."

"Whatever. Stop interrupting my vision!" Carlo said eyes wide open. "No wonder you have trouble getting laid. You're so analytical. The romantic music is ready: the Beatles, The Doors, or Getz and Gilberto."

"Cream," David offered.

"Excellent choice," Carlo said as he shut his eyes, barely seen under the Tibetan bowl. "You can get lost fucking to Cream."

"I can dig it," David said. "I appreciate the advice, but I need to respect however she is feeling. She's hurting. A few weeks ago, her brother killed himself. Before that, she broke up with a guy she'd known for years."

"You may never see her again," Carlo countered. "You could be drafted tomorrow, soon dying in the jungle."

David said, "No, I'll move to Canada."

"Your regiment leaves at dawn. Whether Canada or Vietnam, this is your moment to make love with her!"

David said, "If I take it slowly with Linda, you may yet have a chance with Rachel."

Carlo opened his eyes wide and then returned to his trance. "Now, I'm visualizing Rachel in her Barely Legal bikini. You're right. You should go slowly with Linda."

17

Santa Barbara

Rachel soothed the terrified bird trembling in her hand, "Everything will be all right." She was saving birds tar-covered and dying from the oil-spill disaster that blackened the California coast. Using a solvent, she carefully brushed the tar from the stranded sea gull's feathers. "Someday this will be a sanctuary. Those ugly offshore oil platforms will be gone."

Gray fog covered green mountains. The dark mist hid the ocean that could only be heard; the black petroleum shroud spread over everything that suggested life. Crying creatures, covered black, lay in sharp contrast to Santa Barbara's white sand, immaculate lawns, and shuddering palm trees.

For months, Rachel had been saving birds in a desperate battle as the oil slick expanded to cover 800 miles of pristine coast. From the ocean floor, oil was still escaping and adding to the death toll. Her sadness deepened as she looked at a dolphin corpse lying on the beach, knowing that it had died slowly and in pain as inhaled black tar caused their lungs to hemorrhage. Rachel could understand the physiology of life; she could not understand this senseless death in the name of oil.

In the weeping mist she labored on. Helping her, Linda and other volunteers hovered over the desperate birds, seals, and dolphins that might be saved. David walked to Rachel, carrying two large empty cages and said, "You're crying again."

"It's so sad," she said. "So senseless. Beautiful birds. Majestic dolphins. Gone forever." She looked at the once gorgeous beach, now a battlefield for the dead and the dying.

"I dropped the last sick birds at the Santa Barbara Zoo's emergency treatment center. They're overwhelmed, but doing their best. Looks like you've got more for me."

"Yes, more seagulls, cormorants, and look at my long-necked grebe with her funny flattop." She finally smiled.

David cautiously mirrored her smile, lifted the cages full of birds, and left Rachel with new empty cages. Another plane flew over the ocean dumping chemical detergents in a futile effort to break apart the vast oil slick.

The environmental nightmare had started on January 29 with a blowout on a Union Oil offshore platform. When the blowout was finally capped, pressure increased under the ocean floor. Multiple faults ruptured beneath the ocean. Methane massively released into the ocean then rose to the stratosphere to trap more heat from escaping the earth.

While the volunteers desperately tried to save creatures, at his Santa Barbara home 10 miles up the coast, Governor Ronald Reagan was horseback riding in the hills, taking the day to escape the press and Sacramento meetings. He did not need to hear another accusation about how the oil company had been given permission to cut corners and operate a platform that failed federal and California safety regulations. As far as Reagan was concerned, less regulation was needed, not more. He believed that a free market would take care of this and that California's economy depended on oil. Tall in the saddle on a high hill, he avoided looking at the beaches below.

Rachel vowed to herself, *I will take on the oil companies that are destroying our planet. My PhD thesis will detail how oil drilling and the use of toxic chemicals destroy ecosystems and kill.*

A church bell penetrated the gray mist. Under the grieving sky, she washed another seagull. She looked at the frightened bird and sang the Beatles, "While My Guitar Gently Weeps."

Rachel remembered watching the evening news on television. The president of Union Oil said, "I don't like to call it a disaster, because there has been no loss of human life. I am amazed at the publicity for the loss of a few birds."

The American public was outraged about the environmental assault witnessed on the evening news, while the oil industry attempted damage control.

For months, hundreds like Rachel had volunteered to save birds along the coast. Many volunteers joined Get Oil Out; GOO was a new non-profit organization that urged the public to cut down on driving. Standing near busy Union gas stations, Rachel and other GOO members urged drivers to destroy their oil company credit cards and boycott Union Oil stations. GOO gathered over one hundred thousand signatures on a petition banning offshore oil drilling.

Public outrage grew across the nation as television news stories continued and as major newspapers and magazines printed stories of oil industry cover-ups. The destruction of the spreading oil continued; the story could not be buried.

President Richard Nixon, inaugurated only days after the blowout, confronted the disaster with a nationwide address, "What is involved is the use of our resources of the sea and of the land in a more effective way and with more concern for preserving the beauty and the natural resources that are so important to any kind of society that we want for the future. The Santa Barbara incident has frankly touched the conscience of the American people."

After rescuing birds, Rachel, Linda and David stayed in Santa Barbara to hear United States Senator Gaylord Nelson, a visionary, a leader, and a lover of the lakes and forests of his native Wisconsin. When Kennedy was president, he asked Nelson to lead in addressing environmental destruction. The two had traveled the nation together giving conservation talks. Six years later, Nelson continued to be the Senate's leading voice for conservation and the environment.

At his Santa Barbara speech, Senator Nelson spoke of millions choking from the black air and of children's lungs being assaulted by tiny particles from plant furnaces, diesel trucks, and the lead and gasoline fumes of cars. He praised Rachel Carson's *Silent Spring*. Chemicals and pesticides were silently killing millions of birds, fish, and people. Senator Nelson called for a stop to needless destruction and killing.

Nelson was encouraged by the warm response he got in Santa Barbara, including his conversation with local environmental leaders like Rachel. The Senator told her that environmental teach-ins were needed across the nation that could match the impact of the anti-war teach-ins that had gained major television coverage. High impact. He needed leaders like her. In less than a year, she helped make his vision a reality. It was called Earth Day.

Two thousand protesters descended on San Clemente Beach. Two of Nixon's Secret Service were in lifeguard headquarters all day with David. When he had entered the university in 1965, his Republican father and his Democrat president told him that if Vietnam fell to communism, then all of Asia would become communist. In 1965, David believed them. Now, after seeing TV broadcasts of United States soldiers burning villages and killing children, the nation wanted out. Like most Americans, David no longer believed the communist domino theory. Nixon had promised to end the war; instead, he expanded it into Cambodia and Laos. As more young men were drafted, David knew that he could be next.

Sitting next to the Secret Service, David silently cheered for the protesters. David daydreamed about rescuing the president as he asked for an exemption from Vietnam. *Where would he be next year? Next month? Next week?*

18

Cliff Rescue

"Cliff rescue needed between towers three and four." David heard his orders from headquarters through the vehicle two-way radio.

"Ten-four," David replied as he accelerated his vehicle. It was after 5 p.m. and riding with him was Carlo who turned on the flashing red light while David maneuvered near the surf to avoid crowds.

"There she is," David said, pointing at a girl wedged in the cliff 70 feet above ground. People were starting to gather above and below her. David studied the location of the girl. He hit the horn to get people to move. He drove faster. Finally, they were able to leave the sand and take the road up the hill to where he would make the rescue.

When they arrived above the cliff, David saw a crowd at the cliff's edge, looking down. He knew that would be the point of his descent. Park ranger Doris introduced David and Carlo to the girl's parents and then the ranger started clearing the crowd. The mother was sobbing and unable to talk. Her father looked at the guards and asked, "Can you get Julie off the cliff?"

"Yes, I'll get her," David assured them. Just as in the 130 ocean rescues that David had executed as a lifeguard, David was relatively calm and centered.

From the vehicle, David removed two stakes, rope, and the cliff rescue harness including the genie. For the stakes, he picked a spot near the cliff's edge and ten feet to the girl's left. He instinctively knew not to descend directly above young Julie. That would only intensify her fear. He started pounding the stakes into the ground. The hammer slipped in his sweaty hand. He hoped that the ground was solid and that the stakes would not release when bearing his weight. He wrapped the rope around the stakes and tied a knot, regretting that he had forgotten everything about knots that he had learned at the military academy. David snapped on the sling.

"You sure you want to go?" Carlo nervously whispered to David.

"Yes," David said flatly. "Does that knot look right?"

Carlo shrugged. David pulled hard, the knot looked like it would hold.

The father walked to David and said, "Julie broke-up with her boyfriend today. Christ! She's 15 and has a boyfriend. I could kill the little prick."

David told Carlo, "Radio HQ and request police backup. Keep everyone well away from those stakes and the rope."

Between sobs, the mother said, "Please save her. She tried to kill herself with sleeping pills 3 months ago. It's so difficult being a teen..." Her remaining words drowned in the sobbing.

David now felt his body shaking. He hoped that no one would notice. Adrenaline surged. Carlo got the crowd to back away, but a teenage girl broke through and ran to David who was harnessed at cliff's edge ready for the descent.

"I'm Julie's sister. Julie's pregnant."

Trying to absorb the implication, David asked, "Your folks know?"

"No! Pop would kill her. She told her boyfriend two hours ago and he went crazy."

"What's your name?"

"Beth."

"What should I say to Julie?" David was worried that Julie would jump.

Her sister looked back at her parents then whispered to David, "Tell her we love her. I'll protect her from dad. He can't force her to have the baby."

"Anything else?" David was desperately trying to formulate his approach to stopping a suicide.

"Julie loves animals. She volunteers at the animal shelter. Loves dogs."

David took a last look at the knot he had tied. He prayed that it would hold his weight and his life. "Carlo, keep an eye on the stakes and knot. In military academy, I got a C-minus in knot tying."

David descended backwards over the cliff. The rope held his 180 pounds; he hoped it would hold the weight of two people. Rather than rappel down the cliff, David slowly descended walking backwards down the face of the cliff, feeding the thin nylon rope that held his life. He did not want to frighten the girl. After descending 30 feet, he was level with her he said, "Hello, Julie. I'm David."

"Oh, God," Julie softly sobbed. "Just leave me alone."

"Beth told me that a lot of people love you."

Staring at the rocks 70 feet below, Julie stated in a voice that sounded distant and void of emotion, "No one loves me."

"That feeling must really hurt."

No reply.

He did not know what to say. He tried a new tact. "Sometimes I think everything is hopeless. Right now, they're trying to send me to Vietnam. I don't want to die. I won't. I want to live a long life." No response. *What would Dr. Grace say?*

"Julie, do things look hopeless to you right now?"

Julie looked at David suspended on the cliff. She looked back at the ground and said nothing.

David swung three feet closer to Julie. As he did, the rope jarred loose a sharp ten-pound rock at the top. It flew by David's head, missing by inches. David considered that Julie's life was not the only one that could be lost in this rescue attempt. David recalled being a small child praying at the edge of his bed, *Our Father who art in heaven...*

Shapes and colors were vivid. It was like when he dropped acid. He could see each granite rock imbedded in the limestone cliff. He saw the fading sunlight pierce the thin nylon rope that held his life in suspense. He saw each person's face at the top, looking down. He saw the crowd standing at the bottom of the cliff, many standing on the train tracks.

"Carlo!" David shouted to the top of the cliff.

"Yes."

"Radio to have the guard in tower four clear everyone off the tracks. Keep everyone on top ten feet back from the cliffs." David was frustrated that he needed to give these orders when he already had his hands full.

He returned his attention to Julie. An unstable rock outcropping held the frightened child. He was now close enough to see the fear in her eyes, almost hidden under her fallen brown hair. The fine layer of limestone dust on Julie's face was streaked with tears.

"Sometimes everything can seem hopeless. I once sat on the Golden Gate Bridge and thought about jumping," David lied. "I'm glad I didn't. I worked through the problems. I realized I had choices. People need me."

"Just go away. No one needs me. I'm trouble," Julie spoke in fragments between crying. David took a sideways step closer to Julie.

"Go away!" screamed Julie, "Or I'll jump."

David was still. He saw the sun sink lower. A full moon had edged above the horizon. He had little time. The rescue would be more difficult in a grey twilight.

"I believe you, Julie. That's why I'm here. I'm a lifeguard; I save lives just like you save dogs."

"I try to save the dogs that no one wants." Julie sobbed. "But they end-up getting killed."

David looked at Julie. He tried to think about how he would get her down the cliff alive. "Your sister told me that you're wonderful with dogs. I'm sure that you've helped several get adopted. It's easier with people. There are so many couples that can't have a baby and want one. Babies can always be adopted by nice people."

"She told you? She told you!" Julie cried. "I don't want a baby. Pop will kill me."

"I promise that he won't hurt you. Your parents love you. You have choices."

"I don't have any choice. It's hopeless." Julie buried her head as she cried. David saw that she could easily lose footing. He quickly fed the rope and swung next to her. He grabbed and held her as she cried. Suddenly she lurched pulling David sideways and half out of his protective harness. He and Julie started to plunge to the jagged rocks below.

The girl's mother screamed; her father looked on with horror. Terror swept through the crowds. The rope pulled against the stakes, strained by the weight of David struggling with Julie. Above, Carlo grabbed the rope.

David used every lateral muscle to upright himself. He

grabbed the burning rope with his right hand and ignored the blood as it cut into his hand until he stopped the rope and their fall. They fell ten feet before David regained his footing. He never let go of Julie, holding her tight with his left arm.

Julie collapsed in David's firm grip. David now had enough adrenaline pumping into his muscles to lift a 300-pound person. With one arm, he wrapped Julie around him as he had been taught in rescue training. He rappelled toward the ground holding Julie tightly. With each arc across the cliff, David fed more rope. They descended.

Finally his feet hit the ground. The crowd cheered. David released Julie and removed the harness and rope from his body. He felt pain in his right hand and remembered that he was bleeding. To control the bleeding, he closed his fist and rested his hand on his head.

Carlo drove the parents and sister down the path from the cliff top to Julie below. Julie's parents hugged her. Her sister held her as if she would never let go. David looked into the crowd and was amazed to see Linda. She must have made an unexpected visit to the beach.

Julie's family, the paramedics, and the police surrounded her. *Too many people are around Julie. I don't need to join the crowd.* Carlo gave David two thumbs up and nodded toward Linda. David acknowledged.

Linda gave David a glowing smile and looked at him with wide-eyed admiration. He grabbed her hand, quickly guided her away from the crowd and pulled Linda into a cave hidden in the cliff.

Linda continued to glow with admiration. "That was truly heroic. You risked your life for her. I was terrified. You saved her life."

David had never felt so admired. He held her closely as they shared a long kiss. He held his hand high in the air, making a fist to stop the bleeding, but holding the hand at an angle so no blood would drop on Linda's bikini and blouse.

David said, "Such beautiful words from a beautiful woman; a beautiful person. I'm glad that you were here for this. I'm always glad when I'm with you." They returned to a lingering kiss. "Follow me. I need to see Carlo."

As they walked, she screamed, after noticing that David's hand was bleeding.

Carlo cleaned and bandaged David's bleeding hand. "I'll fill out the report. You're done for the day. At least you're done with work," Carlo said smiling as he nodded his head toward Linda. "By the way, I'll be staying with my folks tonight. The place is all yours."

In her car, Linda followed David to his home so that they could change for dinner. After parking, she carried her large bag containing a skirt and make-up kit. As they walked to his small home, Linda said, "Cute. You live in a little cottage like I do."

"Yeah, I love it." As David reached for the door, he said, "I've got to warn you. The clean half of the place is mine. The disaster area is Carlo's."

"I can dig it. I grew-up sharing a one-sink bathroom with my brother."

"The bathroom is all yours. Let me get a clean towel. Care for a glass of water? Wine?"

"Wine would be groovy."

"Linda took in the art posters, the books, the record albums, the organized areas, and the orange construction tape on one of the bedroom doors."

"OK. I found extra towels," David called from his room, which was separated from Carlo's by the full bath with shower and one sink.

Linda peeked into David's bedroom, then stood leaning against the doorframe, staring at David as he stood and turned holding the towels. He looked at Linda in her bikini and translucent blouse. He put the towels on the bed and walked to her.

They kissed so long that the streaming sunlight softened to pastels of an approaching sunset. David amorously looked at her and asked, "Would you like to take a shower together?"

"Yes. My roommate's an environmentalist. We should save water."

David removed her blouse and his white tee shirt. Linda rested her hands on his shoulders broad from years of surfing. Her hands descended to his muscled chest and then to his arms that were strong enough to hold a person while descending a cliff. Feeling her touch and seeing the fire in her eyes, David was reassured and aroused.

Their shower was full of giggles and laughs, shampoo and soap, tentative hands that were followed with confident touches and caresses and strokes. They lingered in a passionate kiss. He undid her bikini top, then slowly knelt, kissing her breasts and then stomach. He slowly removed her bikini bottom, savoring the touch of her legs. He removed his lifeguard trunks. As he soaped and rinsed her entire body, he lingered to kiss her breasts, and then pleasure her with his tongue. She stroked his hair and screamed with delight.

After showering, they grabbed towels, semi-dried, and then raced to bed. David felt completely connected with Linda as he entered her. Her passion quickly built to an orgasm. After their orgasms, they lay together for a long time.

David drove them to a romantic Italian trattoria. They dined, talked, laughed, and under the table, with hands and bare feet they touched, massaged and aroused. They returned to David's home to again make love, this time in slow motion, and to spend the night together.

19

Walking on the Moon

"It's been quite a week. I saved a life, I almost got killed in the process, and I made love with Linda." David started his session with Dr. Grace. "I keep dreaming about the girl I rescued. She was ready to kill herself. She was 15, pregnant, on the ledge of a cliff, seriously thinking about jumping. I had to rappel down the cliff, talk her out of jumping, grab her, and then carry her down the cliff. She seemed so alone and void of hope."

"Empty of hope?" Dr. Grace asked.

"She was at my beach on a camping trip with her parents. This girl, Julie, told her boyfriend that she was pregnant and he freaked. She worried her father would kill her, saw no way out, worked her way down the cliff, threatening to jump, and I was called in to make the rescue."

"What was that like?"

"She seemed hopelessly alone. She had to choose between having a child that she didn't want and trying to get an abortion. When I reached her during the cliff rescue, she kept talking about killing herself. I keep thinking of how sad and all alone she was."

"She may have felt abandoned," Dr. Grace said.

"Abandoned with nowhere to turn. I keep replaying the rescue and how sad and lonely Julie looked."

"It must be difficult to go through life feeling abandoned," Dr. Grace said.

"All alone and nobody there for you," David repeated softly.

"David, I think that abandonment is a core issue for you. You lost your mother when you were five. Your father left you with grandparents, then military academy. You must've been a lonely five-year old."

David looked at Dr. Grace. He felt stunned and started to say something, but no words came out. Finally he said, "My life has been lonely. I don't know what love is. Never have. I'm kind a dangling on an emotional cliff."

"How does that feel?"

"Lonely." David said as his eyes filled with tears. "Yeah, I'm lucky I've got Carlo as a friend. I feel a real connection with Linda, but I've just started seeing her and she warned me that she wasn't ready to get involved. I've never dated anyone for very long. I've no idea how long things will last with her."

"As a young child, you lost your mother. Since then, you've never had a relationship with a woman."

"Yeah, and who knows how much longer I'll be here. Any day now, I could get the Report for Duty letter from Uncle Sam. Then I'm off to Canada. I'm not going to Vietnam. I've been thinking about how I could've died on that cliff or made one mistake and killed Julie. I don't want to die and I don't want to kill people. I'm not going to be like my dad with his schemes, secret bombings, crippling villagers with napalm."

"You're showing courage," said Dr. Grace. "We've talked about all the years where you tried to win your father's approval in military academy. Many people who fear abandonment never stop trying to win their parents approval."

"I ruled out any hope of getting his approval when I rejected acceptance by the U. S. Naval Academy after all his campaigning inside the navy and with some members of congress. That bridge is burned to the ground."

"How do you feel about your father?"

"He killed my mother and abandoned his only child. How should I feel about him?"

"He killed your mother?"

"He was driving the car when we crashed and she was killed." David started crying and going through one Kleenex and then another.

Finally, David said, "I just remembered my mom and me a few days before the crash. She wouldn't let me play with a toy." David looked at the wall, trying to remember. "It was a toy gun. She took it away. I threw a tantrum and told her I wished she were dead." David was crying harder than any time that he could remember.

After the crying subsided, Dr. Grace said, "It's perfectly normal for a five-year-old to get angry and say something like that. It's also normal for a five-year-old to have feelings of megalomania. When your mother died, deep in your unconscious you may have blamed yourself for her death, holding a childlike belief that your words had the power to kill her."

David, mouth-hanging open, stared at Dr. Grace. "That's crazy. Of course, I'm in here because I'm crazy."

"You're not crazy. In therapy, with courage and insight you confront deep feelings and make steady progress. With your feelings of abandonment, you have difficulty seeing that people care about you. You said that you don't know how long your relationship with Linda will last. That will depend primarily on your willingness to trust her."

After the play was over, David and Linda strolled out with the crowd. They were at David's alma mater, and Linda's new university, UCI, to see Shakespeare's *Much Ado About Nothing*. They strolled the campus, holding hands.

"I loved the banter between Beatrice and Benedict," David said. "Boy meets girl, girl rejects boy, and then they fall in love."

"Get married and live happily ever after," Linda said.

"It was hilarious to watch their friends set them up so that they fell in love." They walked under the stars until they reached a bench overlooking the park in the middle of campus. David had an idea. "You know that Rachel is Carlo's Beatrice."

Linda pulled her hands to her mouth. She looked at David and then laughed. "Heavy. Getting her to go out with Carlo. What a challenge. She does need to start dating again, but Carlo?"

"Yeah, even getting them through one date would be a challenge, so I think we should do it," said David.

"Remember Big Sur? Rachel doesn't quite get into any of it, but Carlo's all in dancing with a Tibetan bowl on his head. Hilarious. He's the college dropout and she's the scientist going for her PhD."

"Definitely a challenge. Carlo, of course, would go out with Rachel in a second. He's very attracted to her."

"Totally, but he comes on too heavy."

"True."

"Rachel has said that she thinks Carlo is handsome and funny. Wesley has moved back east, so she's been moping around and not seeing anyone.'

"Carlo used to have a good relationship in Santa Barbara with Susan and she was a scholar."

"If nothing else, I think they would have fun. She takes life too seriously. He would lighten her up." Linda warmed to the scheme. "When we talk on the phone, we could talk just loud enough so that our roommates could hear."

"Like when we're in our bedrooms with the doors shut."

Linda warmed to their conspiracy. "Like the play, I could repeat Carlo's qualities and interest in Rachel's saving birds, but warn that she is too hostile to men."

"Far out. And I could be on the phone with you, talking about her qualities and hidden interest in Carlo, but warn that he is too immature," David said as he looked up at the stars thinking.

After walking in silence, David said, "I've got it. Rachel will be totally into watching Apollo 11 on TV, right?"

"Totally."

"A couple of days before the moonwalk on July 20, I'll remove a vacuum tube from the TV at your place. She'll freak. She'll hear you call me about the no TV problem. I'll invite the two of you to join me and Carlo for dinner and watching the moonwalk at our place."

"Ingenious," said Linda as she threw her arms around David and kissed him. "I actually think this might work. You're blowing my mind. I didn't know you had a deceptive side."

"I'd better get one if I hope to stay out of Vietnam."

Over the next few days, David and Linda executed their cupid's plot with all the precision of the Kennedy Space Center. On July 19, when Rachel was out, Linda sneaked David into her place to remove a TV vacuum tube. Later, Rachel returned to a broken television and started loudly swearing in Spanish.

Linda called David about she and Rachel watching the moonwalk at their place. He casually asked Carlo if Linda and Rachel could come over the next day for dinner and watching the first moonwalk in history. Carlo eagerly said yes. Cupid's arrow had been launched from space.

Carlo looked at the disaster areas in their house. This was his last chance to connect with Rachel. Everything had to go well. Launch minus-24 hours; terminal countdown began; at T-24, the house became Mission Control. David and Carlo went to the market and bought cleaning stuff, a mop, and the dreaded toilet scrub brush. At T-22, the place was actually clean for the first time. Framed posters finally got dusted and hung. Carlo converted his disaster area into a bedroom.

At minus-21 hours and counting, Carlo realized that Rachel would be expecting real food. Swanson's TV dinners would not get this rocket off the ground. His space probe entering her lunar module would never happen. Carlo took the only possible course. He bought flowers and went home to see Mama. He pleaded his case and she rescued him by making her famous lasagna.

David opened the San Clemente State Beach headquarters tower and looked a mile to his left at President Nixon's summer estate at Cotton's Point. San Clemente brought the hippies and the marines, the beautiful and the brave, the change agents and those forever changed.

The sea was flat as Nixon's latest speech that promised an end to the war. Both ocean and sky were the same gray. The beach was nearly empty. No rescues would happen with the ocean this calm.

In his small tower, Carlo attacked the boredom with a

desperate vengeance. He constructed two armies with plastic soldiers. He devised strategies, battle plans, and gave orders to the subordinate generals. Carlo was not allowed to bring his trumpet into the tower, so he snuck in the mouthpiece of the trumpet and blew a call to battle. In the middle of the combat, a fly entered Carlo's tower. Carlo engaged the fly in an aerial dogfight with Carlo attacking with his Bactine spray bottle. In the end, Carlo was the victorious flying ace.

One by one, the guards lifted their telephones, desperate for a human voice to cut through the silence of boredom, and talked of surf and sex, war and peace, and how Carlo should woo Rachel.

Linda and Rachel arrived in the morning at the guys' place, so that Rachel would miss none of the Apollo broadcast. Linda used the house key that David had given her, since David and Carlo would not return from lifeguarding until evening. Linda was relieved to see the place clean and Rachel liked the cottage. Linda brought a salad and Rachel, in a gesture of peace, brought a bottle of Chianti.

Rachel immediately turned on CBS to watch Walter Cronkite's continuous Apollo 11 coverage. Four days earlier the massive Saturn V rocket had lifted off the ground at the Kennedy Space Center in Florida. Now, tension was high in the command control center.

On TV, the lunar module named Eagle was on the far side of the moon where no communication with earth occurred. Around the planet, people prayed for its successful separation from the command module, Columbia.

Finally, lines of pixels painted on the screen, revealing the Eagle. No longer hidden on the dark side, communication was restored. Everyone at the Space Center cheered.

"It's running long!" The Eagle was on a trajectory to land miles west of the intended site. Program alarms displayed on multiple screens. Minutes passed until a message to proceed with the landing was displayed after a tense debate at Houston. With only seconds of fuel remaining, the Eagle landed on the moon.

Around 5:30, David and Carlo arrived from the day of lifeguarding. Linda ran to the door and gave David a big hug. Rachel, somewhat cautiously, shook hands with David, and then Carlo, thanked them for the TV coverage, and excitedly summarized the lunar landing.

The men took turns quickly showering and changing from lifeguard uniforms to jeans and shirts. The four squeezed onto the sofa facing the TV. David and Linda sat in the middle, with Carlo and Rachel at opposite ends, as all saw replays of Apollo 11, watching the astronauts guide toward a landing site full of dangerous rocks and craters. Armstrong took manual control of the lunar module to avoid disaster, with fuel disappearing rapidly.

"Houston, Tranquility Base here. The Eagle has landed", Armstrong announced as the lunar module landed on the moon's surface with only 25 seconds of fuel remaining. The four cheered.

Carlo, determined to be a gentleman, set the table, food and wine, and invited the four to dinner. The four dined, praising Linda's salad, and complementing the lasagna for which Carlo gave his mother full credit. The Chianti Classico was enjoyed and the bottle emptied. A second bottle was opened and poured.

The four talked about the exploration of space and of life on earth. Carlo took a subdued role and listened carefully as Rachel discussed science, including her research in marine biology. Talk inevitably shifted to Vietnam. All agreed that the war must end. David encouraged Carlo to tell of his daring escape when his Reserve unit was shipped to Vietnam. Carlo acted out the drama in three acts. Everyone laughed and applauded, including Rachel.

As the four returned to the sofa in anticipation of history's first moonwalk, David and Linda sat at one end of the sofa, leaving Rachel no choice but to sit next to Carlo. As Linda and David had plotted, David brought out a bong and invited everyone to smoke grass in anticipation of the moonwalk. David inhaled, then Linda. Rachel shrugged and took a strong hit, as did Carlo.

The time had arrived. Commander Neil Armstrong descended the ladder from the lunar module to become the first person in history to step on the moon. He announced, "That's one small step for man, one giant leap for mankind."

Across America, people young and old joined in a common celebration as the vision of the decade was realized. Apollo 11 signified the promise of a new era when people could reach for the stars, oxygen could be created in the vacuum of space, and energy could be created from solar power.

For most watching, this was their first view of earth from space - a small beautiful blue sphere in the sky, a home to the miracle of life, a home to be shared in peace.

20

Woodstock

Linda and Alicia stared at the *Woodstock Music & Art Fair* poster, which promised three days of peace and music. The poster featured an image of a dove perched on the end of a guitar. The list of performers included many of their favorite groups including Creedence Clearwater, The Who, Janis Joplin, Joe Cocker, Jimi Hendrix, Jefferson Airplane, and Santana. Three days in upstate New York from August 15 to 17 promised to be epic.

While Alicia visited in Laguna, they discussed and debated going. Alicia wanted the great adventure of hitchhiking across America with backpacks. If they were going, Linda favored driving. Alicia kept playing the music that they would be hearing and talking about a great adventure. When Alicia said goodbye, Linda promised to consider the journey.

Linda was exhausted from her day at Montessori. Two four-year-old boys fought, screamed, and cried all day. It started with a power struggle over a toy truck and never ended.

When she returned home, there was a letter from Brad, return address of Fort Ord, U. S. Army. Full of dread, she read the letter, and then angrily threw it away. Just as she had warned him, he was being shipped to Vietnam. Once a leader in the anti-war movement, he was now a trained killer. The major who promised Brad a deal to work in the VA hospital was transferred to Vietnam. Now, Brad was going, most likely into combat.

Full of anger and sadness, Linda started walking. Streets

connected to trails until she was in the hills above Laguna. She thought of her brother John sitting in a wheelchair staring at every passing car. She was again haunted with the image of him lying dead, holding a shotgun.

Then there was David. One day he talked about his hopeless schemes to stay out of the war; the next, selling computers to the military-industrial complex; the next, splitting to Canada.

You barely know the guy. He could be gone like Brad. Why did I daydream of being married to David, raising kids and teaching, while he is doing his suit-and-tie computer job? Our whole life planned, just like Ozzie and Harriet.

Linda sat on a hill and looked down on the distant streets of people coming and going, buying and selling, drifting and driving. She wondered what to do with her life. Did she really want to teach screaming kids and spend thirty years stopping boys from fighting? Maybe she could become a professor like Rachel and champion a great cause. She could spend a year in Europe, wait tables and see the wonders of Paris, Amsterdam and Rome.

At the very least, she could see America with Alicia and hitch to Woodstock. As she sat on the green hill, her conviction grew.

Linda and David sat on a cliff in South Laguna, looking at the ocean and waiting for sunset. A distant typhoon in Asia had launched big waves that crossed the Pacific, crashing in explosions on California shores.

Linda said, "These weeks with you have been groovy."

"I've never been more happy."

Hearing this, Linda's body tensed, as from pain. She said, "My friend Alicia from Berkeley wants me to go to the biggest rock festival ever. I'm going to Woodstock with her."

"I haven't heard about it. Where is it?"

"Upstate New York."

"New York for a concert?"

"I've got to get away. I'm having a bummer. I just got a letter from Brad that he's going to Vietnam. I can't stop thinking of John's suicide. Kids fight at school and I'm not sure I want to be a teacher. I'm a mess."

David started to talk, then stopped and waited for the big set to finish, with each wave exploding more loudly than the previous. "It sounds like you're getting hit with a lot."

"I miss John terribly. This war is madness. I've got to get away."

"I'll miss you," David said. "How long will you be gone?"

"I guess I could do it in ten days, but I need a break. Our romance has been wonderful, but I can't handle a relationship now. I'm depressed and confused."

David looked shocked. "What are you telling me, Linda?"

"Please wait until I call you," Linda said as she started to cry. "I need a couple of months."

It was the story of his life. David felt abandoned.

The auto shop estimated five hundred dollars to replace the clutch and put a rebuilt engine in Linda's dying VW Beetle. She didn't have five hundred, but she was now determined to go to Woodstock. She took a bus to Berkeley where she and Alicia started their great adventure of hitching across America. They quickly got a ride in Berkeley, taking them to Lake Tahoe. They passed towns that had once been ruled by Spain, Mexico, independent republics, and even Russia. They passed vineyards and levies and cities born of the Gold Rush and then ascended into the mountains.

After being dropped off in Truckee, near Lake Tahoe, they stood at an intersection, taking turns standing with a thumb out. Linda wore a Mexican blouse covered with bright flowers; Alicia, a translucent turquoise gauze blouse. Alicia wore a flower-bead headband; Linda, beads and bangles. Both stood on the roadside barefoot. Discouraged with no one picking them up, they walked into the Truckee Depot asking people if they were going east. Soon they had a ride as far as Reno.

In Nevada, they stood on the road, holding a bold sign that said New York. A pink Cadillac pulled over. Two prostitutes drove them for hours across the desolate windswept Nevada desert. They were going to Salt Lake where the hookers were working a bowling convention.

One said, "That's right. While they're bowling for dollars, we'll be balling for dollars. You two look like you could use some good money. Why don't you join us?"

Alicia raved about the adventure of being hooker for a day, until she saw Linda's withering look.

Next, a rancher took them across the high plains of Wyoming to Cheyenne. For a few fitful hours, under the stars, they slept in their sleeping bags in the flatbed of his pick-up truck.

Across Nebraska they traveled with a couple that had just said goodbye to their daughter starting at the University of Colorado. They worried about her and the war and a nation being torn apart. They drove through a thunderstorm, which once depleted, unveiled a rainbow over furrowed fields, grain silos, and red barns. As they approached Council Bluffs, the man talked about how the transcontinental railroad had transformed America. The couple offered them a room in their home for the night. The girls luxuriated in hot showers and clean sheets and a home cooked breakfast.

After a lonely three hours at an I-80 on-ramp a marine vet picked them up in his old Ford sedan. The gunnery sergeant had been part of the Khe Sanh siege where five thousand marines held out for two months against an enemy of forty thousand. It was after that siege and the televised broadcast of dead and wounded from the Tet Offensive that most Americans had turned against the war. Now out of the marines, the gunnery sergeant was headed home. He talked of fighting for the freedom of his country, but not seeing whites fighting for the freedom of blacks. The vet talked of joining the Black Panthers, but he'd seen enough killing for one lifetime. He dropped Linda and Alicia at a Chicago Metro station. They rented a cheap room nearby.

The next morning, they were picked-up quickly. Alicia and Linda jumped in the back of the Chrysler sedan. The driver was unshaven and looked to be in his late thirties. He said, "Must be tough to be standing in the rain."

"It was," Alicia replied. "We weren't ready for the downpour. Thanks for the ride."

Through the rear-view mirror he looked at Linda and Alicia's breasts, revealed by their wet t-shirts. "Where you going?"

"New York," was chorused in unison with giggles.

"You read about those hitchhikers in New Jersey getting killed." There was something flat in the man's voice, something strange. Linda looked at the man's face reflected in the driver's cracked rear-view mirror. His eyes were narrow, dark and almost empty.

"Creepy," Alicia said. "Why do people do that?"

"Killer's mother was a drunk and a whore who wanted nothing to do with her son. Guy never had a break." Linda pulled her shawl tight over her t-shirt. She wanted to ride in silence. The conversation made her shiver.

"The guy's going to prison. I hated prison."

Linda tried to sound friendly and polite. "Do you have any music?"

He played the Beatles *White Album.* They listened to Paul McCartney singing "Helter Skelter." She heard the sound of the balding tires cut through the pools of water on the lonely road. John Lennon sang about being lonely and wanting to die.

His words enveloped Linda like a dark storm. She looked around, nervous that the city had disappeared behind them. The road was half-empty. They should have taken the Greyhound bus, instead of going with Alicia's hitchhiking fantasy.

"Hell, when you're thrown out on the streets as a kid, you got no choice but to steal. At least in the Big House you get fed your three squares." He stared down the road. "No one gives a shit."

Linda tried to deflect the conversation, "Where you headed?"

Charles formed a thin sardonic grin, "Going to hell, just like the rest of us." He chuckled. "Where you from?"

Alicia answered, "Berkeley."

"Wild out there. You live in a commune?"

Linda quickly replied, "No, we're good girls." Alicia looked at her and rolled her eyes.

"Revelation. The end is coming. You watch. Nixon will drop a nuclear bomb on North Vietnam that will accidentally take out a Russian ship. The nuclear missiles will fire automatically. Nuclear war. The end. It's all in the Book of Revelation."

Linda looked at the dark wet empty road as the silence stretched for miles. When she read the road sign announcing

South Bend. "Charles, could you stop at the drugstore? I need to get something for my infection."

Charles looked in the mirror at his beautiful guests. He said nothing and the narrow eyes above his unshaven-scarred face revealed nothing.

When they entered the town the car slowed to the 35 mph speed limit. "Please, Charles, I need to buy the medicine."

"Need gas anyway." He pulled into the gas station next to the drug store. "Don't be long." He got out of the car to fill-up. Linda and Alicia jumped out of the car with their cotton bags and started running. He watched them with his dead eyes.

Linda and Alicia ran into the drug store. Linda asked, "Is there a police station here?"

"Oh my. What's the matter?"

"No big deal. Sorry, it's personal. Which way is it?"

"Two blocks down the street. Next to the post office."

Linda saw a screened door in the back of the store. She grabbed Alicia's arm. They walked briskly to the door. She pushed the door. It would not move. They heard the front door open.

Carlo staggered into the kitchen, raised the shades, and then recoiled from the piercing sunlight the way a mongoose recoils from a striking cobra. It was morning. He was hungry, so he opened doors to view the almost empty cupboards. There was a box of pancake mix. He had never made pancakes.

Carlo squinted in the sharp sunlight to read the directions - pour milk, break eggs, add pancake mix in a bowl, stir, and then pour into a heated skillet covered with butter. He opened the refrigerator and smiled broadly. This would be his day. All the ingredients were there.

He had a flash of insight - a breakthrough. Julia Child meets Albert Einstein. He realized that for all these years, millions of people had unnecessarily created an extra dirty dish. He sorrowed for their toils through the eons. Now, he, Carlo the Magnificent, had a better way. He started mixing the milk, eggs, and pancake mix directly in the skillet. Never again would a mixing bowl be wasted.

The mix quickly spread to cover the entire ungreased skillet. Carlo considered this, and then decided that he would simply have one large pancake. This would add to his fame. He turned on the flame to medium and left the kitchen to shave.

Lying in bed David smelled something burning. He walked into the kitchen and saw that it was black with smoke. Choking, he opened doors and windows. On the skillet was a gigantic oozing bubble that could get a starring role in a horror movie with Steve McQueen. David turned off the stove and shouted, "Carlo, what the fuck have you done?"

Carlo ran from the bathroom into the kitchen, half shaved, wide eyed, and naked. He stared at the remains of his giant pancake – the top was oozing giant bubbles and the bottom was black carbon welded to the frying pan. Uncharacteristically for Carlo, he was speechless as his half-awake brain pieced together what had happened.

It is said that making pancakes is a good way for a guy to learn to cook. However, if the guy is hungover and still asleep, this may not apply.

Linda and Alicia were alive in New York City. After their escape from Charles, running to a helpful policeman, and a night in a cheap hotel, Linda prevailed and they took Greyhound, completing their journey of thousands of miles through majestic mountains, soaring cities, and plains of golden grains. These two pilgrims had traveled the cities where Martin Luther King had preached of dreams, won civil rights, and had died. They journeyed where Robert Kennedy spoke of women's rights, evoked hopes for peace, and had died.

They had crossed a nation that had shipped a million young men to fight in a distant land, only to return to unwelcoming hometowns where fathers were divided from sons, mothers clashed with daughters, and where the dreams of one generation were discarded by the next. Their odyssey had carried them across a nation of war and peace, and of music and love.

Linda and Alicia walked through the sea of people approaching the music beckoning from the soundstage. They were at the Woodstock Music Festival after hitching, taking the Greyhound, and from Manhattan, the New York Port Authority bus to the festival. A portion of a 600-acre farm had been converted to Festival grounds.

In the parking lot, Linda and Alicia walked through masses, mostly young, that were walking, tripping, and hanging out. Most wore jeans and tee shirts; some flowers, beads and tie-dye. From the back of a pickup truck, a guy was selling hashish for five dollars. Alicia made the purchase; loaded her pipe, and she and Linda were soon tripping.

They sauntered into festival grounds, weaving, stepping over people, smiling, and giving the peace sign. After days on the road, Linda and Alicia looked like wandering pilgrims in bell-bottoms, bare feet, disheveled hair, no makeup, and each carrying two cloth bags that carried their meager wardrobes and belongings.

As the late afternoon sun continued to warm the meadow, Richie Havens was finishing "Hey Jude." The crowd finished singing with him, cheered and gave a thunderous applause. Then the conga drummer created growing tension and Havens sang of freedom with his haunting rendition of an old spiritual, "Motherless Child." In singing of freedom, he evoked that Woodstock was more than just about music. It was a ritual gathering for the common cause of peace, love, and freedom.

Alicia, smoking more hash than Linda, sat immobilized for hours taking in the music. Linda wandered among the crowds that seemed like a biblical gathering. She endured long lines to use a portable toilet, secure water and food, and by some miracle find her way back to Alicia.

In the dark of night, Ravi Shankar played an unforgettable sitar set. Shankar had gained fame by teaching George Harrison the sitar; Harrison expanded Beatles music into a fusion of East and West. Although the Beatles were not at Woodstock, several performers played at least one of their songs in homage to their influence. Rumor was that Lennon wanted to be at Woodstock, but U. S. Immigration would not let him in the country, seeing his anti-war stance as a threat to the nation.

The Shankar sitar set was cut short by rain that started with playful drops and then turned into a complete downpour. It rained so hard that a young Noah was gathering two of each species. Holding Alicia's hand, Linda guided her to an area where people had tents.

It seemed like a miracle that Linda bumped into a friend from Cleveland. She and Alicia squeezed into the tent of her friend and her friend's boyfriend. Sheltered from the storm and hearing distant music on and off through the night they had a fitful sleep.

Saturday morning as the sunlight streamed, Linda smelled wet alfalfa, marijuana and pungent incense. The crowd stretched beyond the pasture and into far hills. One hillside that had seated thousands of wandering pilgrims was now a mudslide that invited people to descend its mud shoots. Alicia stripped naked and soared down the long mudslide. Linda striped to panties, bare breasted, and screamed with delight down the long descent. At the bottom the two looked at each other and laughed, as they were completely covered in mud. After more slides, more screaming, and more mud, they followed a path to a lake on the farm. They waded in with many others and waded out clean.

Saturday continued the celebration with some of the greatest music of their generation. For Linda, none was better than a group she had known from her trips to San Francisco. Santana mesmerized the sea of people that had swelled to an estimated 500,000. With the group's fusion of Latin and rock they brought the festival to its feet. Santana's guitar magic combined with exotic playing of keyboards, congas, percussions, and drums. At age 15, Santana had migrated to the United States from Mexico, making minimum wage washing dishes. Now at age 22, he was a superstar with a major recording contract. America.

Before midnight, under a sky with a red glow from the lights of the festival, Linda and Alicia wandered back to the tent city. Unable to find their friends they slept under the stars. Linda awoke in the middle of the night, hearing Janis Joplin in the distance singing Gershwin's "Summertime," and then with searing passion, "Piece of My Heart." Linda drifted back to sleep.

Sunday morning, Linda was dancing to Jefferson Airplane. She kept looking at a handsome guy nearby. His face looked pure and enlightened. Beads swayed across his naked chest while his long hair flowed in the morning breeze as he danced barefoot in the muddy earth. He looked at Linda and smiled.

She felt that he was seeing into her soul. Jefferson Airplane sang "Somebody to Love" as he walked to Linda and said, "I love the flow of your dance."

Linda slowly inhaled and exhaled as they locked eyes and then she said, "It's a beautiful morning. Isn't this an amazing celebration?"

"It will be with me everyday for the rest of my life. My name is Child of God."

Linda heard herself reply, "I am Wind Spirit. Enchanting to meet you." Linda looked directly at him. They danced and their bodies kept touching. Electricity flowed down to her toes, stimulating her everywhere.

Child of God whispered, "I just took pure mescaline. I can already see the clouds dancing to Grace Slick's lyrics."

"You're in a state of grace," Wind Spirit replied.

They laughed. "This mescaline is wonderful. I'd be glad to share," he offered.

Linda accepted and sucked the orange tablet into her mouth while continuing to look into Child of God's sky-blue eyes, "Delicious. Thank you." Still dancing, she turned her gaze to Jefferson Airplane.

Music soared, soon enhanced by the drug's psychedelic effects. Colors intensified and time slowed. Wind Spirit and Child of God strolled through the crowds, smiling, each holding a flower that had somehow been placed in their hands. Everywhere there was peace and love. Renoir had painted this scene, making careful use of light to warm each face.

The couple found themselves on the periphery of the crowd as they walked to explore the farm that had been transformed for this epic celebration. They walked through woods on dirt paths marked with makeshift signs that read Groovy Way,

High Way, and Gentle Path. In a glimmering pond, they saw people cleansing themselves. It was a baptismal. It was the purification of the Ganges. Wind Spirit and Child of God reached the edge of the pond where everyone was naked, natural, and pure. He took off all his clothes and she, hers. Naked in the pond, they groomed each other. Each touch lasted forever, fusing them in passion.

They swam until they were hidden in the bushes at an edge of the pond. Wind Spirit walked to the wet grass and lay on her back, smiling at her lover. Each motion together was experienced in complete detail under the timeless sun. The kisses on her breasts and clitoris brought her to ecstasy. They were one with each other. They were one with life at this celebration of peace and love.

As Linda walked, carefree and smiling, heads turned, some because she looked like Grace Slick, others because she was naked and beautiful. By afternoon, Wind Spirit and Child of God separated with the same ease with which they had fused.

Remember high school, Susan and her catty calling you a goody two-shoes. Now it's People's Park, psychedelics and Woodstock. You're not in Ohio any more.

Strangers shared, smoked, and talked in mystical terms of their new community of peace and love. News of Woodstock reached boxy suburbs, violent cities, and napalmed jungles. The festival was a message in a bottle from the love generation.

Joe Cocker passionately sang "With a Little Help from My Friends." Those in the audience helped each other with food, water, and dope.

Dark clouds warned of another impending downpour. Thousands started trudging to their cars for their reluctant return to reality. Others awaited the baptism from the sky.

Linda was at peace with the crowds, the stench of damp wool, sweat, urine, and stale food, mixed with incense and grass. She felt her bare feet in the mud as she walked around people and trash. Her trip was real, beautiful, accepting of everything and everyone, and unfolding in slow motion.

Navy veteran, Country Joe, protested the war by singing, "I-Feel-Like-I'm-Fixin'-To-Die Rag." The young men at Woodstock were living for the day, not knowing if they would have a tomorrow. Linda took in the music of Ten Years After, The Band, and Blood, Sweat and Tears. For her, the harmonies of Crosby, Stills, Nash and Young (Neil Young refused to be filmed) probably best captured the spirit of the festival, of the time, and of the generation with works such as Long Time Gone, Wooden Ships, and Cost of Freedom.

By five in the morning, she finally slept a few brief hours. She wandered in the greatly thinned crowd until she found Alicia. They shared a long embrace. They finished the festival listening to army veteran Jimi Hendrix sing of love, trains a-coming, and his electric rendition of "The Star-Spangled Banner."

Woodstock was a lifetime compressed into three and a half days. At the festival, two children were born, and thousands were probably conceived. Many fell in love; a few were married. Drugs were more available than food, water, and shelter. Despite these conditions, there was no violence. It was truly a celebration of peace and love.

Woodstock was a music festival, a Dionysus, an Eden, a love-in, a beginning, a wake, and an end.

21

Laurel Canyon

The Laurel Canyon neighborhood was near the Hollywood recording studios, where much of the sixties' greatest music was recorded, and near the world's leading movie studios. It was the mecca for groups and groupies, artists and enlightened, the tuned-in and turned-on. David and Carlo drove to a party in the epicenter of Laurel Canyon.

"I am totally bummed about Linda splitting," David said.

"What a shocker. You two were so connected, now she's back east."

"I dug her more than anyone I've dated."

"She's gone through heavy losses, man. It's not permanent. She said, like, two months, right?"

"Yeah, but I've heard that before. It feels like she's gone for good," David lamented. The traffic crawled through the monotony of the Los Angeles basin, as one town of strip malls and industrial zones spilled into the next.

"Maybe she's gone, but maybe it's in your head. I thought you said you've been making progress on this in therapy."

"Linda didn't talk to my therapist."

For a while, they crawled through LA in silence. "In six weeks, send her a beautiful card and note, then call her. The irony is that you and Linda set-up Rachel and me" Carlo said. "I really appreciate that man. Bella Donna. She's a stone fox."

"So, how did you uncover our set-up plot?" David asked.

"We were laughing about it last night, replaying the events. Her TV stops working, then after the moonwalk it's suddenly fine. Musical chairs on the couch. Masterful. Did you and Linda scheme all that?"

"We did. We thought that you two might be good together."

"Most appreciated! Yeah, I've got the hots for Rachel, but I'm trying to dial it back. I know that I've come on too strong in the past, so I'm trying to pace myself. Listen more. Talk less. Not tear her clothes off."

"After all the advice you've given me about women, can you handle some advice from me?" David asked.

"For sure."

"It's about foreplay with Rachel."

With Carlo driving, the wagon swerved and he fought it back into the freeway lane. "Man, you can't say 'foreplay with Rachel' while I'm driving. OK, you can. Tell me."

"*Silent Spring*. You've got to read *Silent Spring*. She totally cares about the environment. You've got to start with that book," David said.

"You call some hardcore book foreplay?"

"Rachel is a hard-core environmentalist. For her foreplay is either stopping oil drilling or controlling toxic pesticides."

"Bummer, man. Foreplay should include a romantic dinner, wine, dope, throbbing music, kissing her breasts, stroking her everywhere, whispering words of passion. God, I want to fuck her. Can't I just beg?"

"*Silent Spring*, man. You've got to get in her head."

As they drove, the sunset turned LA's choking smog into a

light show. On the radio, Buffalo Springfield was singing "For What It's Worth." Demons fought inside David's mind in a fierce struggle of agape and abandonment, trust and betrayal.

After 90 minutes of mind-numbing driving, Carlo exited the freeway and enjoyed a few minutes of motoring at normal speed, before the evening traffic of Hollywood Boulevard slowed them to another crawl. They passed famous theaters, restaurants overflowing with tourists, and streets littered with broken dreams.

They turned and followed Laurel Canyon Boulevard as it wound into the hills like a serpent goddess through cliffs covered with shrubs and flowers. They passed bungalows hidden behind sycamore and California bay laurel. Carlo turned left onto Lookout Mountain Avenue and followed the winding street until he parked at the end of a long line of cars. He and David walked a couple of blocks to their destination. Even without an address, they could easily have found the sprawling two-story house spread across the steep hill, because the house was throbbing with music.

They ascended steps, past Harley choppers on the walkway, opened the front door, and seeing no one to talk with, walked in. Carlo went to the kitchen to find his connection and deliver drugs, while David walked in the direction of the music, where performers were circled, playing guitars, conga drums and singing. David loved the fusion of rock, blues, Latin, and African rhythms, the like of which David had never heard.

After a while, David wandered to the kitchen and mixed a rum and coke. When he turned around, one of the singers was standing next to him. David said, "That was amazing music."

"Thanks. We were having fun jamming," she answered and enticingly stared at David.

"Hi. I'm David."

"Hello, David. I'm Angela."

David was star struck. "Were you jamming with Stephen Stills of the Buffalo Springfield?"

"That's him," Angela said. "Springfield is history. He's just put together a new group with David Crosby, Graham Nash and Neil Young. I know a lot about harmony, and let me tell you, their harmonies are amazing. Crosby, Stills, Nash and Young were big at Woodstock. Didn't you see them on Dick Cavett?"

"Sorry, I don't watch much TV," David said sheepishly. "Woodstock. Wow!"

"Artists are back from New York, doing deals, celebrating. You're not a musician are you?"

"I bet my haircut gave it away. I'm a lifeguard in San Clemente, but I do sing in my tower, sometimes."

Angela laughed. "So you're like those guys I see on the beach in Venice and Santa Monica."

"Exactly," David said.

"Saving any lives, lately?" Angela's voice sounded playful, as she looked at David, standing inches away.

"Yeah, I've been keeping count. I've made 143 rescues, mostly weak swimmers caught in riptides getting pulled overhead. I made the newspaper two weeks ago with a cliff rescue."

"So you're famous?"

"In my own mind," David replied. "Most rescues are pretty routine. You can see people with weak strokes drifting toward rips. I'm usually rescuing Camp Fire Girls and marines, never a beautiful woman like you."

"You're sweet," Angela said. "So you ever have to bust

people for drugs?"

"Fuck, no. I just try to avoid getting busted. I love to smoke dope like everyone else," David said.

"Then you need to follow me," Angela said as she slid her hand inside his arm and led him out the kitchen and down the long hallway.

"You with a group right now?" David said, a bit star struck.

"I stay pretty busy with studio work and Hollywood Bowl gigs. When you see those lovely ladies doing the harmonies and backups, you just might be seeing me. I moved here from Detroit. I did a lot of Motown studio work with Marvin Gaye, Stevie Wonder, and Smokey Robinson."

"Totally cool," David enthused. "I'm sure I've got some of your albums." He followed her lead up the stairs and into a small room where a few people were passing a thin glass-blown pipe. They sat next to one of the women with whom Angela had been singing.

"Pace yourself, Angela," her friend warned with a smile. "This is strong hash."

Angela took the pipe and inhaled strongly, and then passed the pipe to David who took a strong hit, held it in, and passed the pipe. David looked at the circle of people, many with mellow smiles, and some lost in the distant corners of their imagination. After the pipe had circled four times, with he and Angela inhaling deeply, they looked at each other and acknowledged they were stoned. She rested her hand on David's shoulder and slowly stood. Then David started to stand, felt lightheaded, and had to kneel for seconds before carefully standing. Arm in arm, they left the room, walking down the long upstairs hallway.

They looked into one bedroom and saw a couple having sex. Looking in the next bedroom, a man had one nubile riding his penis and a second his tongue. With the hash, David experienced everything in slow motion with his body, the floor rolling in waves with the music, the body weighted like an astronaut, the delicious feel of Angela's body pressed to his as they slowly walked.

The next room was empty. Angela fell on the bed, pulling him on top of her. As they kissed, he was lost in the taste of her full lips and the erotic swirl of her tongue and through her thin cotton covering, he felt her eager response to his hand sliding down her stomach to her legs. His lips descended from her lips to her breast.

Coming up for air, David and Angela rolled on their sides, smiled at each other and laughed. Angela started singing "Hey Jude," which many were singing in the living room below. David remembered singing the song with Linda.

David rolled farther from Angela and then held her hands in his. "Angela, you're so desirable, I can't believe I'm saying this. I'm hung up on someone else. I need to go."

In a flash across her face, there was shock, then anger, and then calm. "It's totally cool that you love someone. I'm into my main man, but he's on tour, probably doing it with some groupie, and you're here and looking good. Your kissing is dreamy and I love what you've been doing with your hands. I want you and I know that you want me."

David could not take his eyes of Angela. He sank into the bed, feeling heavily stoned and dizzy with desire. The seconds passed slowly as they looked at each other, and then his lips again merged with hers, their hands were everywhere caressing and stroking. They eagerly undressed and made love.

Long after her orgasms and his, he pulled out from her. Slowly they both dressed and kissed goodbye. She walked down the hall to rejoin her friends.

David slowly walked out of the bedroom, down the hall, and down the stairs. Languidly descending half way, he stopped, lost in the music. He looked at his bare feet and then returned upstairs to the room of hash smokers. Walking in with a sheepish grin, he picked-up his shoes and socks, and then reached down to Angela to again kiss goodbye. He again walked the hall, descended the stairs, and searched for Carlo. As he was leaving the party, he saw Joni Mitchell in an animated conversation with Graham Nash.

In the cool night air, David took the road less traveled, walking uphill. Fading in the distance, he could hear a recording of Cream singing "Tales of Brave Ulysses." Hearing the riffs of Clapton's guitar, David's feet carried him up the hill. He ascended past the scattered houses, cabins hidden in the laurels, and bungalows embedded in the steep hills. He walked upwards toward the billion stars in the Hollywood sky. He finally rested on the edge of a cliff, looked below at lighted streets that crisscrossed Hollywood, and then beyond to the miles of city lights stretching to the distant ocean.

22

Together

Linda opened the door and threw her arms around David. She radiated with the happiness that he remembered from Big Sur. There was no sadness in her turquoise eyes that matched her Native American necklace. She was wearing a black bolero lace top, leaving exposed her flat stomach, and wore lavender bell-bottom corduroy pants. Although usually make-up free, she wore Revlon Moondrops lipstick.

David looked at her and all thoughts vanished of long talks about hurt feelings. She had been depressed with the loss of her brother, she saw America and returned, and she was beautiful. Only weeks had passed, not months. She was back.

Little time passed, from the lingering kisses and hugs in the doorway to passionate lovemaking in her bedroom. They reached the restaurant for dinner two hours later than planned.

David stopped by Linda's Montessori school. As agreed, he was taking her to lunch and then to one of Laguna's art festivals up Laguna Canyon Road. From the entrance, he watched Linda in reading a story to mesmerized listeners aged three and four.

She turned the book around to show the children a picture. David could not hear her words, but he could see that the kids were answering her questions, observing, pointing, and showing excitement.

One boy in Linda's semicircle was squirming as he sat between the legs of a guy Linda's age. The guy whispered something to the young boy, pointed, and the group started laughing. The guy said more and all were laughing and having fun. Linda was laughing and looking at this handsome guy who was looking at Linda.

David turned and walked out the door and started walking down the street. David could feel his face flushed. He felt angry.

Linda's different since Woodstock. Bright, beautiful, and confident. Something happened. I want to ask, but shouldn't. Jealousy, thou art a green-eyed monster.

David walked blocks, wrestling with his emotions, before he could turn around. The narrow street lacked sidewalks, forcing David to walk around parked cars. The homes were an eclectic mix: first a shack hidden beneath a jungle of overgrowth, then a white Spanish hacienda with red rhododendron, a ranch house with manicured yard, and then a cottage embraced with flowers.

After a long walk, he returned to the white house with steep gray roof, brick chimney, towering cypress, oak, pine, and Montessori School sign. David took a deep breath, walked through the front door, and then walked softly toward Linda reading to the group. He caught the corner of her eye and she beamed at David, and then motioned him to sit. He sat five feet behind the circle of kids and tried to smile and focus on her storytelling.

The teacher who had been working with kids doing their individual art, study, and playing with toys, asked everyone to take their place in a bigger circle. She summarized the day. The children went to their shelves, gathered their belongings, and lined-up at the door to depart with their parents.

Soon, David and Linda were alone on a bench overlooking the ocean. David said, "The children seemed mesmerized as you read the story. With your acting talent you should have been on stage." David hoped that he sounded encouraging as he internally wrestled with feelings of jealousy. "I never tire of watching you." David took Linda's hand and said, "Those kids were hanging on your every word."

"I do love storytelling. For sure, teaching feels like what I want to do, at least when the kids aren't fighting and screaming."

"I must have seen about 20 kids at the school. With all their energy, I was surprised at how calm everyone was during the reading circle and doing art."

"Betty's an amazing teacher," Linda said. "There were 18 children there today, all ages three to six. She gets help from me and Rod, but Betty keeps it all together."

"So Rod was the guy helping you," said David, trying to sound nonchalant.

"Rod blows my mind. He's so funny. Rod was holding Jesse, who is hyperactive. Being held seems to calm Jesse."

"So Rod is a teaching assistant, like you."

"Yeah, and he's in my teaching credential class. He's great with kids."

They continued talking as David drove Linda to the art festival. They walked among the sawdust grounds taking in booths of watercolor impressions of nature, acrylic portraits that unveiled every human expression, funky pottery, and handmade jewelry that Linda frequently stopped to admire.

The next day, dark clouds blocked any hope of seeing the sunset as David drove to Linda's home. In the flat light, trees and houses looked black and white. As he walked to her front door, he heard her talking with Rachel. After knocking, he heard running, and then Linda opened with a warm smile. They briefly kissed, conscious of Rachel's presence.

"Hello, Rachel. What's happening?" David asked.

"All kinds of stuff going on."

David smelled lavender from the bath, tomato and garlic from the kitchen. David looked at Linda and said, "Let me change out of my guard uniform and I'll join you two in a minute." David walked into Linda's bedroom, closed the door, and quickly put on jeans and a Madras shirt. He walked out barefoot.

"We've been talking about the environment," Linda said. "This magazine article shows my favorite river in Ohio, the Cuyahoga. It's so polluted that it's on fire! Look at these photos. Unbelievable. As a kid, I hiked the river and falls."

"A river on fire!" David exclaimed as he looked at the photo.

Rachel said, "It's tragic the way steel mills, coal power plants, and oil companies use rivers like open sewers. The environmental articles in *Time* will help mobilize the nation to insist on change."

"Rachel was telling me about Earth Day," Linda said.

"Senator Nelson is organizing a nationwide network of teach-ins for next spring," Rachel explained. "He's calling it Earth Day. I think it will raise consciousness across the nation. Coast to coast, there'll be teach-ins about how we are destroying our environment, how we can stop pollution, and live more sustainably. When I talked with him in Santa Barbara, I gave him my paper about the oil spill. Today, I got a letter from him, complimenting my paper, and asking me to get involved with Earth Day. I've drafted my reply, stating that I have been one of the leaders of GOO, and that I would like to be a leader of Earth Day in California. I'm excited!"

"Earth Day could mobilize students and media coverage. We need to protect our air and water," David said.

"I'm so proud of everything that you are doing," said Linda. "All the birds you've saved after being covered with oil tar. Now you're fighting that chemical plant that dumps DDT, killing bald eagles. What could be more American than the bald eagle?"

"I'm doing my best," Rachel said. "The stakes are higher than I imagined. Last week I took part in a symposium at UC San Diego. I learned that when you burn coal or gasoline, CO_2 is emitted and traps heat in the atmosphere like a greenhouse. I was startled to see graphs showing earth temperature increase correlated with CO_2 emissions. I'm tempted to change my PhD thesis to impact of this greenhouse effect on marine life. It's a new field with a big future."

Rachel looked at the puzzled looks of Linda and David. "I can see that I'm getting too serious." After a silence, "Changing subjects, thanks for scheming to get Carlo and me together."

"Carlo told me that you two quickly figured it out," David said.

"I got suspicious when you sat on the couch forcing me to sit next to Carlo. When my TV worked the next day, your plot was obvious."

Linda teased, "You figured it out before Neil Armstrong walked on the moon and you made out with Carlo of your own free will."

"I admit I'm attracted to him," Rachel said. "He's all man, funny, and handsome. He's taking me dancing. Were going to a place in Santa Ana that plays salsa music. How I miss the music of my childhood."

"You're right about Carlo being funny," David said. "He and I are clueless in the kitchen. He decided to make pancakes for the first time. To have fewer dishes to wash, he mixed the batter in the frying pan. In two minutes, he had a pancake as big as the

Blob filling the kitchen with black smoke."

"Funny! *Por dios*. I'll ask him to tell me the story. He gets so involved in his storytelling, acting out all the parts, exaggerating every detail. I'll be crying with laughter."

David drove the Scout down the beach on the hot morning. Waves crashed loudly. He could taste the salt water in the air. The beach was already a collage of beach towels and umbrellas of every color. He stopped by Carlo's tower and shouted, "Up to six feet with strong rips. Rescues today."

"Fine with me," Carlo said. "In this heat, I'll be ready to jump in the water. Look at that shoulder." Carlo pointed at the perfectly shaped wave. "Want to surf after work?"

"Sure. You're not seeing Rachel?

"No, she's off to some save-the-whales rally."

"OK, let's grab some knarly waves after work, if it's not blown out." David drove down the beach.

Carlo watched a march of young girls lead by a woman overflowing from her one-piece bathing suit. The woman was equipped with a whistle, megaphone, and rescue buoy. She commandeered a section of beach, then ordered mothers to place food containers, first-aid kits, chairs, and beach umbrellas in specific locations. After the maneuvers were executed, the woman walked to Carlo's tower.

"Hi, I'm Doris. We bused in 42 Camp Fire Girls from Corona. We'll keep a close watch. If there's any problem, me and the moms have these rescue buoys to help out."

Carlo said, "Thank you for stopping by. With six-foot waves today, we're having strong side currents that will pull your girls into riptides. Please warn them of the situation and ask them to stay close to shore."

"How does a riptide happen?"

"The large surf brings in extra water. The ocean floor isn't smooth. It has grooves where more water can flow back out to sea after a wave crashes. We lifeguards know where the rips are located. We can see them. Can you see where the waves are flattened by brown dirty water that looks like a river heading out to sea?"

"I'll have the moms positioned at the riptides with their rescue buoys."

"Please leave that to us," Carlo said. "I have pulled in up to five kids at one time. I've got backup from the other towers and the vehicle driver. We don't want to rescue both the kids and the moms."

She walked back and delivered a megaphone speech to the girls, who immediately started racing in all directions, shouting and laughing. A number ran to the water, some with surf mats and some with tire tubes.

Carlo sat on the deck of his tower in a half-lotus, breathing deeply, and watching everything. He focused on swimmers with poor elbow-in-the-water-first strokes, tracking them as they drifted toward riptides.

Soon, a riptide was pulling out two girls. He followed standard procedure and lifted his phone off the hook to alert HQ, grabbed his rescue buoy, and then jumped to the sand eight feet below.

As he started running to the riptide, he could not feel anything in his left leg. It had fallen asleep. Also running into the riptide was Doris with her rescue buoy. Carlo snapped his buoy open as he hobbled into the ocean. He dove under each wave, pushed off the bottom, and quickly passed Doris as he swam to the girls. Carlo was so fast in the water, that the girls on the beach started cheering.

Carlo quickly reached the two girls, now over their heads in a powerful riptide that had pulled them 80 yards offshore in a few seconds. He threw them his orange buoy connected by a rope to the strap over his shoulder. "You are in a riptide. Just hold the buoy and I will take you safely to shore." The girls grabbed the buoy with frightened looks.

To escape the rip, Carlo swam at an angle toward the shore. Soon, they were out of the riptide that was only a few yards wide. As he continued to rescue the two girls, he heard a desperate cry for help. It was Doris, screaming, as the riptide pulled her out to sea. As Carlo scanned the water, considering his options, he smiled with relief. The Scout was parked in front of the rip and David was rapidly swimming out to save Doris. Within minutes, Carlo and David had all safely on shore.

"You were there with perfect timing," Carlo told David after the rescues.

"Today we're definitely going to earn our $3.50 per hour."

"Good thing this didn't happen two weeks from now. We're going to be down a guard after Reagan's budget cuts hits the park system. I wish he'd stop complaining about government workers not earning their pay."

Days later, sitting on the lifeguard tower, Carlo and David scanned the ocean, looking hundreds of yards left, then right for swimmers in trouble.

"How did it go with Rachel?" David asked.

"Amazing!" Carlo enthused.

"I notice you didn't come home last night," David replied to his roommate. "So, are you and Rachel now lovers?"

"At this point in our story, we don't know," Carlo said and then paused for dramatic effect. "She wore this hot strapless dress. Her gorgeous legs were everywhere. When she got in my car, her dress was so short that she had to hold the bottom of it with both hands, and do a turn worthy of the Bolshoi ballet. I went into heat, but tried to play it cool as we drove to this Spanish restaurant. Awesome meal, fine wine, laughter, flirtation, and then we went to this dance place."

"Man, you're grinning ear to ear."

"I couldn't help watching Rachel's breasts while we're salsa dancing. Then they played this slow ballad and we're pressed together in a slow sensual Samba," Carlo said as he embraced the air, acting out the evening. "I felt her wanting me. We headed to her place, which we've had to ourselves."

"So that's why Linda wanted to stay at our place last night. Those two had it all planned out. I'm always the last to know," David said.

"We sit on her couch. She poured a brandy and brought out dope," Carlo said. "In two minutes, were making out and our hands are everywhere. She was into it, man."

"I can see that your dreams were about to be fulfilled."

"Then she put on this record album where the orchestra is so lame it sounds like elevator music at Macy's. I would have played the Moody Blues, Cream, or The Doors. But it was her music, so OK, man, whatever she wants. Music playing, she's sensually dancing in front of her bedroom door, staring at me. Seconds later were in bed, I'm kissing her everywhere when there's this banshee wailing coming from the record player!" Carlo exclaimed.

"Banshee wailing?"

"A mind blower. This record alternated between the Macy's elevator orchestra and a recording of humpback whale mating songs!"

"You've got to be kidding."

"I wish. For real. Even though she's a marine biologist dedicated to saving whales, I never saw this coming. Have you ever heard mating humpbacks? On the record, one whale sounds like it's in grief; a second, a parakeet being strangled; a third screams this ten-second banshee wail. I look at naked Rachel. Total stone fox! I'm completely aroused, then I hear this soprano humpback five-second moan, followed by a ten-second-baritone humpback call for mercy. These whales are in a Verdi opera, where everyone's going to die."

"Now we're in an opera?" David asked while laughing. "Why didn't you just ask her to play a different album?"

"Because she had removed the last of my clothes, she's stroking me, and giving me this look that says take me now. I look at Rachel and I'm hard as a rock, then another banshee wailing and I was at half-mast." Carlo paused until David got his laughter under control. "While I'm licking her, she has an orgasm, saying 'oye, oye,' not 'oh, oh.' I've never heard 'oyes' in a Macy's elevator accompanied by banshees. Then I let my eyes take in all of this stone fox. I'm mind-blower turned-on. She pulls me inside. I'm on fire. Just when I worry about coming too soon, we leave Macy's elevator for more humpback moans and screams. Ultimately, the humpbacks did me a big favor, because every time I was about to come, they screamed, and I couldn't get there. By the time I climaxed, Rachel had reached ecstasy many times, and these humpbacks had a full orgy."

23

Chokehold

The hot air, dry as a thirsty desert, carried smoke and ash from the inland wildfires as David drove on scorching sand. His throat was parched and choking from the smoke in the Santa Ana winds. In past centuries, Spaniards, moving north from Mexico to conquer California, called these the devil winds.

A bit suffocated, he hummed a raspy version of the theme song to *Lawrence of Arabia*.

The eight-foot surf was coming in sets of seven to nine waves, followed by lulls of up to ten minutes. With the big waves there was a strong side-current that would carry people to riptides that pulled the unsuspecting 200 yards out to sea. Because it was past Labor Day, and because of Governor Reagan's budget cuts, there were half the lifeguards on the beach that were needed for a day like this. Carlo was in tower one, Clark in tower 3, David driving the Scout, and Martinez up in HQ where he could scan the beach with binoculars, but could not help with making rescues.

The Santa Ana winds brought people from inland, escaping the heat, brush fires and smoke. The beach crowd included a group of marines, easily spotted with their close-cropped haircuts, drinking beer, telling stories, and daring each other.

David parked his Scout halfway in the 600-yard gap between Carlo and Clark. He had the Scout facing out to sea in front of a large riptide. David stood on his vehicle seat, and scanned the swimmers, moving his head slowly left to right, then right to left, noting the swimmers with weak strokes that side-currents would soon deliver to rips. David predicted that his next rescue would be the two that were 80 yards to his left.

In a few seconds, the current pulled them into the powerful rip. David radioed Martinez that he was going on a rescue, grabbed his buoy, jumped out of the vehicle and started running. A big set of waves was coming in. David hit the water, diving into the riptide, snapped his buoy, put on the shoulder strap, and then dove under the first wave. David grabbed the bottom and then pushed off, he felt the wave strongly pulling on the buoy that trailed ten feet behind. The force of the riptide was stronger than the waves. David worked his way out to one man who was trying to swim towards shore, and a second, farther out, who was yelling for help.

David pushed his buoy towards the first buzz-cut marine. "Hold this!" David shouted. "I'll swim to the other guy, then come back and pull you both to shore. Don't worry; you're in a riptide. We pull out guys all the time."

"Got it," yelled the marine as he tightly held the orange buoy. "Get Chuck. He's in real trouble."

David rapidly swam toward Chuck, the second marine who was now 30 yards farther out to sea, being pulled by the fierce rip. David swam head-up to keep a close eye on Chuck. In less than 20 seconds, David had closed the gap and was near Chuck who was screaming for help. The large buzz-cut marine was thrashing, spitting water, and had a wild panic in his eyes.

This guy is dangerous! David's stomach tightened. He tasted bile. A couple of times each year, David had made rescues where he had to leave his buoy with one person and then swim to the next. David knew what to do, but he had never had someone with this level of panic. "Don't worry, Chuck," David yelled. "I'm a lifeguard and I'm going to pull you in.

"Lord, I'm drowning!" Chuck yelled with a Southern accent. His voice was booming and panicked.

David started the standard procedure of diving under water, grabbing the victim's legs, turning them around, then putting an arm over their shoulder, and sidestroke to safety. The procedure works in a swimming pool where one can see in the clear water. David dove under water. Blackness. Damn! David surfaced, swam behind Chuck, and put his arm over Chuck's shoulder. "I've got you. I'll pull you in."

In a flash, David's neck was head locked by the muscled and terrified marine. *He's going to break my neck!* David grabbed the squeezing headlock, but could not pry the arms lose. As David was choking he desperately tried to kick Chuck in the groin. David squirmed and weakened. No air. *Don't black out!* David tried to pull both of them underwater; sure that Chuck would let go. No luck. David could not move in the killing headlock.

As David faded into blackness, he remembered being under water in the coral reefs at Pipeline with Carlo. He was lost in an embrace with Linda. His father was wildly cheering, hugging him, and pointing to Jackie Robinson stealing home plate. He saw his mother reaching to comfort him. He was floating into a white light.

The clock of life ticked with measured slowness - one second, two, three, four, five. It was the second hand of a funeral dirge - six seconds, seven, eight, nine, ten. *Missa Solemnis* - eleven seconds, twelve, thirteen, fourteen, fifteen. Suddenly, David was awake and underwater. He was alive. There was no death grip. Carlo had swum out to help. Sizing up the situation, Carlo shoved Chuck underwater, causing the Marine to panic, release David, and surface for air. "Grab the buoy!" Carlo yelled at the Marine as Carlo pulled David five feet away from the strangler, then ten feet.

"You OK, man?" Carlo asked as David gasped for air. Color slowly returned to David's ashen face and life returned to his eyes.

"I'm alive. I thought I was gone. You're the Lone Ranger," David said.

Carlo released David and swam a few yards away. "Swim to me, David. I want to make sure you can swim."

David slowly swam to Carlo. "I'm OK," David said weakly. "I'm getting enough air."

"Can you pull in this guy while I go back for the other Marine?"

"Sounds like a plan," David said as he warily swam closer to Chuck.

"I'm going to pull you in, Chuck," David said. "But you've got to get your panic under control."

The massive marine clutched the buoy, saying, "I'm sorry, man. I'm sorry. I lost it. I shouldn't a lost it."

David needed to retrieve the shoulder strap connected to the buoy by a 10-foot rope, but the strap and rope were underwater. "I'm going to put on the shoulder strap and pull you in. David, on full alert, got within three feet of Chuck. David reached out carefully, felt for the rope until he found it. David started moving away from the marine, extending the rope, and then putting on the shoulder strap. David then started swimming at an angle to shore, pulling the panicked marine at the end of the ten-foot rope.

David swam backstroke, pulling Chuck, watching for the riptide's boundary and incoming waves. David swam slowly, very tired, and pulling a heavy weight. The rip was about 30 yards wide. When David escaped the rip and its menacing pull, he took a few heads-up crawl strokes to see that Carlo had his rescue under control. Carlo was moving to shore much faster than he.

David returned to his backstroke pull and saw a big set of

waves approaching. Normally, he would have snapped the buoy around the person being rescued in eight-foot waves and then hold the person through each wave. With Chuck, it was far too dangerous to secure the buoy on him.

"We're out of the rip, Chuck," David tried to reassure.

"Damn, thank you, sir. Sorry I lost it. Sorry."

"It happens. We're making progress to shore. The waves will help us to shore, but they'll hold you under a few seconds, so you hold on to that buoy and it will float you to the surface."

"No way am I letting go of this," Chuck said.

"Good. Hold it tight. Don't worry, the seconds under the wave will feel longer. You grip that buoy, and it will float you to the top, and I'll be right with you. Hold on!"

A massive ten-foot wave crashed down on both of them. David relaxed and let the wave tumble him toward shore. He felt Chuck's body brush his as the wave churned them both underwater. David pushed to the surface and was relieved to see Chuck pop-up, clutching the buoy. The rope connecting the two was still strapped over David's shoulder.

"Lord, help me. Thought I was gone," Chuck said with panic back in his voice.

"You did great, Chuck!" David reassured. "Hold that buoy tight, here comes the next." Another massive wave crashed on them, forced them underwater, and tumbled them like an industrial washing machine. They finally surfaced. The process repeated three more times. Each wave brought its own terror. Each wave pushed them closer to shore.

"I can't take this!" Chuck screamed.

"Stand up!" David yelled. Chuck looked at him dumbly.

"You're in three feet of water. Stand up," David yelled.

Chuck finally understood and stood. Like a dog on a leash, David walked to shore pulling Chuck until they were on dry sand.

"You OK?" David asked, as he scanned Chuck, looking for indicators of shock. The marine looked like a six-foot, three-inch, football player.

"I'm OK. You saved my life," Chuck said as he extended his hand.

Cautiously, David shook hands and then said, "You better put on clothes to warm-up; lie on your back, feet elevated, for a few minutes. You don't want to go into shock." David got an affirmative nod and then asked, "You play football?"

"I was an all-league champion in Alabama. I played tackle."

"I believe it. Good luck to you, Chuck."

"Thank you, sir. I'm off to 'Nam. It can't be any worse than that ocean of yours."

24

Celebration at Big Sur

"This will be like Woodstock!" Linda said to David as they walked on Pacific Coast Highway approaching the Celebration at Big Sur. "Many of the same musicians, but look at this setting." She pointed at the Pacific Ocean and gave David an enthusiastic hug. This two-day music festival took place one month after Woodstock.

David had just ended lifeguarding. In four years, David had rescued 142 people and delivered over one thousand first aids. In two weeks, David would start his new career, as a system engineer for Digital Equipment. Between jobs, this weekend with Linda was a perfect time to celebrate. Also, Linda was ready to party before starting the full course load of her master's program in early childhood development, as she continued to work with children at Montessori.

They walked past all the cars crawling on the highway including a '56 Chevy with three surfboards stacked on the roof, a VW bus covered with painted flowers and windows fogged with the cannabis cloud of its inhabitants, and past a family in a Ford Fairlane with children in the back seat giving them the peace sign.

They walked past a Salinas Sheriff's patrol car as two officers took in the pageantry and ignored the omnipresent dope. David, fresh from a summer of lifeguard vehicle radio communication, recognized the emergency responder codes that interspersed with the walkie-talkie conversation: 10-9, repeat; 10-38, your destination; and 10-66, suspicious person.

"Those two are all the cops I see at this festival! What a

contrast to People's Park!" Linda said. They had walked two miles from their Big Sur campground.

Cars disappeared and reappeared in the morning fog that splashed over the massive Big Sur cliffs. The sun danced between the waves of fog. The fog thinned into a mist that yielded to the warming sun, as they entered Esalen, the festival's venue. Above the highway noise and crashing waves, they could hear "I Shall Be Released" sung in haunting a cappella by Joan Baez. The words echoed off a hillside covered with spruce, pine, and coastal redwood.

David and Linda found a perfect place to sit, with only the Esalen swimming pool separating them from the stage where favorite musicians would play, sing, and spontaneously collaborate. Behind the stage was the vast Pacific Ocean. Miles up and down the coast, they could witness massive green hills descending hundreds of feet to the ocean.

The Celebration at Big Sur was a joyful composite of folk revival and psychedelic rock, gentle forests and savage surf, Salinas farmers and San Francisco hippies.

David and Linda spent their Big Sur nights camping under stars and days nourished with song and sunlight. They joined in singing, "Get Together," as Joni Mitchell, David Crosby, Stephen Stills, Graham Nash and John Sebastian invited all to join. Later at the festival, David was lost hearing Joni Mitchell sing, "Woodstock."

Your Garden of Eden ended when you lost your mother. It's not that you've never known love. You lost feeling in love when she died. You buried your heart in military school. It's time to love again.

David looked over at Linda. She was smiling, seemingly swept away. David put his arm around her, drew Linda close, and kissed her cheek. She slowly turned, looked into David's eyes, and then into his soul.

"I am so glad to be sharing my life with you," David said. "You're a deeply caring person and a beautiful woman." His next words fought some inner struggle to be given a voice until he whispered, "I love you."

"I am so glad, because I love you."

David prepared for his Digital job by driving to the L.A. garment district. With a loan from Carlo, David bought two suits, one blue and one gray, to add to the old suit he had worn for job interviews. His days of working barefoot over; now would begin long days of working in dark suits, white shirts, uncomfortable ties, and polished dress shoes, attire anathema to hippies and college students. He felt like an outlier, but the excitement about his job outweighed his feelings of selling out.

David was on a plane for a week of training at Digital headquarters in Massachusetts. He arrived early enough to hike on the Appalachian Trail, seeing trees of orange, red, and gold. He did well in his studies and presentations. He made a point of going out for drinks with three guys from Toronto. Should he get his U. S. draft notice, he would try to transfer to Digital Canada. Since degrees in computer science were fairly rare in 1969, he was optimistic that he could negotiate the transfer, if needed.

While in training, most evenings were spent with his Digital classmates watching the World Series. The favored Baltimore Orioles were playing the New York Mets, a team that was next to last in the previous session. In Game 5, the Mets came from behind to win the World Series and be heralded as the "Miracle Mets."

Back home, each evening he checked the mailbox for a letter from the Army stating that he was drafted. So far, it had not come. Although Nixon had campaigned with the promise of peace, there was none; over 500,000 U. S. soldiers were fighting, bombings were escalating, and it was no longer secret that the war had expanded to Cambodia and Laos. On TV each night, the world could see more jungles napalmed, more bombings reported, and more dead. The rich continued finding ways to avoid going to Vietnam; the poor found no escape.

There were rumors and speculation. They would end the war by dropping a nuclear bomb on Hanoi - Hiroshima deja vu. There was that scary speculation that a nuclear war was too critical to depend solely on the latest politician elected president.

David called his father, proud of his new job with Digital Equipment. The talk was pleasant when they talked of past times together hiking, fishing, and going to baseball games. Inevitably, they talked about the war. David asked for an opinion on when it would end. David mentioned that he had recently seen the movie *Dr. Strangelove* again. It is only a movie his father stated. David asserted that if only the president could authorize nuclear attack, then one missile from a sub could knock out Washington DC, ending the US ability to launch. Surely several generals and admirals must have the ability to launch. The phone went dead. Subsequent calls to his father went unanswered.

With the demands of work and study, David and Linda saw less of each other. Each time together, they played *Abbey Road,* the new album released even though the Beatles had officially disbanded. They talked of work, new friends, and new ideas. They said nothing about their future together.

Linda continued living in Laguna with Rachel who was busy with her research about the impact on marine life of the 800-

mile oil spill and calls to Senator Nelson's office about Earth Day. With Carlo, Rachel took one day at a time: days of delight, dancing, and passion. Humpback whale recordings gave way to bossa nova, blues, and rock.

David continued to live with Carlo in San Clemente. David worked and studied. Carlo was full of entrepreneurial energy as he worked construction with his dad, bought a triplex in a foreclosure sale to begin rental-property aspirations, and used his part-time drug dealing to finance property repairs.

"You can't believe what happened when I was observing a middle-school-special-ed teacher," Linda said.

"I want to hear this," David said.

"I was helping Joshua with arithmetic by using blocks. In walks Vice Principal Prufrock, a very proper man with short hair, dark suit, and a conservative tie. He lets everyone know that Jesus is his personal savior. Prufrock tells Mary, the special-ed teacher, that her kids are writing profanity on the bathroom walls. She politely asks why he thinks it was her kids. He says that they cause trouble, and someone wrote the 'f' word. He has zero proof that it was our kids. I saw Mary getting angry as she listened to him. Mary finally said that she would demonstrate why it couldn't be one of her kids. She said, 'Joshua, go to the blackboard and write 'fuck.'"

"She said 'fuck?' In front of all the kids and the Vice Principal, she asked a kid to write 'fuck?'"

"Mary was indignant and knew that her special-ed kids could not spell," Linda said. "So Joshua, wandered up to the blackboard, scratched his head and mumbled 'fuck.' Prufrock turned bright red. Joshua with primitive writing starts to put the chalk on the board. Prufrock stared at the writing to compare it with the bathroom wall. Joshua finally writes 'PHX,' then sits down."

"The kid spelled 'fuck,' 'PHX?'"

"These poor children have learning handicaps. Mary turned to Prufrock with this I-told-you-so look. He glared. So Mary asks another student, Bob, to go to the blackboard and write 'fuck.' It takes him longer, his writing is more obscure, but he finally writes 'GUD' then sits down." Linda was laughing. "Then Mary asked little Harold to write 'fuck.' He finally wrote 'FKT.' At this point, Prufrock stared through Mary, and still speechless, he turned and walked out."

"So this is your chosen career?"

"For sure, even if the administration does not know what the fuck they're talking about."

25

Vietnam

After four days of marching in the rain, Brad Friedman's platoon was moving in the sun, looking for the enemy, and sometimes engaging in firefights. The platoon was getting smaller as soldiers, mostly boys, were killed or wounded and evacuated.

Brad often thought of Linda. He recalled her warning that he would end-up in the jungle. At times, he thought of staying alive and keeping his buddies alive. Mostly, he didn't think of anything. He just kept moving, or as the soldiers said, humping.

They had humped in the rain past vistas of haunting beauty - rice paddies, jungle canopy, and thick forests. Today, they were moving into the mountains, at times on an open ridge and others in thick foliage that would make them hard to see. This day was killer hot. Brad took an extra salt tablet and downed another quart of water.

Bunkers, hooches, and fresh graves suggested that the Viet Cong were near. Brad's platoon moved through the jungle in near silence.

Suddenly, enemy machine gun fire cut along the ground. Williams, Perez and Graz were all screaming and covered with blood. Brad got to Graz first, dragged him off the road and into a ditch, hoping it would act like a bunker protecting from enemy fire. The platoon intensely engaged the enemy as M16s countered AK-47s, and grenades countered claymore blasts.

Brad tore clothing to make a tourniquet that he wrapped above the knee of Graz's right leg. Brad listened to the rhythm of gunfire and blasts, knowing Williams would be killed if left in the open. During a lull he ran to Williams and started pulling him to the ditch. The firefight renewed and Brad's leg was hit. He used all his strength and his one good leg to get Williams to the ditch before a sharpshooter shot Brad near his heart. Williams thanked Brad and apologized for calling him a draft dodger. Brad opened his mouth to reply, but there were no words, only blood. Brad closed his eyes and the explosions vanished and the machine guns silenced.

He remembered embracing Linda. He remembered speaking of peace to the thousands at People's Park and speaking of love to hundreds at his Bar Mitzvah. He remembered being eight and laughing as he played catch with his dad. He remembered his mom's proud embrace after kindergarten. Brad remembered.

26

Thanksgiving

Two months after the Celebration at Big Sur, when David opened his closet, he saw Linda's clothes - dresses, bell-bottoms, and blouses. He had freed a drawer in his dresser for her and part of a shelf in the bathroom. They had exchanged keys to each other's homes.

He started the year a lonely virgin and now he was enjoying sex day and night with someone he loved and admired. He stared at the tiny closet in his small room.

Why do I sometimes feel lost? Why do I want evenings void of conversation? Being with someone feels surreal. She's great. It's me. After that Bergman movie, why did I tell her I needed to be alone and then leave? Maybe it's the sixty-hour workweeks plus nights studying computer manuals. I'm making more, spending more, and still broke. I'm going to be in therapy forever.

David went into a kitchen that was now clean and organized thanks to Linda. He quietly grabbed fruit and nuts to snack on outside. He was quiet because Linda was immersed in a textbook. Ten minutes later, she closed her book and turned on the TV with excitement.

The half-hour preview opened with an animation of failed rocket launches. "It looks a little like Yellow Submarine," Linda said.

"Are they satirizing Vietnam?" David asked.

"They're just having fun."

Two puppets, Bert and Ernie, previewed Sesame Street, a

new TV program for young children. Instead of commercials, the letters X sponsored the preview, then M, then E. "I like the mellow narrative about the letter E with a sitar in the background," David said.

"This will be wonderful for my preschoolers," Linda said. "Young kids spend far more hours watching TV than being in classrooms."

Both were fascinated by the 30 minutes of puppets, animation, and people as they modeled teaching numbers, schemed to eat cookies, and were introduced to Big Bird and Kermit the Frog.

"I can't wait for my Montessori kids to see this!" Linda said. "Kids are wonderful. I can't wait to have a few of my own."

David watched Linda in silence as color disappeared from his face.

After the Sesame Street preview, hamburgers grilled by David, and an hour of study for both, they reconnected on the sofa.

"I talked with my mom. She's less depressed than when we first lost John. She just put away five boxes of Halloween decorations and is ready with three boxes of Thanksgiving decorations."

"Your mom is really into the holidays. You brighten every time you talk about them."

"I always loved Thanksgiving through Christmas. I was right there with my mom, into decorating, cooking, parties, dressing up, and seeing cousins."

"Little Miss Sunshine," David said.

"That's me. Little Miss Sunshine most wanted by the FBI."

They laughed. She continued, "I told my folks that you're wonderful and that we're in love."

David sat stiffly and said, "Yes, we are."

"My folks have invited you to Thanksgiving. I haven't seen them since we lost John. I really need to be with them and I'd love for you to meet them. I know money would be a challenge, but you're invited to fly back to Cleveland with me."

"It would be tough. I'm still broke, and the pressure's on at work."

"I understand," she said. Linda moved close to David, touched his hand and said, "Holidays haven't been easy for you, have they?"

"No. I always missed my mom and was bummed that my dad usually wouldn't see me. He used the navy as an excuse to not be a father."

"I like knowing more about you. Tell me a holiday story."

David thought that she sounded like Dr. Grace. He took a deep breath, thought of a story that would reveal more of him, and said, "When I was fourteen, the Army and Navy Academy was almost deserted with everyone having left for Christmas with their families. I was staying at Army Navy because Dad was on a ship somewhere in the Atlantic Ocean. Chuck, a bully who was a lot bigger than me, said, "What's a matter Davey, you staying here cause your folks don't want you around?' In a rage, I moved at him, then he lunged at me, fists doubled, I stepped sideways, spun, and delivered a karate kick into his knee. As he started falling, he no longer towered over me and I karate chopped his neck. He staggered and I started driving my fists into his face when we were both seized and had to face the academy president, a hard-nosed retired Colonel. I was suspended from school for breaking Chuck's nose and he was suspended for repeatedly starting fights."

As David described his own violence, Linda looked shocked, leaned away from him, and held herself.

"I know that I'm freaking you with this story," David said. "I've been meaning to admit to you that I got in some fights when I was a kid. Mostly had to. If I hadn't taken Chuck, he would have taken me. The irony of getting suspended is that I spent Christmas with my grandparents in North Carolina. They rented a cabin in the mountains. I tobogganed in the snow. I got into celebrating Christmas with them: hearing stories about when I was little, about my mom, watching old movies, singing carols and eating turkey. On Christmas Day, I built my first snowman."

Black smoke covered the orange groves. Soot rained on helpless cars forced to suddenly turn on headlamps. The smoke's stink permeated David's car before he could shut off the vent. To protect the oranges from a killing frost, growers had fired smudge pots in the orchards.

David exited the freeway and followed the road through the black smoke until orange groves gave way to housing developments. David crossed the busy intersection and drove into the shopping mall. The parking lot was crowded, as people descended from every inch of suburbia for holiday shopping.

David maneuvered around the cars that idled near the mall entrance as they waited for a free parking spot. David drove on to a distant corner of the parking lot and grabbed a free space. He walked briskly to the movie theater entrance where Linda was waiting for him. He was late, so they missed the opening cartoon.

They watched *Yours, Mine and Ours*, a movie where Lucille Ball and Henry Fonda merge their collective 18 children. Linda laughed through the movie; David was sullen.

After the movie, in a restaurant bar, Linda again talked of Thanksgiving through Christmas as a magical time of year, and a time for reaching out with cards and calls and caroling. It was a time of family, feasts and gift giving. For David it felt surreal. At some visceral level, Christmas was a reminder of his not being part of a family. It was a reminder of his staying behind at military school and of anticipating Christmas gifts that his father failed to remember to send.

With Linda's prodding, David described the challenges of work and feeling insecure in his new job.

Linda delighted in talking about the antics of the kids at Montessori. With pride she described the progress of a few boys and girls. She looked across the room. "Look at that cute little girl wearing a ballet outfit with a tutu and a tiara."

David looked at the children and wondered if he could ever afford to have a family. *A lifetime commitment. Would I be a good father? With my background, how could I? Linda keeps talking about kids and friends who move in together. Two kids, four, or six? Two cars, home in suburbia, yard work on Saturday, church on Sunday. You'd always have to do what your manager's demanded. No matter how lame. Locked in. Trapped.*

The restaurant music filled the void created by David's silence. Linda continued, "I wanted to ask you again about flying home with me for Thanksgiving. The whole family is wondering if my cousin George will propose to Carol." David listened as his restless feet squirmed, unable to find solid ground.

"I'm scheduled to fly home the day before Thanksgiving and return Sunday." Linda paused and looked at David for any reaction, then continued, "It would be wonderful if you could join me. You'd get along great with everyone. What's your thinking about joining me?"

"Linda, I'm broke. I doubt that I could get that time off

work."

"I know, David. I already told them about your new job and doubted you could get time off. It's too bad. You'd love my folks and they would love you."

David stared at his feet in silence. Irritation became a mix of anger, sadness, and defeat as he listened to the holiday music. *Why such sadness? Look at how happy she is. Linda deserves a happy person. This is too heavy. I'm too young. We're too young. Linda wants a serious relationship. Does she want me to propose at Thanksgiving? She's ready for the whole Yours, Mine and Ours.*

Linda said, "Thanks for going to this movie with me. I've always loved Lucille Ball. It was cute, great kids, and filmed in San Francisco."

"Sorry, I didn't like it," David said. "It came off like a Department of Defense propaganda film. I'll bet Fonda's daughter didn't like it."

"Jane Fonda hated it. Their father-daughter relationship must be fireworks."

"I don't think Rachel would like it either," David said. "One of her favorite books is the Population Bomb. This naval officer leaves 18 kids and a pregnant wife to take off for six months at sea. I think that he was a poor excuse for a father."

"I guess it touched a nerve."

"Didn't abandoning his wife and eighteen kids outrage you?"

"What's wrong with you?"

"I guess I've got some open wounds."

"We all have wounds. That shouldn't stop us for living a full life."

David looked at Linda through his reddened eyes and held

her hand. "Linda, you are a wonderful person. You deserve someone better than me who can have a serious relationship."

As if awakening from a dream, she looked into David's frightened eyes. She heard the quivering uncertainty in his voice.

"Linda, I think that we should take a break from seeing each other. You deserve quality time with your friends and family. I've got to get my life together. Financially. Emotionally. Hopefully I won't get drafted but I could. I...this isn't the best time for us. Let's say goodbye for now."

Linda started crying. She hugged herself as she started to quiver. "Please, David, don't throw away all that we have. I love you." She sobbed and then suddenly stopped. Her jaw tightened. She stared at David with anger. "When I saw you make that cliff rescue, you were incredibly brave. But when it comes to relationships, you're just a coward."

"Linda, I am so sorry. You're more than I deserve." David looked at Linda who could no longer look back. David left money for the drinks and slowly walked away to the far corner of the mall parking lot, fading into the blackness.

27

Pandora and the Pusher

Pandora opened her apartment door to Carlo, revealing her long body, barely covered by a bikini and translucent blouse. Santana was blaring.

"I'm ready," she said as she opened her mouth.

Carlo placed the psilocybin on her tongue. He placed a second tablet of the powerful psychedelic on his tongue. They both swallowed.

Since David broke-up with Linda, Rachel had been cool and distant with Carlo. When they started dating, he and Rachel had talked about being open to seeing others, and the subject had not come up again. So, here was Carlo with voluptuous Pandora.

Two hours later, Carlo and Pandora were naked and hallucinating on a beach in South Laguna. It was a good trip for Carlo, but Pandora freaked, terrified of trees that looked like attacking snakes. Pandora kept screaming that they were trying to kill her. The police came and locked Carlo in jail.

On the third ring, David lifted the phone. "David this is Carlo. I don't have much time to talk. I desperately need your help. I'm in the Orange County Jail, 550 North Flower Street, Santa Ana."

"Hang on. Let me write this down." David wrote the address, then said, "Got it. Carlo, what's going on?"

"It's a freak here. I'm getting leered at. These guys are hard-core. I've got to get out of here. I'm being charged with possession of a Schedule I drug and this girl is making all kinds of accusations. I've got to raise five thousand dollars for bail. My dad won't help. He won't talk to me."

"Five thousand is a fortune!"

"I can't say much on the phone. There's a big coffee can in the garage. It's got enough in there to make a big dent in the five grand. Look for money in my room. Can you help me?"

David took a deep breath and gave his friend the answer, "Yeah, Carlo, I'll raise the bail. I've got no idea how, but I'll get you out of there."

"Thanks, man! I can't tell you what it means. The food is poison here. I've got to squat in front of these killers to take a shit. I've got to get out of here."

"I hear you. I'll get you out. What are you doing keeping money in a coffee can?"

"I can't say any more. The guard is ending the call." The line went dead.

David walked out to the garage and brought in the five-pound coffee can. He opened it. *Holy shit!* Inside were bottles of pills. He recognized the LSD Orange Sunshine. He'd never seen most of the other drugs. A large bag contained what looked like a kilo of grass. Another bag contained three bags of chocolate. Chocolate? David smelled. No, this was hashish. *Holy shit!* Carlo could go to prison for this. *I live here. I could go to prison!*

The clock was ticking. David had to help his best friend. Carlo had saved his life. He went through Carlo's room. He found $350. *A can full of drugs and three fifty won't get Carlo out of jail.*

"David? The operator said that this is urgent," David's father stated. The admiral was getting straight to the point.

"I'm glad the operator patched me in," David said. "What part of the world are you in right now?"

"Pacific Theater HQ in Hawaii. Before you say anything else, I need to remind you that we are on a military connection. We can't talk about any of your Strangelove nonsense."

"Yes, sir. I am hoping that you can help."

"What's the situation?"

"My best friend Carlo is in trouble. I am not asking you to give me any money. I am hoping that you can loan me five thousand. I know that's a lot. But you have my word, I will pay it back within months."

"That's a lot of money. You bailing him out of jail?" The admiral continued to be direct.

"Yes, sir."

"David, I've always counted on you to be truthful. Drugs involved?"

David was caught off-guard with his father's directness. "Yes, sir."

"Sorry. I can't give money to help someone with a drug problem."

"Carlo doesn't have a drug problem. I'm trying to get my friend out of jail. September, Carlo saved my life. I was rescuing two marines. One panicked and got me in a chokehold. The marine was a six-three football player. I'd be dead if Carlo didn't save me."

"Thank God he did," Dex Eliot's voice softened. "I admire you two being there for each other. Got to take care of our buddies."

"I'm glad you understand my position."

"Why isn't Carlo's dad bailing him out?"

"Long story."

"David, I'm proud of your new job with Digital Equipment," Dex said. "Don't jeopardize your career being roommates with a draft dodger with a drug problem. It was total bullshit that he got out of the army when his reserve unit was called up."

David was stunned. "Where did you hear that?"

"Son, I've got clearances above Top Secret. I was shown my latest security report and had to answer questions. The report showed how he got out and provided evidence that he might be selling drugs."

"Is the navy spying on us?" David shouted.

"Standard report. Didn't take them much to get the info."

"So even though he saved my life, you won't lend me the money."

"Can't. Carlo should cut a deal with the judge and agree to army service in return for having the case dropped. Happens all the time."

"So that's what this is about," David's voice was angry. "This stupid unwinnable war that Nixon said he would end."

"Nothing stupid about stopping all of Asia from falling to communism like a bunch of dominos. What's stupid is your friends smoking dope, singing songs, and going on peace marches while my brave seamen and airmen are dying for their country."

"It so happens that I spent the last year working long hours and studying long hours to graduate with honors in computer science. I worked those long hours because you cut me off and I had to pay my own way at the university. Now you won't even give me a loan to help a friend in real trouble."

"Sorry, Carlo's got options and he needs to pick one and solve the problem of his own making."

"OK, Dad, you've made yourself clear. I'll say goodbye."

"Sorry. Goodbye."

David returned to the five-pound coffee can full of drugs. He searched Carlo's room and found the box containing Carlo's coin collection, organized in books of coins, including Indian Head pennies and old silver dollars. The day after David dropped acid, he disavowed material possessions and sold his prized coin collection to Carlo, the culmination of years of collecting through his childhood, for only $200. It was probably worth a multiple of that.

David found Carlo's phone book, the proverbial little black book, mainly full of women's phone numbers. David found the number he needed and called Sam the Shaman. With drugs hidden in the coffee can inside a blanket, David drove on the Ortega Highway. David's hands were sweaty and kept slipping on the steering wheel. David arrived at Sam and Electra's place.

"Far fucking out, man," Sam said. "Carlo's busted. Hark, hark, the narc."

David could not help but smile when facing Sam's enthusiasm and perpetual smile. "Carlo sounds like he's freaking in the Orange County jail. We got to bail our friend out of there."

"Like what's the ransom, man?"

"Five thousand."

"Five thousand! Carlo's in deep shit. He must be up for a multiple felony rap."

"Sam, I'm broke. This looks like our best hope in raising the money. Help me sort this out." David put the five-pound can of Folgers Premium on the coffee table. He spread out the pharmacological contents.

"Yeah, I know this shit. Sold half of it to Carlo. We scored some great shit at good prices."

"Top quality. My acid trip with you opened my doors of perception."

"Like, I'm loaded with shit and about out of cash. I wish I could help Carlo, but I can't take on this stuff. Like, I've got to move my own inventory, man."

David stared into the distance, thinking, and exhaled a discouraged sigh. David replied, "I hear you. I know you'd help if you could. Help me figure what this stuff is worth. Do you know someone that would cut me a deal?"

"Yea, I could make some phone calls while you're here. We gotta free Carlo from the iron bars." Sam was sniffing the hash bars like an eager dog on a hunt.

"I remember this hash. Great stuff. Pure. Concentrated. Sold it to Carlo for one hundred fifty a bar. I could buy this back at cost."

"The three bars?" David wanted clarification.

"Right on, I'll take all three. Electra you got bread for Carlo's collection plate?"

"I'll get it. What do you need?"

"Four fifty."

"For sure, we got to bail Toto from the pound."

Sam started working the phone. He called, he cajoled, and he negotiated. David's pulse started returning to normal. He wanted to get rid of these drugs and raise the money as fast as possible. He was angry with Carlo for putting him in this position.

Within an hour Sam had it all arranged. He and Electra divided the loot into three brown paper lunch bags, matching the three agreed-upon deals. Sam and Electra moved in unspoken unison, having done this a hundred times. It was like they were working behind an ice cream counter. In each bag, Electra added one of her trademark chocolate chip hash cookies wrapped in a pink ribbon.

Sam told David how to get it done, "Like here's the deal, David. You wear this L.A. Dodgers cap so they will know to connect with you. Faust will meet you at the counter at Denny's at nine, then you connect with Rico at the Biker's Bar at eleven, then Jamsheed at the Coach House at one."

"Long night."

"I got stuff that'll keep you wired all night."

David replied, "That's OK, Sam. This drug dealing has already got me wired."

"Just ride the wave, man. Ride the wave."

"So, what do these guys look like?"

"You know, man, you're typical stoners," Sam answered. "First guy calls himself Faust. Don't ask him about his name or anything. He's six two. Heavy set. Heavy brow. Don't fuck with him. Just take him to your bus. He checks out the goods, you count the cash. He's in for six hundred."

"OK."

"Rico at Biker's Bar is a five-eight dark-skinned Mexican. He'll be on coke, acting paranoid. He's the big score at a thirteen hundred fifty."

"Got it," David noted.

"Jamsheed's Persian. He's cool. He's in for nine hundred fifty."

"This gets me most of the way to bailing Carlo. I think I can scramble up the rest. Thanks, Man!" David nodded and wrote names and amounts. He verified each bag with Electra and wrote the recipient's first name.

"Carlo in jail. Fucking far out. High-ho Silver. The Lone Ranger to the rescue!" shouted Sam.

David carefully put the three brown bags in the coffee can. He drove off to make his connections and collect the cash. When he got to Denny's, he sat at the counter and ordered a hamburger with fries.

A hand gripped his shoulder. It was Lieutenant Gonzalez with the San Clemente Police Department.

"David, how are you doing?"

"Lieutenant Rich Gonzalez, good seeing you." David tried not to act nervous as he shook Gonzalez's hand.

"David, your hand's cold and sweaty. You OK?"

David was worried. He knew Gonzalez from guarding and surfing, but that wouldn't help in a drug bust. Be cool was David's silent mantra. "Think I'm fighting a bit of a cold. Sorry, I shouldn't have shook hands. Been hitting the surf?"

"Absolutely, great sets at Cotton's. Glassed-off the other night. Great shape."

"Life is good. Hey, thanks for all the times you covered for us."

"That's what we're here for. To serve and protect. Well, gotta run. Take care." With that Lieutenant Rich Gonzalez was gone without again shaking hands."

David's heart was pounding. He could feel his own cold

sweat. His food arrived and he finished three bites of his burger when a guy who fit Faust's description sat down. David looked at him and asked, "You Faust?"

"What's your name?"

"David."

"Yeah, I'm Faust. Let's head out to your car." Faust said evenly. They started out.

"Where you going?" The waitress asked.

David replied nervously, "I'll be back." He found a ten in his pocket. "You can close the bill and bring change."

She replied, "That's OK. You can pay at the cashier later."

"For sure." David and Faust walked out. David led him to the bus; they sat in the front seat. David gave him the bag marked Faust. The other drugs in the coffee can were hidden in the back under blankets.

Faust acted shocked, "What the fuck is this? I thought you were going to show me surfboards!"

David was incredulous. "I was there when you talked with Sam."

"Listen, cop, I don't know what the fuck you're talking about. What's in this bag you just handed me?" Faust handed David the bag, unopened.

David was trying to understand why the deal had unraveled. "I'm no cop."

"You got a cop haircut. I saw you talking with a cop."

"Yeah, he said hi. Know him from surfing. He'd bust me in a heartbeat if he knew what I was doing. I dropped this acid with Sam and Electra. This is pure Orange Sunshine. It's incredible. We're giving you a deal 'cause I'm raising money to bail my friend."

Faust glared at David. "Are you a member of any law enforcement?"

David answered "No."

"I asked you directly. If you are this is entrapment."

"What a mix-up," David said. "I'm friend of Sam. This is pure acid for six hundred. You want it or not?" David offered the bag to Faust.

Faust's paranoid eyes lasered into David. Time stopped. Faust put a gun to David's temple. "I hate narcs. I'd rather die than go back to prison. Better yet, I'd rather you die."

Each step up the cemetery hill was slow and heavy for Linda as she walked like a mountain climber, empty of oxygen, forcing herself toward an unattainable summit. The ground was barren and desolate. The sky was grey with choking smog. With a final step, she reached his gravesite.

Linda kneeled and placed the flowers on Brad's tombstone. "I miss you so much, Brad. I still love you." She choked on her tears.

It was two minutes before she could continue. "I saw your mom last night. I went to temple with Ruth. The rabbi said wonderful things about you. Your cantor sang with such beauty. I didn't know you had a woman cantor. I guess your temple is pretty liberal. Your mom's going to make it. She's been so sad losing you. She told me it was your dad that talked you out of prison and into the army deal. After my night in jail, I should have known that you're too beautiful a person for prison."

It was minutes before Linda could say more to Brad. "I've written letters and got thirty-eight Girl Scout Troops to sell cookies at anti-war rallies and donate part of their sales to ending the war. Can you believe it?" Linda tried to laugh. "If I ever have sons, the first will be named John, for my brother. The second will be named Brad. I'll miss you forever." Linda sat in the stillness. "I wrote an op-ed that got published in the Berkeley Barb." Linda pulled out her clipping from the paper and read:

> For our generation, 1967 was the Garden of Eden. Forbidden fruit was tasted and then consumed in abundance. In 1967, sons buried their fathers. In 1968, fathers buried their sons: Martin Luther King Jr., young soldiers, and protesters in the streets. In 1969, we are lost and wandering pilgrims in search of a spiritual path back to the Garden. Those who went to Woodstock saw sunlight stream from Heaven onto the Sacred Ground. Those who went to Vietnam saw the young dead swallowed into the Fires of Hell.

David awoke shivering. *I'm alive!* David felt his swollen temple. There was blood on his hand. He twisted the rear view mirror to look at his cut and bruised face. *I'll live.* Faust was gone with his bag of drugs and without leaving the $600. Everybody was gone. It was almost 11 p.m. and the parking lot was deserted.

David removed the layers hiding the coffee can. The rest of the drugs were there. David wanted to go home, sleep, and have nothing to do with criminals with guns, but Carlo was in jail. Carlo had saved his life. Weary and wary, David drove to the next deal.

By the time David dragged home at 2 a.m., he had barely talked his way out of two fights with guys in the bikers' bar that saw his baseball cap and declared that they hated the LA Dodgers. He had accumulated threats of a broken leg and broken neck if anything was missing. He was exhausted, but he had $2,300 for the drug sales, plus $450 from Sam, plus Carlo's money.

David was relieved to have unloaded all of Carlo's drugs. *It better be all. They could search the house.* He had even dumped their half-ounce of pot in with the kilo. It was all gone. The house was clean, he hoped. After this was over, he would tell Carlo that it was either no more drugs, or no more David as a roommate.

In the morning, with little sleep, he went to a coin shop in Santa Ana. By 11:45 a.m., David had sold the treasured coin collection for $750. David hoped that they wouldn't notice him missing at Digital, his employer. He was still shy of the $5,000 by $1,150. David had $177 to his name.

David went to a pay phone and called Sam the Shaman. David told of Faust pulling a gun on him and stealing the drugs without paying. David reminded Sam of Big Sur, their tripping, and how Carlo needed his help. At first Sam said that he could not help, but finally agreed to lend the $1,000 necessary to free Carlo. David made the long drive to Sam's and returned with a roll of twenty $50 bills.

David called the Orange County jail and learned that he would need a cashier's check. At five minutes before his bank closed, David had a cashier's check for $5,000.

At 7:30 p.m., Carlo walked out unshaven, haggard and depressed, but he walked out. He and David hugged.

Having little money, they dined at Taco Bell. Carlo claimed to be innocent of anything more than dropping psilocybin and getting naked on an almost deserted beach. David talked about selling the coin collection and drugs to raise the bail; how Faust put a gun to his head, knocked him out, and then stole drugs; and how Carlo owed Sam the Shaman $1,000. David drove Carlo through Laguna streets and alleyways until they found Carlo's wagon. Another long night came to an end.

Los Angeles Airport (LAX) was unusually crowded when David arrived on the Sunday after Thanksgiving. He drove endless aisles in the massive lot until he found a parking space. It all took time, but he had left an hour early.

Saturday, he had driven to Laguna and had talked with Rachel, angry with him for dumping Linda. David explained some of his history and asked for forgiveness. Rachel listened, sympathized, relented and agreed that David could surprise Linda at LAX and go in Rachel's place to give Linda the ride home.

Carrying a dozen roses, David checked the airport sign and then walked to Linda's arrival gate. He gave the gate supervisor Linda's flight to verify her arrival. After typing into the computer the first leg of Cleveland to Minneapolis, the supervisor looked shocked and said, "Just a moment, sir."

A man in a coat and tie escorted David into a private room and said, "I'm very sorry to tell you that Linda Hope's connecting flight from Cleveland to Minneapolis did not arrive."

"You're kidding," David said with disappointment. "Do you know when she will arrive?"

"I'm so sorry, but that commuter flight crashed. No one survived including the twenty-two passengers."

The roses fell onto the hard floor. David cried.

"I'm so sorry. Shall I arrange for someone to pick you up or drive you home?" David declined by shaking his head. "You can stay in this room as long as you would like. Shall I call the airport chaplain?" David again declined with a shake of his head.

Eventually David stumbled out of the room. He placed the dozen roses on a chair, hoping someone would get use from them. In a daze, he looked up at the sign showing all flights. He looked at the several Canadian Air departures to Toronto and Vancouver. *I should buy a one-way ticket and leave. I don't want to live here anymore. Be decisive. Leave.*

David walked slowly to the ticketing area at the entrance to the LAX. He passed a U. S. Navy recruiting booth. He stopped to look at the brochures. *Maybe I should just get this over with.* A friendly guy in naval dress uniform started a conversation. When he learned that David had a degree in computer science, he talked glowingly about naval computer training and opportunities. *I bet my dad could get me interesting computer science work at the Pentagon. I don't want to live here anymore. There's no way out. Sooner or later, you'll get a draft notice. I could at least complete the officer application. It's either Canada or computers at the Pentagon. There's no way out.*

"David Eliot," was announced through the airport paging system. He found the phone to answer the page and was connected to Rachel.

"David," Rachel said loudly. "I missed you at home. You must have left early. I've been paging you every half hour. I have Linda's new flight numbers."

"Then she may be alive."

"What are you talking about?" Rachel asked.

"Her connecting flight to Minneapolis crashed."

"Por dios. Then she is very lucky. She called me from Charlotte."

"Charlotte?"

"She arrived at the Cleveland airport early and they gave her some incentive to take an earlier flight through Charlotte. She's on flight seven eighty. It should be there by now."

David was ready to race to the gate, but then he thought to ask, "Does she know that I'll be picking her up?"

"I told her and she's furious with me. You'd better run to her gate."

On the massive electronic sign, David located flight 780, and then ran to the gate. As he neared, he saw Linda approaching him. She glared.

He stopped in front of her and started sobbing, "I thought you were dead. I thought I'd lost you forever."

"What on earth are you talking about?" Linda was angry and incredulous.

"I got here over an hour early. They took me into a room, told me that your connecting flight to Minneapolis had crashed with no survivors, and offered to get me a chaplain. I thought that you were gone."

Linda melted at seeing David distraught and crying. She dropped her bag. They embraced. Minutes passed as throngs of busy people passed around them. They found empty seats so that they could talk.

"Terrifying. I'm so lucky I got to Cleveland airport early and changed flights. They had to talk me into the change. I'm lucky to be alive," Linda looked at David's poignant tears and her distrust, anger, and hurt were gone.

"I brought you roses, but then gave them away after they told me. Thank God, Rachel had me paged. I don't know what I'd have done."

Linda held his hand. They embraced and both cried.

David looked at her and said, "I am so sorry. You deserve much better than the way I treated you. Thanksgiving and

Christmas have always been so lonely for me. I panicked. I've been trying hard in therapy to trust love. It's so hard for me. My instinct has been to retreat inside myself. I was wrong. I'm here for you. Please take me back."

Linda held David tightly as she heard each welcomed word. "I understand, David. You really hurt me and I'm mad at you, but I understand. I know about your struggles. I've had my own conflicts losing John and Brad. I guess I did the same to you when I split for Woodstock."

David and Linda walked arm in arm on the beach. Their bare feet in the sand did not experience cold; the fire between them was sufficient warmth. David delighted in Linda's stories of Thanksgiving with family and friends. David promised Linda that he was making progress in therapy. He was working on accepting his childhood and forgiving his dad. He told her that he would be with his dad on Christmas Eve to try to reconcile.

Waves splashed a million water drops skyward, refracting sunlight into a dance of rainbows. David suddenly embraced Linda, spinning her around at water's edge, gently lowering her, and saying, "You're wonderful, I love you and I won't leave you. Will you take me back?"

28

New Beginnings

"Bald Eagles mate for life," Rachel explained. "In their courtship they soar, lock talons, fall toward earth in a death spiral, and then free their talons at the last minute, usually avoiding death."

"How romantic," Linda said. "Remember, you and I attended that lecture at Berkeley."

"Of course. Our animal behavior class."

"Sorry to interrupt. No doubt you wanted to tell me one of Rachel's parables."

"Neither you nor David are ready to commit for life. You go to a movie about 18 children, talk about marriage, and then wonder why David panicked."

"Fine. Take his side. He hurt me."

"I hear you. Is what he did so different than you splitting for Woodstock?"

"I was upfront with him that I was grieving and not ready for a heavy commitment. Besides, that was back in August."

"So you see the situations as very different?"

"Maybe." Linda sounded doubtful. "You've got a point." Linda folded her arms and stuck her tongue out at Rachel.

"He ran away, then right back to you. He loves you. Why not date him without worrying about where the relationship is going. He's just not ready to lock talons for the death spiral."

The draft lottery on December 1, 1969, would determine David's future. He sat in front of the TV with Linda waiting for the lottery broadcast to begin.

David guessed that birthdates not selected in the first 200 would be safe if Nixon kept his word about troop reductions. If David's birthdate was one of the first selected, he argued that his 45-step plan and legal resistance could buy him months, maybe years, of freedom. Linda, after losing John and Brad, felt that his rights would be ignored. If he fled to Canada, he would need to renounce his United States citizenship and never return.

David struggled with questions and scenarios. *Will Linda and me stay together? I'm not ready for marriage. Would Linda move to Canada without a commitment? Is she ready? Am I ready? If I am refused entrance to Canada, will I die in the war?*

Linda reached for David's hand. It was cold and wet from perspiration.

David sat with Linda, watching his fate on the television as a senior Republican on the House Armed Service Committee reached into the large glass bowl. Capsules drawn at random were determining his fate. It was the nation's first draft lottery, determining the fate of men aged 19 to 25. The first number selected was day 258, for those born on September 14. *Only 365 capsules to go.*

Millions across America watched the televised first draft lottery that night. The congressman drew the next birthdates: April 24, December 30, February 14, October 18, September 6, October 26, September 7, November 22 and December 6.

The next day, newspapers told stories of the boys with lowest draft numbers. Most of the rich found ways out, most of the poor enlisted, a few left the country, and a few committed suicide.

After the congressman's first selections, young men and women were used to randomly select numbers, as the TV live broadcast slowly continued. Three of the young men made comments in protest. A fourth refused to remove a ball and walked out. During the entire broadcast, no one mentioned that the draft only applied to men and not to women.

When David's birthday finally was announced as 279, he was excited, relieved, and exhausted. David would be in the lottery for one year; if not called-up, free from worrying about being drafted after the year. He embraced Linda. Each showed tears. David was lucky. He was born on the Fourth of July.

Linda noted to herself that Brad's birthday was 331 on the list. He would be alive and free, had he not protested the war, been framed by the FBI, selected the army over prison, and been killed in Vietnam.

When the drawing ended, David opened champagne and they celebrated. They played the Beatles, singing and dancing. Holding each other close, they slowly started to realize that the draft was no longer a threat to their relationship. They controlled their future.

Carlo's lawyer got all charges dropped after Pandora explained that she had freaked out; Carlo had not mistreated her. The $5,000 bond was returned. Carlo repaid Sam and David, and permanently stopped selling drugs. Carlo worked overtime on one of his dad's construction crews. Carlo's triplex was cash-flow positive, fueling Carlo's ambitions to expand his ownership of rental property.

Linda read the magazine article about the Rolling Stones concert at Altamont. Over 300,000 attended the free concert that included Santana, Jefferson Airplane, and Crosby, Stills, Nash &

Young. The December 6 concert stood in sharp contrast to Woodstock. Altamont was marred with stolen cars, considerable violence, and four dead.

"Yes, we're totally committed to have at least one hundred Earth Day teach-ins in Southern California," Rachel said into the telephone. "I'm getting enthusiastic support from members of GOO, WWF, schools and universities." She listened and wrote. "I'll drive up to see Congressman McCloskey." She listened and then said, "Thank you. Goodbye."

Linda asked, "What's going on?"

"Earth Day! April 22, 1970, we'll have thousands of environmental teach-ins across the country, including over one hundred in the region that I'm coordinating. The date is when most of schools have spring break, so we can use the schools for these teach-ins. I was on the phone with Linda Billings, one of Senator Nelson's staff who is taking the lead on Earth Day. They're getting telegrams, letters, and calls for support across the nation."

"As an Earth Day leader, you're in the middle of something big."

"President Nixon will establish an Environmental Protection Agency on January One! Oil and chemical companies have been fighting this for the seven years since *Silent Spring* was published and now they've lost. Environmental action is getting strong support from Republicans and Democrats."

"Who is Congressman McCloskey?"

"He is the leader in Congress for environmental issues, just as Nelson leads in the Senate. Together, they co-chair an Environmental Steering Committee, so that legislation supporting clean air, clean water, and better health stay on a fast track. His district is in the Bay Area, but he can introduce me to congressmen in Southern California. If we get congressmen and mayors to speak at the teach-ins, then we can get TV coverage."

"Wow. You're connecting with heavy people."

"McCloskey must be smart; he went to Caltech and Stanford. He's anti-war even though he served in World War II and Korea and was awarded the Navy Cross and Silver Star. I'm totally excited about Earth Day!"

Linda stroked David's hair, now a bit longer than in his lifeguard days. He smiled through his week-old mustache.

"I'm proud of myself," Linda announced. "I'm done with my finals for the quarter, submitted my big paper, finished my shopping, organized sightseeing plans for my folks, and written my New Year's resolutions."

"I'm still working on last year's resolutions. My best hope is an incomplete," Carlo said.

"Is everyone ready with their New Year's resolutions?" Linda queried with a smile.

"Linda the teacher. Everyone get ready for their next homework assignment," David moaned.

"Not homework," Linda said. "Resolutions are about your dreams. Share them with friends and you're likely to reach them."

"Linda's right," Carlo said. "It's about dreams. OK, everyone. What are your dreams? Think big!"

"Dreams and resolutions," Linda continued. "Dreams tell us what, and resolutions tell us how."

"Beautiful," David said. "Linda, tell us your dreams and resolutions."

Linda squirmed as the others looked to her. She held out her glass. "More wine, please." David poured her more.

"I dream of every baby having a home. I dream that every child is loved. I dream that every person learns and grows to their greatest potential."

David said, "You're full of compassion." He kissed Linda. Rachel and Carlo applauded.

"*Amore,*" Carlo said.

"Linda, you expressed an admirable vision," Rachel said. "Now, what are your resolutions?"

"I resolve that by September 1970, I will have my teaching credential, my master's degree, and my own classroom."

"Perfect," Rachel said. "I'm confident you will achieve those." All raised their glasses in a toast.

Rachel broke the silence, "I'll be next. First, thank you so much for volunteering for Earth Day: Carlo, you're presenting passive solar and sustainable construction from the *Whole Earth Catalog*. David, you'll be talking about how computer models are used in environmental research. Linda, you're coordinating a hands-on children's area. Thank you, thank you, thank you."

"Totally."

"Groovy."

"For sure."

"OK, my vision." Rachel continued, "I dream of a world where people live in harmony with nature and with each other. I resolve that our first Earth Day will be so successful that one billion people will be aware that they can make a difference to this fragile and remarkable planet."

"Beautiful."

"Awesome."

"Wonderful."

"I dream that the people of this world will all be able to communicate with each other and learn from each other," David said. "At UCLA, a computer science professor that uses our computers showed me ARPANET, which connects computers at key research centers. He called it the Net and thinks it will eventually connect hundreds of major universities. I dream of writing software that would allow millions to share information on the Net."

"Follow your dreams!"

"It's a pretty off-the-wall idea," David continued, "My New Year's resolution is more down to earth; I resolve to no longer be broke." Everyone laughed.

"I also resolve to open my heart to Linda, this wonderful woman I love." Linda beamed, then melted in David's arms.

While Linda smiled admiringly at her fully decorated Christmas tree, David smiled at her.

"I couldn't wait until Christmas," Linda said. "This is for you."

He awkwardly accepted the wrapped gift. "Open it now?"

"Yes, of course."

David opened his gift. It was a teddy bear wearing a pinstripe business suit. "This is funny."

He carefully examined the bear. It had a pull string on the back. He pulled the string, and the bear announced, "You are the greatest."

David laughed. Linda applauded and announced, "It's an

executive teddy bear. Just like you." She hugged David as he held the bear. She said, "You're my executive teddy bear."

David pulled the string again, "You're one of a kind."

David sighed, "At least that statement is accurate." He pulled the string again. Teddy exclaimed, "I love you."

David held Linda close, kissed her cheek, and said, "Thank you. I love my gift. I love you."

"I love you." They hugged and kissed.

"I am so excited about Christmas," Linda said. "The tree, the lights, the wreath on the door. I'll put up a little more once Rachel flies home for Christmas."

"Rachel's flying all the way to Venezuela?"

Rachel shrugged. "Familia."

Silence.

Linda said as she looked around, surveying the living and dining area, the tree and Christmas lights. "I miss my nutcracker."

"Your what?"

"Nutcracker. Like the prince in the ballet *The Nutcracker*. As a girl, I had one just like in the ballet, until the dog destroyed it. I miss my prince." She held her hand to her mouth. "But I have you. You're my prince."

David made a mental note to get her a nutcracker. Rachel and Carlo went for a walk.

"I'm excited for you," Linda said to David. "You're seeing your dad on Christmas Eve, then spending Christmas in Laguna with me and my folks."

"I have been wondering if Christmas is the best day to meet your folks...."

"Not, again, David. Not more of your second thoughts and second guessing!"

"What do you mean?" David asked.

"We see a stupid movie and you bail on our relationship! I get such mixed messages from you. You bring flowers, you listen, and you tell me that you love me. Then you push me away."

David listened with his mouth hanging open. He leaned forward as if to start talking, then leaned back.

"My folks have already agreed that you and they won't be exchanging presents. You don't have to join us for opening presents, although I've always loved that part. But I want you to spend hours with us. A big Christmas dinner. Talking. Getting to know them. They're eager to meet you." Linda started crying.

David held her and whispered, "I'll be there. I'll be with all of you on Christmas."

For minutes he held Linda as she cried.

"I'm sorry. This is our first Christmas without John. Since his suicide, it's been rough."

"How could it not be," David said. "I'm sorry you and your folks are going through this."

"Thanks," she said softly. "Family is really important to me. It's important to everyone. David, you need to forgive your father. He's the only family you've got."

"Hard to call us a family," David sighed. "I was the one to reach out to him. I'm driving down Christmas Eve. We'll see how long it lasts before the inevitable blow-up."

"It's been bad for five years, hasn't it."

"Yeah, bad my whole life, but especially since I turned down the Naval Academy after he had pulled a bunch of strings."

"You did the right thing," Linda said. "You could've spent your life in the war machine, taking orders from The Man."

"I made the right choice."

"Although I hate what he is part of - a war that killed my brother - that's killed a million innocent people, he's your dad, your only family."

"A very distant father who refuses to tolerate an insubordinate son who speaks up and makes his own choices."

"He's got no control over you," Linda said. "He has zero control over you, legally or financially."

"Right. I don't need his OK for anything."

"So why did you call him about getting together Christmas Eve?" Linda asked.

"In my therapy, we talked about how I might be stuck unless I forgive him and forgive myself."

"I love that you're open to look inside. I hope you have a breakthrough with him, for your sake, and selfishly, for our relationship."

29

Prodigal Son

On Christmas Eve, David drove south from San Clemente, California, where he had lifeguarded four summers. He had saved lives, earned enough to stay in the university, and graduate. He drove to see his estranged father.

He drove past President Nixon's "Western White House," the sprawling hacienda on the ocean where the fate of our nation was debated, the fall of communism plotted, the bombing of Vietnam, Laos and Cambodia escalated.

As he merged onto the freeway, his 1960 VW bus slowly reached its top speed of 58 before it started shaking. He saw little joy in the faces of exhausted fellow travelers in cars that thrust, stopped, and then inched forward in angry traffic, some crawling toward remote shopping centers, and others in journey to family gatherings. He listened to The Beatles singing, "Eleanor Rigby."

David drove past the massive Camp Pendleton where the Marine Corp trained men, boys really, to kill or be killed in Vietnam, a war that killed over a million, mostly civilians burned, bombed, and napalmed.

Like most Americans, a few years earlier David had supported the war. Freedom meant stopping the falling dominos of communism. Then came the nightly live TV broadcasts, starting in 1968, of the blood-drenched dead in the Tet Offensive and the anguished mothers holding their dead infants as they ran from napalmed villages in flames. Most of the nation then turned against the war. David would not fight his father's war.

David hoped to reconcile with his father, Admiral Dex Eliot, war hero, former Pentagon strategist, executive officer in the Pacific Theater, and keeper of secrets. Admiral Eliot could lead men with distinction and launch weapons with lethal precision.

A pickup truck passed David displaying the bumper sticker "America / Love It or Leave It." A VW bug moved past him, adorned with painted flowers, peace symbols, and an ironic bumper sticker "Kill a Commie for Christ." This was a nation divided with an open wound that refused to heal. David's vehicle displayed a singular bumper sticker that said "Peace" framed with peace symbols.

He drove past the Carlsbad exit where he had spent much of his youth boarded at the military school.

David drove past the Point Loma exit, remembering the lonely road to the funeral of his close friend, John Eastman, age 22. He remembered the military funeral with marines in blue jackets, red trim, white caps, flashing sabers, and a gun salute that put every bird in frightened flight.

As David exited the freeway in San Diego, Mission Bay stretched out before him. Sailboats heeled over in the cold water, trying not to capsize.

Looking at Sea World, he remembered when his father had invited him to the grand opening in 1964, his last year in high school. David rejected the idea, having no interest in doing things with his dad. For most of his life, David had kept his father at a distance. He had kept people at a distance. *You've carried the sinking weight of your father all these years. Voices of what he wanted you to be howled down by the wind. Footsteps to follow washed away.*

David looked at a lonely fishing boat motoring out to sea. *Let it go. Let people in.* David thought of his long years of struggling to win his father's approval and trying to win his love. Whatever he did, it was never enough. Yet, when his father reached out, like inviting him to Sea World, he rejected the invitation.

He was trying. Maybe he was as clueless about being a father as you are about being a son. You need to forgive him. You need to forgive yourself.

While driving, David recalled March 1965, when he stood wet and shivering in the military school hallway, taking the phone call from his father.

"Sorry for the delay in getting back, Son," Admiral Dex Eliot said. "It's been non-stop meetings here at the Pentagon, including a meeting at the White House."

"Understood," David said. "You meet the president?"

"Affirmative. Johnson and the Joint Chiefs. I didn't talk much, but I answered all of McNamara's questions to his satisfaction, and his command of data is quite comprehensive."

"I'm in awe." David did not know what to say next. This was like playing chess. Best just to say it. "Dad, I've been accepted at U.C. Irvine. Exciting new university. Top flight. I appreciate everything you did to help me get accepted by the Naval Academy, but I've decided I want a career in business."

The phone was dead for long seconds as David shivered in his swimsuit, just returned from surfing in the cold Pacific. Dex finally spoke, "You could serve only six years in the navy after the Academy and then have a great career in business. Top education. Navy's the greatest institution in the world. Being a graduate from the Academy would open doors. You could stay in reserves and get a pension on top of your business career."

"Yes, sir. I hear what you're saying, but I've decided on UCI. Sorry, I know that everything would be paid for at the Academy."

"It's not about the money. It's about getting a great education, opening doors, starting your life with a leg up."

"Thanks for all you did," David said.

"I wish you'd decided this before I pulled all those strings with the Academy, with our congressman, and recommendations from other admirals! All those years at the Army and Navy Academy! The tuition. Damn!"

In March 1965, David refused his appointment to the Naval Academy. Looking back he could see that he chose to live his life not his father's dream. Now, in December 1969, he was refusing to fight his father's war.

David found the address and parked in front of his father's temporary quarters. David had initiated this Christmas together with a phone call to his father's office in Honolulu. A few days later, his father returned the call from San Diego, where he had flown to review programs at the U. S. Navy Fighter Weapons School in Miramar. The elite pilot training program was informally known as Top Gun.

David sat frozen for minutes, and then slowly walked to the door. He hoped that this visit would last longer than Christmas 1968, when an argument about the war escalated to insults about David's beard and peace sign. Their last Christmas together ended in minutes.

David rang the doorbell, and then rubbed his hands together, trying to erase their cold perspiration. David thought, *Dad, you and your dreams that I would be the four-star admiral for which you long aspired. Five years have passed. Time to let it go.*

David's father slowly opened the door and looked evenly at David. Both men stood military straight, six-feet in height, similar in looks.

Dex Eliot said, "The prodigal son returns."

David stood apprehensively in front of the entrance. He was wearing blue jeans, flannel shirt, leather jacket, and tennis shoes. He did not wear a suit and tie; he would not be paraded as in his youth wearing a dress military school uniform for another on-ship formal dinner. With hair barely long enough to touch his ears, and with a new moustache, David looked clean-cut enough to be a computer system engineer, his new job. His father had already planned a casual meeting. Dex wore a golf shirt, sweater, and khaki pants.

"Come in." Dex did not offer a handshake. David was relieved. His hands were cold and wet with perspiration.

As David walked in, his father said, "You've been on the road for a while, head's down the hall."

David replied, "I'm OK."

Dex seated himself in a stuffed chair. David sat nearby on the sofa.

"Your friend, Carlo, get out of jail?"

"He did. He's doing well working with this dad in construction and bought his first rental property."

"Already bought property. Guess he didn't need that five grand."

"I raised it, got him out of jail, he paid me back."

"Still roommates?"

"We are."

The two fell into a tense silence.

"I'm excited about Digital Equipment," David said. "I got some great training back in Massachusetts. I caught it at the height of fall colors. I hiked the Appalachian Trail. Beautiful."

"Do you remember when you and your grandparents came to visit me in Washington D.C.? I think you were eight. We drove through the Shenandoah Valley in the spring and hiked on the Appalachian Trail."

David looked stunned. "I'd forgotten." He sat trying to remember. "I think I vaguely remember."

The two sat in the flat light of the military apartment. A long silence was finally shattered with choppers flying overhead.

"I can fix you a Bloody Mary if it's not too early," Dex offered.

"No thanks, but help yourself." David sat in silence, searched for something to say, and then asked. "Any golf or fishing lately?"

"Both. Got an 83 at Torrey Pines last Saturday. I've been playing more. Short game is on the money. I'm on my eleventh putter. It seems to be the best."

David relaxed and smiled, "Eleven putters!"

Dex also relaxed and said, "Yes, Son. You can tell a serious golfer by the number of putters he owns. I love the game and golf's been good for the career. I probably would never have been promoted to Rear Admiral without hours on courses with the stars and bars."

"Talking with you on the phone, it sounds like you're really busy," David said politely. "Saigon one day, San Diego the next."

"Heavy travel. If Admiral McCain is too busy to go somewhere, I seem to be his point man. That trip to Saigon was a sad one, visiting Bill Cunningham in intensive care. He's been like a so..." Dex checked himself. "I've mentored Bill since he started his career as a naval pilot. No matter how dangerous the mission, it's 'aye aye, sir' and he is on his way."

David stared at his father and thought, *"Like a son. I'm your son."*

Not noticing any change in David's demeanor, Dex continued, "Bill may not live. His plane was shot while he was carrying a cluster of napalm bombs. When he crash-landed, the plane caught fire. His whole body is burned so badly I could barely look and I've seen it all." The words choked in Dex's throat and his eyes watered.

Trying to control his jealous anger, David said in a slow measured voice, "He's like a son to you. I haven't been here eight minutes and I'm reminded that your reports have been like sons to you while I was parked in that military academy without a mom or a dad!"

Dex was jolted back from being lost in sadness to the present. He stared at David before replying. "Yes, Bill is like a son to me and he's dying. You're here with me on Christmas Eve. You're my son. Can't you handle me giving a damn about anyone but you?"

"I'm sorry that Bill is fighting for his life," David said, trying to check his anger. "Of course you should care. It's tough to hear about you and others, when I've spent my life seeing little of you."

"You haven't made it easy," Dex said. "You didn't remember my taking you on the Appalachian trail. I left important negotiations and took a red-eye flight back from the Mediterranean for that hike. NATO negotiations are important to this nation that I serve, that I risk my life for!"

The air in the room felt like a charged sky before a violent lightning storm. The two men, of equal height and build, both with martial arts training, sat alert and stared at each other.

"Sorry," David said, trying to reveal no emotion.

"It's been this way for five years," Dex said. "You get angry, blow-up, and you're gone. What's the point?"

"It's been this way since I turned down the Naval Academy and your dreams of me being an Admiral. Well, I'm me and this is my life."

"You're one ungrateful and insubordinate sonofabitch!"

David stood, walked slowly and deliberately to the door and left.

He walked somber streets leading to nowhere before returning and getting into his VW, shutting the door and screaming. Then he sat in silence. Then the silence was assaulted with loud chopping of six large marine cargo helicopters flying overhead as they headed north.

David could not bring himself to turn the ignition key. He worried about his relationship with Linda. He had to get past this. He and his father had to get past this. This was their last shot. This was Christmas Eve.

David returned and knocked on the door. Dex opened it.

"I'm sorry," David said.

"Hasn't been easy for a long time," Dex said and stepped aside so that David could enter.

David sat in silence, until he finally said, "Thank you for taking the long-flight back for that hike on the Appalachian Trail. In some ways, we've both made a long journey to be here today. I want to try harder to make something work between us."

Surprised, Dex looked at his son. A few times he leaned forward as if to say something and then hesitated. Dex asked, "Sure I can't make you a Bloody Mary?"

"I'll take a Tequila Sunrise if you've got tequila and OJ,"

David said while thinking that this was the time they should smoke a peace pipe. He daydreamed of them smoking dope together. Stoned and laughing while he wore the Admiral's hat.

David visited the head and returned to his seat. Their hands barely touched when his dad handed him the drink. David gripped the glass tightly so that his father would not see his hands shaking.

"Thirty years," Dex mussed. "The United States Navy has been my life. I probably gave my career too much; you and your mother too little." He paused to look at David. "I don't think I'll be promoted to two-star if I stay around. Nixon plans a reduction in force. Budget cuts. You'll see brass retiring. Little room to move up."

"You really think there will be a reduction in force?"

"Yes, I've seen the RIF plans," Dex confirmed and fell into silence, seeming to be somewhere else. After a while, Dex asked, "Did you follow Apollo 12 on TV last month?"

"I did. Just amazing. Walking on the moon, again."

"Remarkable achievement," Dex said. "The space program is America at its finest. We established clear goals, planned the mission in detail, recruited the best and brightest, and let them do their job. Your computers were part of it." Dex paused and looked at David and then continued, "It was the USS Hornet that retrieved the astronauts. Back in 1944, I came on that carrier as a commissioned officer. The enemy threw everything at us in the Philippines. We stopped them cold. Our pilots were amazing, showing all the courage and skill we're now teaching at Top Gun." Dex seemed far away as he looked at a framed photo of his former aircraft carrier.

"We were under enemy attack fifty-nine times in sixteen months," Dex continued. "The Japs could never hit us. Our aces and our gunners were that good."

Anger flashed in David's eyes. "Last year I dated a Japanese American."

Dex sat ramrod straight and his fists clenched. "Damn, you're tough to talk to. The Japs, Japanese as you like to call them, attacked us and tried to kill us! I'm proud of what we did and you should be too. Any American should be proud."

David maintained level eye contact with Dex. Silence was broken with the sound of jets screaming overhead. "You've every right to be proud of World War II, giving us freedom over tyranny," David said. "I'm proud of your Silver Star."

Dex looked at David then away. Dex's eyes were red and moist. "Thank you, Son. I am very proud of the way we fought in both fronts. Think about D-Day. Those boats in the Normandy invasion were death traps. Brave men risked their lives to stop Hitler, a monster. This country is worth fighting for. You may not believe it, but there's always a monster that wants to destroy us, to end democracy. We have to stand up to the Nazis, the commies, the tyrants, the bullies." Dex paused, realizing that he was lecturing.

The soft light of afternoon streamed through the curtains.

"Believe it or not, I think about you. I try to understand your generation's opposition to this war," Dex said as he got up to refresh his drink.

"When our country was founded, they made the president the commander in chief because George Washington was a brilliant military leader," the admiral continued. "Now our military is run by politicians whose strategic thinking goes no further than the six o'clock news. McNamara wanted us out of Vietnam in 1967. I sat in meetings with him. In Vietnam, we're pissing into the wind. We've had a long parade of politicians change their minds more than their underwear. They won't let us win." Dex tightened his fists.

"Incredible."

"Yes, I'm proud of serving my country, especially in World War II, but it's time to retire."

In the afternoon shadows, the room was silent as a prayer. David had never heard his father talk this way.

"Sorry I lost my temper last Christmas," Dex said. "You saw secret maps that you should have never seen. My negligence."

"I'm sorry. I shouldn't have walked into to your study. Honest, Dad. I was there a minute. No idea what I saw."

Dex studied his son. "Not your fault. Those papers should have been locked away." Dex paused, deciding what he could say. "I guess I can tell you this much. I'm being asked to plan bombing that is...well it's... it's flat-out wrong. As I talk with you, I've reached a decision. I've been thinking seriously about this. I'm retiring. I want nothing more to do with this. Bombing's been pretty much decided by Johnson and now Nixon." Dex struggled in his chair.

"Wow. You are retiring!"

"I've always saluted smartly and said 'aye aye, sir.' When I did, people knew that I would get the job done. Always did. I'm proud to have served my country. Nothing makes me prouder than that Silver Star." Dex paused. "I mean, career wise, nothing makes me prouder."

"Without the sacrifice of your generation, my generation would not have our freedom of speech and protest."

Dex emptied his Bloody Mary. "Funny. We've barely talked in years. Now I'm saying things to you I can't say to my fellow officers. Haven't said to anyone. Guess I'm twenty years overdue in getting to know my son." Dex leaned forward. His shoulders relaxed from their military erect posture. "Tell me about your new job."

"I'm excited to be with Digital Equipment. At UCI, I got to program PDP Eight's. I was amazed with what can be done with mini-computers without needing a big mainframe. In interviews, Digital was my first choice. It turns out that having a degree in computer science is a real advantage."

"Congratulations on your new job. Computers. Big future. Digital Equipment is an excellent company. Navy is a huge customer of theirs."

"Your congratulations mean a lot. All my life, I've been trying to get your approval. I almost went to the Naval Academy trying to get it."

"I wish you had. With your brains, the leadership you showed as a cadet officer, and computer science, you would have gone far in the navy of the future."

"That's your dream. My dream is being me. I want you to know the real me and I want to get to know the real you."

Dex took a long look at David. "Fair enough. I don't think that it's too late to get to know my only son."

David's eyes were red. He fought tears. "It's not too late. We're doing pretty well right now."

Dex smiled. "I'm only fifty. That gives you fifty years to figure me out."

David laughed.

"You said you wanted my approval," Dex said. "For the record, I am proud of you. Graduating with honors. New job. Guess I'm also proud of your determination to be your own man."

They sat in silence with awkward grins. Dex fidgeted, then said, "It's been many years since I've taken you to Mary, I mean to your mother's grave. Since it's Christmas Eve, I was thinking we could make a visit."

"I'd like that," David said. "I visited her in April."

"Point Loma?" Dex asked.

"Yes, I attended the funeral of John Eastman. Remember him from the Army and Navy Academy?"

Dex hesitated. "Not sure that I do."

David looked disappointed that his father did not remember his best friend of years.

Dex drove David to his mother's grave, a mother he lost at age five, a mother he could barely remember. On a hill, her grave faced the Pacific that stretched to Asia. As the two walked to her grave, the ocean breeze carried distant voices and warning cries of migrant birds in flight, exhausted from their long journey in search of home. The wet air chilled.

Dex laid a bouquet of flowers on her gravestone. "Hello, Mary, it's Dex and our son. You'd be proud of David. He graduated with honors in computer science and has started his career with one of the top computer companies."

"Hello, Mom," David said awkwardly. "I haven't been with you since April, but I think of you every week." David choked on the words.

"I never stop thinking of you Mary." Dex faltered. "I'm retiring from the navy. It's time for deep-sea fishing and golf. I'll probably buy a place somewhere around here." Silence fell, as both Dex and David were lost in thought. "It's sad that David couldn't grow-up with you, Mary. You were such a loving mother." Dex started crying.

Seeing his father's tears, David started crying. He wiped his eyes, trying to stop the tears. He hesitated, then slid next to his father and put his arm on his shoulder. Pressed together, their tears flowed.

"She really loved you, David. I, I, I remember," Dex stopped, unable to continue. A flock of pelicans showed their grace in flight. Sounds softly whispered in the wind. Dex said, "Mary loved to hold you, feed you, and read you stories. You both laughed and sang through the day."

After a silence, Dex looked at David and said, "I was so lost after that car crash. I replayed the accident a thousand times, thinking of what I might've done differently. There I was with a five-year old, grieving for his lost mother, and all my responsibilities as the executive officer of a carrier. I had no choice but to be at sea. That's why I left you with my folks in Mobile."

David's memory carried him back to a small Baptist Church in Alabama. The choir was singing "Amazing Grace." *I once was lost, but now am found.*

"When I was transferred to the Pentagon, I moved you to Mary's folks in Raleigh, so I could see you more often."

David remembered playing hide and seek with all the kids in the neighborhood. He could see his grandmother smiling as they sat down to a generous southern dinner. He pieced together forgotten fragments of his life, a half-finished puzzle.

"When I put you in the military academy, I dreamed you'd be a model cadet officer and you were. I dreamed of Annapolis and you being a four-star Admiral. I had my dreams. I forgot to ask you yours."

Both sat in silence at the grave, as the ocean appeared then disappeared in the thin fog.

Looking at his mother's grave, David said, "There's something I've always been ashamed of." He struggled to continue. "Days before Mom died, I told her that I hated her."

"I remember that," Dex chuckled. "You had a teddy bear that you took everywhere - sandy beaches, the backyard, in the dirt.

Mary couldn't stand it, so she washed your teddy bear. It was ruined and you were mad. Furious. You're not the first five-year old to get mad enough to yell 'I hate you.' Son, don't let that bother you another minute. You loved your mother and she loved you."

After their Italian dinner together, when it came time to say goodbye, the two men, military-trained to guard feelings, stood in awkward silence, looking at each other. David started to extend a handshake; instead he hugged his father. The two embraced at length as the distance between them vanished, the acceptance grew, and wounds of years began to heal.

Dex inhaled deeply and said, "You've got a right to be mad at me for not seeing you more. Yes, the navy made big demands on me, but...." He fought going on. "Whenever I saw you, you reminded me of Mary. I couldn't take it. I wasn't there for you."

"I for...." David whispered and then inhaled deeply. "I forgive you."

30

Farewell to the Sixties

David opened the box his father had given him. He studied the old photographs - age nine, standing on a fishing boat with his dad, smiling proudly and holding a caught fish; Thanksgiving with his dad and grandparents; a two-year old boy holding hands with smiling parents. He lifted his mom's Tibetan pendant. For the first time, David noticed that behind the mounted stone was a thin locket, which he worked with his fingernails to pry open. Inside was a photo of his mother holding an infant in her arms. He noticed an engraving in the silver and held it to the light, reading, "David, you are in my heart. I will always love you." Slowly, he closed the locket and secured the pendant around his neck.

In the early morning sunlight of Christmas Day, David walked the deserted San Clemente beach, reliving memories of past years as he recalled rescues, surfing and romance. He looked up at where he had made a cliff rescue and saw himself as a hero mirrored in Linda's eyes. In the crashing waves he could almost hear the Beatles singing, "All You Need Is Love."

He drove on Pacific Coast Highway to the flowered gazebo of his first real date with Linda. He stood above the rocky beach where they had first kissed. High tide enveloped the beach; surf smashed against rocks, and distant seals barked plaintive cries.

He drove past the Montessori school to Linda's home where they had talked of dreams, sang off-key, delighted in love making, cared for and accepted each other.

Arms full with a bottle of champagne, Marie Callender's apple pie, and Linda's gifts including a nutcracker prince, David knocked on the door. In seconds, Linda opened the door and started to hug, then seeing his arms full, smiled, and carefully took the pie box. The home was rich with decorations, stockings, lighted Christmas tree, Burl Ives songs from the record player, and the aroma of turkey and stuffing from the kitchen.

He shook hands with Linda's father and hugged her mother. Like Linda, her parents were warm and full of stories. Her folks marveled at all they had seen in the past three days, including Hollywood, the mountains, the ocean, and the Newport Harbor parade of boats covered with Christmas lights. They enthused about rides at Disneyland.

Hours of conversation included Linda's childhood of ballet lessons, soccer, earning the nickname of Little Miss Sunshine, the Girl Scouts of her youth, and the Girl Scouts of her Berkeley fame.

Linda smiled as David talked about enjoying Christmas Eve with his dad, visiting his mother's grave, and being surprised about his father's retirement. Linda's dad was impressed that Dex was an admiral. All agreed that it was long past time to end the war.

The Christmas dinner filled the small table. David almost reached his fork toward the turkey, when he saw the bowed heads. They held hands and prayed and included John Hope in their prayers. They feasted, toasted, talked and laughed. In addition to the apple pie dessert, David surprised Linda with a box of Girl Scout chocolate mint cookies.

Linda was delighted with David's Christmas gift for her, a nutcracker that looked like the prince in the ballet. She loved his gift of a Navajo silver and turquoise necklace that matched her eyes. David loved her gift of a watch that he desperately needed for his new job.

As the two parted, Linda enthused about how much her parents liked him and how she loved him. He talked about the warmth and love he saw in all of them.

Linda, David, Carlo and Rachel admired the lights that danced on the water as their sailboat glided down the middle of the harbor on New Year's Eve as midnight approached. People could be seen partying in homes covered with Christmas lights that lined the shore. Music floated across the water. They were sheltered in the harbor, protected from the rough seas and pounding surf. The sky was clear and stars were everywhere.

Dressed for the celebration, David and Linda had flowers in their hair. Linda's Mexican blouse was embroidered with flowers, and David wore a turquoise-colored gauze Tibetan shirt and his mother's turquoise necklace and pendant. Rachel wore a blouse of brilliant tribal colors from a jungle village of Venezuela. Carlo wore a long-sleeve fencing shirt and a bandana. With the plastic saber of his youth tucked into his waist-sash, he looked like Errol Flynn in an old pirate movie.

Carlo held the tiller as he expertly navigated the borrowed 22-foot sailboat. Sitting next to Carlo, Rachel poured more champagne for all. Linda and David were both sitting on the boat's starboard rail to keep the boat from heeling too far.

"I love it when you wear your turquoise pendant." Linda unbuttoned the top of David's shirt, held the Tibetan piece in one hand, and she rubbed David's chest with her other.

"I feel kind of a sacred peace and love when I wear this."

"I'm glad that you reconciled with your dad," she said. Linda rested her head on David's chest and whispered, "You make me so happy."

"I love you."

"I love you."

The boat glided past a decorated pavilion full of people celebrating as the New Year approached.

"Someday I'll write a novel about this year," David said.

"Why a novel instead of non-fiction?" Carlo asked.

David smiled and looked directly at Carlo, "To protect the guilty." Carlo self-consciously smiled broadly, and then raised his glass in a toast.

Spontaneously everyone toasted, "To the guilty."

"In your story, be sure to include our hopes of peace."

"And to protecting our environment."

"And our aspirations for a better future."

"And love for every child."

The four started singing the Beatles' "All You Need Is Love."

Fireworks exploded. Crowds from all over the harbor chanted the countdown for the New Year, "Ten, nine, eight…." David embraced Linda as they fused into a loving kiss. It was the end of the sixties. They were in no hurry to let go.

Biography

John Addison is the author of this novel. In 1969, John was an ocean lifeguard in San Clemente near president Nixon's "Summer Whitehouse." As a recent university graduate, he struggled with the daily uncertainty of being drafted. John has authored two nonfiction books and hundreds of articles.

Thank You

Thank you to my wife, Marcia, for her reading and improving the stories in this novel. Without her encouragement, laughter, and love, this novel would still be unfinished. Thank you to those who had lived in the sixties and shared their stories. Many thanks to Susan Blatty, Gary Bulmer, John Adsit, Pamela Travis-Moore, Bob Eubank, Claudine Marken, Gary Jaffe, and Tim Flood for reading early drafts of this novel and offering valuable improvements.

Printed in Great Britain
by Amazon